DESTINY'S HEIR

CASEY NEUMILLER

First printing, 2013

ISBN-13: 978-0615936598 (Shamrock Concepts)
ISBN-10: 0615936598

Shamrock Concepts
1310 4th Ave
Washburn, ND 58577

To my wife:
Thank you. This is only possible because of you.

1

THE CARRIAGE RUMBLED FORWARD OVER the cobblestone street, jarred roughly from side to side. The team of horses moved only as swiftly as the insistent driver forced them. Days of constant travel had worn down the pair, and the prospect of reaching home, no matter how close, was not enough to inspire them to give anything but their least effort.

The carriage was large enough to seat six easily, but the cabin remained empty. The driver sat in his seat with whip in one hand, reins in the other. He snapped the heavy leather lash at the horses occasionally, if only to prevent them from slowing in their exhaustion.

The driver at last allowed the horses to stop when they reached the wrought iron gates at the end of the cobblestone road. The gates hung from stone walls nearly ten feet high, almost obscuring the even taller trees beyond.

A page hurriedly swung the gates open. "Welcome home, my lord."

"My holdings have not fallen apart in my absence?" Lord Rittin spat from the driver's seat.

The page did not meet his gaze, his head stooped in subservience. "No, my lord." He hesitated before asking, "Was your trip productive, my lord?"

"Enough so. Take my carriage to the stables, and then return with my chest." The noble laid his hand on a carved wooden trunk. "You would do well to neither look inside, nor keep me waiting."

"Yes, my lord."

Lord Rittin studied the sky for a moment. "Is the evening meal prepared, and my bath drawn?"

"Your manor awaits your arrival, sir."

"As it should," Lord Rittin grunted. He flicked the whip forward against the team. "Ho!"

The horses reluctantly broke into a forward trot again as the page swung the gate shut behind the carriage. The page secured the gates, then hastily broke into a trot to catch up to the carriage.

The noble ignored him, of course. The great house rose up among the trees now, majestic in size and scope. While it was no castle like the fortress at the center of Jepitsa, it was the envy of every noble under High King Hazael.

The lord allowed a small smile of satisfaction to touch his lips as the horses stopped before the house. He allowed himself to slide from the driver's seat to the cobblestone road below. Without looking back, he marched up to the house, the doors swinging open before him as the servants within noted his approach.

The page watched in discontent as Lord Rittin disappeared into the hallway. Gasping for breath, he took the reins of the nearer horse and led them at a walk to the stable, a hundred yards away.

The horses were content with the far more leisurely pace. The page had regained his wind by the time they reached the two-story stable. It was a far longer walk than on any other estate around Jepitsa. Lord Rittin had insisted the stable be constructed far enough away that no trace of the scent or noise of a stable would disturb him in the great house.

The page led the horses, still harnessed to the carriage, inside the stable, backed the carriage into its customary place, then freed the horses from their traces and led them down to the open box stalls where he could rub them down and provide them with the care they so obviously needed after a harsh journey.

Silence reigned over the carriage for long moments. After several minutes, there was a faint rasp of a knife on leather as a blade was drawn from its sheath. A few moments of sawing later, and three figures dropped from the underside of the car onto the stable floor.

Ben gathered his feet under him and crouched in the cover afforded by the carriage. Eyes watching and ears listening for any sign they'd been detected, he stretched his arms and back, trying to work out cramps and knots that had tortured him for the last few hours.

The sixteen-year-old thief froze in place as the echoes of footsteps reached his ears. He spared a glance for his companions – the dark-haired Corin and the skinny Zeke. They, too, were frozen as still as statues.

Ben waited patiently, but the steps faded away. *Safe for now*, he decided. *Time to get this show on the road.* He carefully stepped out from beneath the carriage and straightened.

His legs and back screamed in protest. Ben ignored the pain as best he was able, but the cramps were nearly debilitating.

"Next time," Corin whispered from the ground beside him, "we find a better plan than whatever Alan comes up with."

Zeke grunted his assent from the far side of the carriage, then added, "You notice how our fearless leader is never the one who has to tie himself to the axles of a carriage for three hours, or hold his breath for sixty seconds while swimming blindly to find a trap door, or let himself fall two stories onto a wagon of straw that *may* provide enough cushion?"

Ben shook his head. "Now's not the time for this, guys. Let's get the goods and get out."

"What *are* the goods, anyways?" Corin asked, her voice brightening.

"Alan didn't tell me." Ben stood and breathed, centering himself. The cramps were mostly subsiding now, and he was fairly certain he could run if the need arose. *Better than two minutes ago*, he decided. *This plan was absolutely crazy.*

Zeke quietly scaled up to the top of the carriage and started rifling about. "Three chests here. Two of them aren't locked. Not much inside — some clothes, some garbage…oh, apples!"

Ben looked up in time to see a red missile shooting down at him. His hand darted forward of its own volition and snagged the fruit. Corin similarly caught an apple and immediately started munching on it. Ben studied it, shrugged, and took a big bite. He closed his eyes at the simple pleasure. *It's been way too long since we had anything this good*, he decided. *Maybe with my cut I'll buy a whole bag of apples, and eat nothing but those until they're gone.*

When he opened his eyes again, he saw Zeke had moved to the front of the carriage now. "This one's locked," he hissed. "Corin, this is your specialty."

"It's why you keep me around," she said cheerfully as she hauled herself up the side of the carriage. She was already drawing a pair of slender wires from her pocket. "Looks like our friendly noble decided to spend enough money to get a decent lock," she announced as she studied the chest with a critical eye. "This may take a few minutes."

"Make it less," Ben whispered. He dropped to his knees and crawled to the end of the stall, looking up and down the stable alleys for any spying eyes. At the far end of the stable, he could just make out the single page brushing down the horses. Ben stopped and calculated. *Another two minutes to finish tending for the team*, he decided, *and then he'll be back here to get one of those chests to take up to the manor. For some reason, I doubt Lord Rittin is worried about his apples. No, it'll be whatever is in that chest that Corin is cracking.*

Corin was humming quietly to herself as she worked. Ben studied her for a moment. Like Ben and Zeke, she was dirty. Filth and grime from the hard street life caked her nails, smudged her cheeks. Her dark hair was unwashed and greasy. Her clothes were ragged and stained.

Yet underneath all the trappings of the street life, Ben still thought she was beautiful. He'd never told her as much – he didn't know how she'd respond – but he thought of her more all the time. Ben stopped and shook his head at himself. *Now's not the time.*

"Corin," he whispered, "you've only got another minute before we have to find cover. How's it going?"

"It's...got it!" she hissed in excitement. The girl drew the heavy wooden lid back, and her eyes widened. "Wow!"

"What?" Ben asked impatiently. "What is it?"

Zeke looked over her shoulder, his eyes widening as well. He reached in and pulled out a handful of gold coins, holding them aloft for Ben to see. "There must be hundreds of them!" he said.

"That's not what we came for," Ben whispered in irritation. "And keep your voice down!"

"It might not be what we came for, but it's what we're taking," Corin said as she plunged both hands into the chest. She withdrew the double handful of gold coins and started stuffing them in her pockets.

"Leave it," Ben said sharply, his voice rising above a whisper for the first time. "We had very clear instructions, and we're not supposed to take anything else from the carriage. Do you see the book?"

"Got it," Zeke whispered as he withdrew a leather-bound tome and tossed it to Ben.

Ben fielded it neatly and tucked it inside his jacket. He glanced down the alleyway and swore silently. "He's coming!" he hissed. "We need cover, now!"

Zeke and Corin both stared at him, then looked around wildly for a place to hide. Ben spun as well, but the only available cover was the underside of the carriage – and the page would hardly miss the sight of three teenagers crouching under the carriage. The stall was otherwise empty, and the walls rose all the way to the ceiling. To reach another stall would require moving out into the open alley, where the three of them would be spotted for sure.

The only cover, then… Ben's eyes fell on the carriage itself. *That's so stupid it might work.* "Inside the carriage," he hissed. "Now!"

Zeke and Corin both flipped off the roof of the carriage and into the cab. Ben didn't bother opening the door, either, jumping through the open window onto one of the leather couches inside. He rolled off it and onto the carriage's floor, pressed in tightly with Zeke and Corin.

The only sound in the carriage was very quiet, very strained breathing as the page's footsteps echoed into the stall.

In his imagination, Ben could see the page walking down the alley, turning into the carriage's stall. He could see the young servant as he placed his foot on the step, hauling himself up onto the carriage with bumps and scrapes. All three thieves held their breath as the carriage rocked from the page's activity.

"Wonder what's in here," the page mumbled. "Lord Rittin sure seemed worked up about it." There was another series of thumps and thuds and scrapes as the page dragged the chest off the carriage and nearly dropped it to the floor, barely able to hold the weight.

"What does he have in here, anyways?" the page wondered aloud. "It's like it's filled with lead!"

Not lead, gold, Ben corrected him silently.

The page's breathing was labored as he staggered away, ladened with the chest of treasure. His steps slowly faded away, and Ben began to breathe more easily. "That," he whispered to his cramped companions, "was too close."

"Yeah, now get off me," Zeke hissed.

"Okay, okay." Ben slowly pulled himself back onto the carriage's leather couch. Once he was in place, he carefully peeked his head out, looking back and forth. "We're clear."

The three thieves piled out of the carriage, breathing heavily and stained with sweat. Corin started giggling as the euphoria of a near-escape overcame her. "Inside the carriage!" she quoted Ben between fits of laughs. "Now!" She doubled over in laughter. "You were so dead serious."

"It was just a page. Not like he was going to stab us all if he found us anyways," Zeke commented.

Ben sighed and shook his head. "I'd just like to get out of here without getting caught. Is that such a bad thing?"

The other two thieves considered, and Zeke finally relented. "No, it's better if we get out before someone knows we're here. Even if he would've seen us, though, we could've made a run for it and made it out of here before anyone would catch us."

"So, now what's our plan now?" Corin asked, finally past her fits of laughter. "Steal some horses and make a break for it?"

Ben shook his head. "The gate will be locked. We'll need to find a way over the wall, or wait until someone else leaves the estate."

Zeke looked at him suspiciously. "It sounds to me like you don't really have a plan for getting us out."

"Uh…" Ben swallowed hard. "Not so much, no."

"Wonderful," Zeke growled.

"Hey, it's fine," Ben protested. "It's not like anyone knows we're here. Let's just scout around a bit, figure out the lay of the estate, and we'll find a way out of here. After all, these places are built to keep people out, not in." He smiled. "Nobles don't like being trapped if something goes wrong. Lord Rittin has to have a way out of here besides the main gate."

"So, scout things out and meet back here in thirty minutes?" Corin asked.

Ben nodded. "Keep your head down, though, and don't get caught."

The three thieves scattered into the shadows, blending in effortlessly. Ben had spent most of his life living in the slums and shadows of Jepitsa; it took no effort to keep himself concealed from casual view. He moved slowly, darting from cover to cover, always alert for any servants that could expose him.

Zeke and Corin had both headed away from the manor, most likely to scout for any openings or low spots in the surrounding wall where three teenage thieves might slip through to safety. Ben, instead, chose to scout the manor itself. *Hey, there's always a chance of an easy mark there*, he told himself. *It'd be nice to fill my pockets with some extra gold or jewels because someone was careless. After all, what Alan doesn't know won't hurt him, and he didn't say anything about not stealing from the manor, just the carriage.*

A careful ten minutes of slinking left him within easy view of the manor. Unfortunately, the glass windows were all tightly shut, and proved resistant to the subtle pressure of a dagger's blade. His scouting did reveal a single open window on the second floor of the manor. There was no convenient access to the upper-level portal, but an apple tree halfway around the house allowed him to carefully ascend to the roof of the manor.

The thief moved slowly across the surface, down on hands and knees, crawling with every scrap of stealth and silence he could muster. Walking across roofs was far more dangerous than anywhere else – he could give himself away with a falling stone or shingle, he could be heard from inside the house, or the roof could give way beneath him, announcing his presence to everyone within a hundred yards.

The roof and Ben's luck held, and he successfully reached the edge of the roof above the window. He lowered himself down headfirst to look inside.

The window opened onto a study – Lord Rittin's personal study, if Ben were to guess. The room was well-lit by a lantern, but unoccupied with a closed door. A massive oak desk took up a third of the room, covered with books and papers. Ben contemplated the sight for a few moments.

Well, there's nothing immediately valuable I can see, he observed. *The papers and books might be worth some coin, but I don't have a way of knowing that unless I steal them first and try to sell them later. I'm certainly not going to walk out of here with a wooden desk strapped to my back. If there's anything in there, it's probably going to be in the desk.*

Assuming it's not locked, of course. He repressed a sigh. *Too bad Corin isn't here. She'd open those locks like they're nothing, and then we'd have our pick of what we wanted. I can pick locks, too, but she's so much better than I am.*

Ben considered for a moment longer. *I really shouldn't do this.*

Then, with a fluid motion, he allowed himself to drop from the roof and swing through the open window.

He landed in a crouch, the thud of his feet impossibly loud in his ears. He froze in place, trying not to breathe as he listened for any indication his entry had been detected. Blissful silence was all his ears could hear, though, and after a dozen long heartbeats he rose to his feet and crossed to the closed desk.

Ben tugged open drawers. The first one he tried was locked, but the rest yielded to his touch. The drawers will filled with more papers, stacks of receipts, scribblings, and other pages Ben couldn't begin to decipher. Giving up on that approach, Ben turned his attention back to the locked drawer. *Well, I didn't come in here to leave empty-handed*, he decided. He withdrew his own lock pick set from his pocket and crouched down to study the drawer. He nodded once and slid both wires into the lock, feeling out the tumblers.

Corin always makes this look so easy, he decided as he tried to trick the tumblers into yielding. *I think she does it just to make us look bad.*

Minutes ticked by, and Ben's frustration grew as the lock refused to yield. *This is taking too long*, he decided. *I need to get back to meet with Zeke and Corin. But I didn't waste all this time for nothing.*

He withdrew his dagger and slid the blade into the narrow gap. Carefully, he pressed down, levering the drawer apart from the lock.

With a loud crack, the lock abruptly came to pieces and the drawer slid open. Ben winced. *So much for Lord Rittin not knowing we were here.* He started to rifle through the drawer, looking for anything of value. Ben was so intent on his task, and a small pouch of jewels, that he almost missed the heavy footfalls coming straight towards the study.

A moment before the door swung open, Ben abruptly realized the danger. *Oh, damn!* With no other cover and the window across the room – it could've been as far away as the moon, for all the good it did him – he rolled himself under the desk.

Really? he asked himself. *Are you* really *hiding under a desk? What are you, Ben, some six-year-old who's never stolen anything before?*

Two pairs of feet entered the room, accompanied by two voices: the page who had retrieved the chest from the carriage, and Lord Rittin himself.

"Put it on the desk," Rittin commanded.

The page allowed the chest to crash to the desk's surface. Ben winced at the sound but forced himself to sit absolutely still.

"Now, the key," Lord Rittin murmured, fishing around in one of the desk drawers.

Ben swallowed hard. *If he tries for the locked drawer, I'm done.* But his luck held as Rittin provided the key from another drawer.

"And now, we unlock…" Rittin frowned. "Wait. This chest is already unlocked."

Corin didn't re-lock the chest, Ben thought with dismay. *Oh, no.*

"You!" Lord Rittin snarled. "My own page, thieving from me!"

"No, sir!" the page protested. "I didn't even know it was open!"

Lord Rittin's tone was unrelenting. "To your quarters," he barked. "If I find so much as a single gold coin there, I'll have your head!"

Footsteps receded, and the door slammed. Ben blew out his held breath. The room was too hot, too close, too *dangerous* to wait any longer. He rolled out from under the desk and headed to the window. He had just gotten a good grip on the frame to pull himself back to the roof when the door swung open.

"...won't risk another one of you stealing by leaving this unlocked," Lord Rittin was saying over his shoulder. As he stepped into the room, his head came back around, and the noble froze.

Caught! Ben heaved himself up onto the roof.

"Thief!" Lord Rittin's shout followed him. "There's a thief! Guards!"

Ben sprinted across the rooftop to the tree he'd previously used, scrambling down as fast as he dared. It was too fast, and he lost his footing and fell the last six feet to the ground, landing in a painful heap.

No time, no time, can't stop to hurt. Ben's mind raced as he jerked himself back to his feet and started sprinting away from the house. *They'll be all over me if I can't get out of here. Need to get Zeke and Corin and get out before they catch us all.* The house grew smaller behind him, but the

14

shouts grew louder. *They'll have guards combing the ground in minutes. Have to get out.*

The stables loomed before him, but he didn't dare duck into the well-lit building. He angled for the wall instead, searching frantically for cover. A glance over his shoulder showed torches leaving the manor now – guards no doubt fanning out to look for traces of the intruder.

Ben's backward glance cost him again, and he tripped as his foot caught in a previously-unseen hole. He crashed into the grass and dirt, and pain shot up his leg. *Ow, ow, ow! No time for this!* He barely had regained his feet when two hands appeared before him, reaching *down* towards him. He instinctively reached up and caught them, and a half-second later was swung off his feet and into the air.

Zeke and Corin pulled him up onto the stable roof. He scrambled up and immediately laid flat, panting for breath. His two friends followed suit, silently watching the ring of torches leaving the manor.

"What, did you just get bored and decided to have some fun?" Corin's voice whispered warmly in his ear. "There's other ways to do that, you know."

Ben's breathing finally slowed, but his heart still pounded in his ears. "Oops," was all he could mumble in reply.

"This will make getting out a bit more complicated," Zeke chimed in with a hushed whisper.

"Yeah, this wasn't what I had in mind," Ben finally managed. "Corin, did you find any way out?"

The girl hesitated. "Well, the outside wall is solid all the way around — there aren't any gaps or anything. And apparently Lord Rittin wouldn't allow any trees to grow close enough to the wall to use for our escape."

"How inconsiderate," Zeke grunted.

"So there's no way out but the gate?" Ben asked, trying not to give voice to the despair he was feeling.

"I didn't say that," Corin hissed back. "But you're not going to like it."

"Anything's better than staying here."

"There's a creek on the northwest corner of the property…" Corin began.

"You're right, I don't like it," Ben interrupted.

"Shush, you two," Zeke hissed, still intently watching the scattering guards.

"How do you know it actually will lead us out?" Ben asked, quieter now.

"The part that's inside the walls is maybe forty yards long," Corin explained. "So it's a real short stretch."

"And?" Ben prompted.

"There's a boat inside the wall," Corin observed. "So there has to be a way out."

"Are you sure it isn't locked?"

"Of course it's locked," the girl answered in exasperation. "And why did you bring me along?"

"Right," Ben said dryly. "Okay, that sounds better than the gate. Let's move."

"Wait," Zeke interjected. "Wait two minutes, and the guards will be inside the stables. Then we can move."

Ben watched the guards move with agonizing slowness, but he heeded Zeke's advice. *If I had been a shade more patient in the house, we wouldn't be in this mess,* he knew. *So yeah, I'll be patient now if it means we get out of the scrape I put us in.*

At last, the handful of guards moving to the stable disappeared inside. Following Zeke's lead, Ben dropped off the low roof, followed by Corin. In near-silence they slipped through the darkness, staying well clear of the torchlight shed by each of the searchers now combing the property for them.

Ben silently berated himself as they crept along. *Stupid, stupid, stupid. You got greedy, and just about got caught by it. If someone doesn't make it out of here, it's all your fault. Even Alan wouldn't have been stupid enough to come out from under that desk before he was absolutely certain it was clear, and he's the most reckless thief you know. Stupid, Ben, stupid.*

Still, their stealthy escape was going entirely unobserved. The hasty search by the guards was uneven and unorganized, and better yet, the bright torchlight made them easy to avoid in the darkness. *Lucky for us, they're not real bright,* Ben thought with a little smirk. *If they used their heads a little more and just put the torches out, we'd be caught for sure. Or they could have scattered to the walls and stationed a few people at the gate, and they'd have us for sure.*

If Corin is right and there's an exit up here, they should have stationed a dozen guards there to intercept us. This place is built like a castle, so if there's any holes to get out of, Lord Rittin and his guards should know them. From the torches,

17

though, it looks like there's only a couple of guards ahead looking for us, and none of them are standing still.

Ben's confidence rose in spite of the pain he felt from two falls and the amateur mistake he'd made. *We really are going to get out of here.*

Then the howls floated to his ears on the night breeze, and only his fast-moving momentum kept him from freezing in his tracks. To Ben, they sounded like demons, some ancient servants of the Dark One, Aither. He couldn't imagine a more dangerous, soul-chilling sound, and his imagination conjured up images of fire-breathing abominations from the depths, creatures too hideous for names or for the safety of daylight.

They weren't, of course; he knew in his mind their true identity.

Hounds.

"Run!" Zeke hissed.

The three thieves abandoned their stealthy escape in favor of a dead sprint for the distant creek.

It will take time for them to track us, Ben knew. *And once we get out, if we stick to the water, they won't be able to track us. If Corin can get the gate open, anyways. If not, we won't have to worry about the guards — the dogs will tear us to pieces.*

The three thieves hit the creek at a full sprint, nearly tripping over their own feet as the water grabbed at their legs. The smaller Corin was immediately ahead of the two, but all three were forced to walking pace as the water quickly reached their waists. They pushed on as fast as they could, the wall looming above them ominously.

"Yes," Corin hissed. "There's a gate. And a lock. We're going to get out of here!"

"Quickly," Zeke urged. "If not, we're all dog food!"

The girl slipped her lock pick set out of her pocket as she reached the iron gates. Immediately she went to work, the slender picks slipping into the keyhole. She grimaced. "Lock is a bit rusted – this could take a minute."

As if to punctuate her words, more howls rose from the manor's hounds. Ben swallowed. *Come on*, he urged her silently. *Come on, get the lock open. You can do this. You can get us out. We're all depending on you.*

Corin's face turned peaceful as she worked. With the pressure of the approaching dogs, and the guards no doubt following them, Ben found her expression oddly disturbing. *How can she be so calm while doom is preparing to fall on us?*

"Ben," Zeke hissed. "Still got your knife?"

The thief jerked out of his thoughts, startled by the question. He dropped his hand under the water, found his dagger by touch, and withdrew the blade from its sheath. He nodded at Zeke, though he knew it would be barely visible in the darkness – a darkness that, only a few minutes ago, had been comforting in its concealment, but was now a source of terror.

"If the dogs come, we hold them off with our knives until Corin can pop the lock." Zeke's tone sounded more wishful than determined. "I mean, how hard could it be to knife a few hounds?"

"If you want to be sporting," Ben joked, "just go at 'em unarmed. I mean, they don't have a weapon — why should you?"

"Shut up!" Corin hissed. "You're distracting me!"

The boys fell silent as they listened to the dogs howl in excitement, clearly closer now than they'd been a few minutes ago. Ben glanced over his shoulder at Corin for a moment. *I wish she wasn't here. She shouldn't have to do this. Me and Zeke and Alan and the others, we deserve lives like this. She should be somewhere safe, somewhere she's protected and cared about.*

Guess I'll have to do the best job I can with that, he decided, tightening his grip on the knife. He turned back towards the manor house. Torches were visible now in the darkness — torches no doubt held by guards and proceeded by dogs.

Alright. Think, Ben. When they come, they'll probably leap for your throat. Get your off-hand up to protect yourself. The leather bracer should take the bite without a problem. Once the dog's latched on, thrust with the knife. Don't hesitate, just strike and throw the dog off and get ready for the next one, because it'll probably be more than one.

"Got it!" Corin whispered. "The lock is open!"

Ben turned back to see Corin shove against the iron gate. The gate refused to budge. *It's all the water*, Ben realized. *The hinges are all rusted tight.* "Zeke! On the gate, too!" he called, wading forward to add his own strength to Corin's.

Zeke joined them, all three shoving against the gate. Slowly, an inch at a time, it started to open. Abruptly, the rust gave way and the gate swung open with a rattling, screeching whine, sending all three thieves sprawling in the cold water.

Ben found his feet first. He could hear shouting, now; the dogs howled so loudly he thought they might already be through the gate. A glance back showed the torches less than fifty yards away, held aloft by guards. The hounds strained against their leashes, held tight by two armored men.

"You there! Stop!" one of the guards shouted. An instant later, the men holding the dogs released their leashes, allowing the vicious hounds to bound forward unrestrained.

Ben knew in a heartbeat there was no escape; the dogs would be through the open gate in seconds, and there would be no fleeing into the darkness with the predators that close behind. As his heart thudded in his ears, a single *possible* solution flickered through his mind like a bolt of lightning in a thunderstorm.

He snatched the lock from Corin's hand and threw himself back towards the gate.

The dogs let out another bone-chilling howl as they descended towards Ben. He hastily reached through the cold water, grabbed hold of the gate, and slammed it shut in the hounds' faces. The trio of dogs smashed into the iron gate, almost bowling the thief over. Pure determination held him in place – determination, and fear

21

of the consequences of allowing the dogs through. Struggling to hold the gate closed, he reached up and hooked the lock closed around the gate, snapping the rusted implement in place.

Ben fell away from the gate, gasping for breath as the cold water continued to pour over him. The dogs smashed into the gate again, and a third time, but the lock held.

"Let's go!" Corin snarled as she and Zeke hauled Ben to his feet. "Before they come around from the other side!"

11

"GAIN!" THE HARSH VOICE BARKED.

The Magi apprentice, Arraya, lifted her trembling arm. Sweat plastered her amber hair to her head, ran down her forehead and stung her eyes. Fire danced between her fingertips. She concentrated and *pushed*, and a narrow gout of flame lashed out from her hand to the candle a dozen feet away.

The flame licked the candle wick, which burst into light. Arraya allowed her arm to fall to her side and barely managed to stay on her feet, swaying dizzily. She raised her chin and forced herself to stand steady.

"Good," the voice said, clearly pleased. "Very good. You have learned your lessons well. When you are confronted by the forces of the Dark One, they will not wait for you to rest and recover. They will strike when you are tired, heartsick, and alone. You must always be ready to wield the power, even when your strength is ebbed."

Arraya nodded once. "Yes, master." She hesitated. "May I sit, master?"

"No." The voice was hard but not unkind. "You must push until you find your limits. Resting now would sacrifice that knowledge for your convenience, and that knowledge could save your life."

The apprentice tried to hold herself straight, but as the magic flowed away from her, so too did the euphoria that accompanied it. In the span of a heartbeat, she became intimately aware of her sore arms and calves and back, stiff from countless hours spent hiking up and down the mountainside with buckets of water. Channeling the true magic and manipulating its flows also took a toll, though it was often more mental than physical. *The last time I slept was…two days ago? Three?*

"Tell me, my apprentice, why do you continue on this course?" This time the voice was unyielding iron. "Why do you continue to fight and struggle to grasp the true power?"

It was a question Arraya had often asked herself in her fifteen winters. "I choose to walk this path to become a Magi," she replied.

"You do, but why?" the voice asked again.

"Because it is my destiny," she answered.

"Destiny?" The voice laughed aloud, a rolling chuckle that lasted nearly a minute. "What do you know of destiny? What do you know about the intentions of the Light One, about the flows of the true power, about the ways of our world?" He chuckled again. "You know nothing."

Arraya *knew*, in a heartbeat of clarity, that a blow was coming: knew when, from which direction, where it would land. Her muscles, locked tight from exertion, refused to respond to her commands, betraying her. The wooden staff struck her calves and swept her legs out from under her, leaving her with her back on the cold stone floor, staring up at the dimly lit training room.

Her master, the Magi Shallum, clucked at her disapprovingly, and she could imagine him shaking his head. "Train and train and train, and still you are defeated by a single blow from a simple wooden stick. Tell me, my apprentice, what would have become of you were you set upon by the Dark One's worshipers? Or ambushed with three feet of steel by a servant of the Imposter-King?" He continued to shake his head. "Were you skewered upon a spear, what would be of your great destiny?"

Arraya knew better than to answer. She merely climbed to her feet – slowly, with great care – and bowed her head to her master.

"How long will you persist?" Shallum whispered to her. "How long will you pursue this training as a Magi, as one of power, before you surrender this impossible quest?"

Red-hot anger flared in Arraya's chest, and she barely managed to bite it back.

"Your power is weak and unfocused. This exercise is for one two years your junior, and yet you nearly failed." The Master's voice was harsh now, flogging her ears like a whip. "Yet you refuse to give up, when others more powerful than you await the opportunity to train."

The heat forced her mouth to open, her lips to give shape to the words emerging from her heart. "Yet *you* chose *me* as your apprentice. You clearly thought I could become a Magi."

"Did I?" Shallum mocked. "Did I think you could become a Magi? Perhaps I wanted to force you to fail, to acknowledge your meaningless powers, so that you would never be a risk to any mortal. Perhaps you have failed to meet my expectations, and I was wrong about your power and will."

"Then why am I still training? Why have you not cast me out?" Arraya's lips seemed to ask independently of her mind. "Is this all just to make a mockery of me?"

"Perhaps it is," Shallum acknowledged sarcastically. "The Magi live far longer even than the Scions. I have many lifetimes to train a worthy apprentice and successor. What is your lifetime to me, should you fail to complete your training?"

The apprentice swayed on her feet. Her legs were trembling under her, but her anger kept her standing. "I will *not* fail."

"Are you certain you haven't? Perhaps this was a test that you had to pass, and now you have failed in it."

"It wasn't." Arraya was finally back in control of her voice, and she forced the words out with a confidence she did not feel. "You would not hinge my apprenticeship on a single test."

Shallum laughed aloud. "Very good, my apprentice," he said without a trace of mockery. "Four days awake, physically exhausted, your powers at the very edge of their limits, and yet you still can think with a clear mind. *Very* good."

Arraya nodded slightly, knowing she should feel good about her victory but unable to muster any feeling beyond weariness. "Thank you, master."

The Magi smiled at the apprentice, stepping in front of her now. He was old in the way all Magi were old, clearly aged but in a nondescript way that made it impossible for Arraya to guess his age. His robes were plain and brown, with almost no decoration. They were heavy, though, thickly padded with sheep's wool for warmth against the cold dreariness that laid upon the Magi's hidden fortress.

"You," he said after a long moment of silent contemplation, "are a unique apprentice, Arraya. You are not the strongest I have seen or trained, and many more powerful than you have failed to complete their apprenticeships. Yet you persist — your strength of will drives you on when others falter."

Arraya hesitated before asking, "Is that why you chose me as your apprentice?"

Shallum was uncharacteristically slow in responding, as though Arraya had asked a question he wasn't prepared to answer. "It is not yet the time to speak of this. When that time arrives, you shall know." His eyes fell upon her again. "I think it is time for you to rest, my student."

"But I have not yet met the limits of my strength," Arraya retorted with just a hint of heat – the most she could manage, given her swaying. "I'm still on my feet."

"My student, if I did not send you to rest now, you would continue to push until your sleep would be eternal," he said dryly. "Go, and rest in the apprentices' quarters. I will retrieve you in twelve hours' time."

"More training, master?" she asked. Her very bones seemed to grow leaded at the prospect of sleep, though the idea of even harder lessons following the respite was dispiriting.

"No. I will speak before the Council, and it is only appropriate for my apprentice to be present," he said. "Now, go and rest."

"Before the Council? Why?" Arraya asked.

"Go, and rest," Shallum repeated again. "There will be time enough for your questions later." He turned away from her, walked over to the single lit candle and blew it out.

***

Arraya slowly walked through the last stronghold of the Magi. Ignis Castle was a long-forgotten fortress constructed deep in the Cosmane Mountains. The apprentice had lived there for nearly ten years – ever since her apprenticeship had begun and she had been whisked away from her quiet life in one of the provincial villages in Werbri.

That was a lifetime ago, she thought as she ambled through the stone passageways. Cold gusts of snowy wind blew in through cracks and crevices, and she tried to huddle deeper in her robe for warmth. The training rooms were in the southern watchtower, the one furthest down the mountain slope. The great hall, where food was prepared and eaten, was in the lowest level of the northern tower. Above it were the apprentices' quarters, and further above those were the quarters of the Magi themselves. *I still don't know why they gave themselves the more inconvenient quarters*, Arraya wondered as she walked along the empty passageways. *Especially given that many of them can't move as well as us apprentices. They have to climb that many more stairs. Well, unless they have some way of using magic to make their way up.*

The great hall was half-filled with apprentices, some commoners, and, more importantly, warmth. Arraya stumbled towards a table near the fire, stopping only long enough to pick up a bowl of stew, before she settled into a seat in front of the fire.

The ambient heat from the blaze warmed her skin, while the hot stew, filled with chunks of meat and heavy vegetables, filled her achingly empty stomach and sent tendrils of warmth radiating outward. By the time she had finished the bowl, she felt warm but was nearly asleep.

She was very grateful the apprentice quarters were just above the great hall as she climbed the stone steps, even more exhausted than before but now warm and comfortable. Arraya found her own quarters, forced herself to place a new log in her fireplace atop the glowing embers, and stirred them into open flame again. Satisfied that the fire wouldn't burn out anytime soon, she slipped between the covers of her bed and was quickly lost to darkness.

Unfortunately, darkness did not bring peace – it brought dreams. Arraya was never certain if her dreams were merely illusions of her imagination, or memories that she could not recall in her waking hours. The most vivid of them, so real she could touch and taste and smell them, she believed were visions: brief glimpses of past, present, and future.

She had asked Master Shallum about such visions once. Arraya could still recall the conversation.

Master Shallum studied her with an intense gaze. "What do these visions show you?"

"I'm not sure," Arraya answered him. "War, blood, fire, death. So much death."

"Do you have any sense of when?" the Magi asked her.

"No. Sometimes I think it's long ago – before I was born, even. But sometimes I think it's the future. Sometimes I think I see glimpses of myself, but I'm never sure."

"Why aren't you sure?" he queried her, his voice gentle.

"If it's me, it's an older me. My face and hands are covered in blood and dirt. My robes are soaked in it. And I see only for a moment, and then I'm gone."

"Sometimes a Magi will have visions of the future," Shallum explained slowly. "Or sometimes, glimpses of a past

necessary for us to proceed to our destinies. But it is difficult and dangerous to act on such visions."

"Why?" Arraya wanted to know.

"In seeking to prevent such a vision from becoming reality, you may inadvertently bring it to pass. Act carefully, with foresight and planning." He smiled at Arraya. "Do you know why we are called Magi?"

The apprentice shook her head.

"We are called the Magi because the true kings believed us wise. We know a great many things about how the world was and is and is to come. Much of that wisdom is from our studies – you understand well the depth and breadth of your education."

The master closed his eyes in contemplation. "But some of our knowledge is what the magic shows us. As a Magi, you will know things that you should not. You will have knowledge that an educated mortal would not."

"I understand," she said, bowing her head reverently.

"No, you do not," Shallum corrected her gently. "But someday, you shall."

Arraya's dreams were not those vivid images of visions. They were the far more common variety, though no less unsettling: nightmares of failure.

In some nightmares, she was cast out by the Magi. In others, she was struck down by servants of the Dark One. Sometimes, she destroyed herself with magic. In all of them, though, she failed – failed to become a Magi, failed to save herself, failed to save others.

***

Light peeked through the wax paper-covered slits in the wall, and slowly Arraya surfaced from her deep sleep like a swimmer from dark waters. The red-headed apprentice normally awoke quickly, but now she slowly opened her eyes, her mind still churning from the disturbing images of her own imagination.

The bed, layered thickly with blankets, was still warm, but her exposed face was cold from the chilly air in her room. A glance showed her fireplace was still and dark, without even the glow of embers to give warmth.

Reluctantly, she slipped out from under her warm covers and quickly placed two logs in the hearth. She poked at the cold ashes in vain, trying to find some trace of a spark but to no avail. Instead, she set the poker aside and summoned a whisper of the magic. She imagined the warmth of the sun, its brilliant light filling her up like a trickle of water into a cup. When she felt she could hold no more, she breathed out and extended her hand.

Fire leaped from her fingertips and brushed the dried brown wood golden. Instantly the dry kindling burst into flame, with the heavier logs following suit. Arraya breathed out more of the power, encouraging the small flame into a blazing fire, the wood crackling with heat as the supernatural fire feasted hungrily upon it.

She fed a third log to the fire, and then retreated to her still-warm bed and its heavy blankets. The apprentice snuggled back in, waiting patiently for the room to warm.

Hunger gnawed at her stomach, but she forced herself to wait for the fire. The angle of the light filtering through her wax paper windows suggested it was morning, and she was in no hurry to rush downstairs to the cold great hall for her customary bowl of porridge.

At last, her face warmed from the crackling blaze in the hearth. She slipped again from her bed, reveling in the luxurious warmth of the fire. The sleepy haze in her head almost completely cleared now, she decided to clean up before she descended to the great hall for breakfast. Four days of filth and sweat clung to her from the last intensive training session, and cleanliness would be a nice luxury.

The apprentice tested the pot of water above the hearth with her fingertip and found it satisfactorily warm. After ensuring her door was bolted shut, she slipped off her soiled robe and retrieved a scrap of clean cloth. Seating herself in front of the fire, she dipped the cloth in the warm water and slowly scrubbed the dirt and sweat from her skin. When she had finished, she plunged the robe and the scrap of cloth into the warm water repeatedly, leaving the water grimy and dark.

She hung the now-clean robe beside the fire to dry and slipped into her other garment. *I wonder what it's like to be a Magi,* she pondered. *I've heard they have as many robes as they like, while we apprentices only have two.*

Allowing the idle thought to slide away, she unbolted her door and descended to the great hall for breakfast.

***

Arraya was surprised to find she had arrived in the hall early. The large pot of porridge hanging over the hearth was hardly touched. She took a moment to find a bowl and spoon, and then ladled her breakfast into the bowl. The heat of the porridge warmed her bowl and her hands while she found a seat near the hearth.

She had barely managed a few mouthfuls of food before her master seated himself across the table from her. "Apprentice," he greeted Arraya.

She swallowed hastily. "Master," she said with a reverent bow of her head once her mouth was clear. The hot porridge burned all the way down to her stomach, but she forced herself not to wince.

"You did not rest well," he commented.

How does he always know? she wondered. "No, master," she concurred as she kept working on her breakfast.

"Visions?" Shallum asked.

Arraya shook her head. "Only dreams," she said. "Enough to disturb my sleep. Not enough to worry about now."

He smiled at her. "You show wisdom for your age." He rose to his feet and returned a few minutes later with his own bowl of porridge and a tankard of milk.

They ate in companionable silence for several minutes before Arraya worked up the courage to ask, "Why are we meeting with the Council?"

"There is one lesson I've never seemed to be able to teach you," he commented wryly.

"Master?" she said, confused by the change in subject.

"Patience." He smiled broadly as he took another spoonful of porridge. "You never want to wait to know. You always want to know *now*."

Arraya was slow in speaking, weighing her words carefully before giving them voice. "Master, I am more useful when I understand what is going on, and why it is happening. If I must only react in the Council meeting, I am more likely to make a mistake."

"And you fear the Council," he concluded. Shallum waited for his apprentice to reply, but when she remained mute for nearly half a minute he relented. "Do you understand the nature of fear, Arraya?"

The apprentice watched him as though looking for an escape from a trap. "I'm not sure what you are asking, master."

"Why do we fear?" he asked. When Arraya's expression didn't change, he explained. "Fear is a natural part of all living things, apprentice. Fear is a survival trait. Fear helps us avoid injury; fear warns us when danger is near; fear checks our ambitions. Fear is a *good* thing." He shook his head. "Save when you allow it to control you, apprentice. Fear is your advisor, not your ruler. You, ultimately, choose your own actions."

Arraya puzzled over the words. "I'm not sure what you're saying, master."

"Your fear of the Council is irrational," he said. "I know very well what you fear, apprentice: you fear failure. You fear rejection. You fear you will not become a Magi."

Shallum's voice was soft and warm. "The Council does not train you, nor do they decide to elevate you or cast you out. Their authority began and ended with their decision to allow me to apprentice you."

"What do you mean, the Council doesn't decide to elevate me or cast me out?" Arraya asked defensively. "Everyone knows the Council of Magi choose their own members!"

Shallum's shoulders shook with barely restrained laughter. "Apprentice, when you started your training, you knew many things. Do you remember when we began your training in the elements?"

Arraya's face burned in embarrassment.

"You *do* remember," the Magi said with a smile.

Wind, fire, water, earth, lighting. There are five ways to express the power of true magic. The lesson floated through Arraya's mind unbidden, the words in Shallum's voice. *You have felt the rush of the wind, the burn of fire, the quenching of water, the unstoppable rumble of the earth, and the brilliance of lightning. The true magic can take on each of their forms, as willed by the Magi. None of them reign supreme; each countered by another.*

And she recalled the instruction that followed as Arraya learned to summon each of the elements herself: the heat of flame dancing from her fingertips, the whisper of a summoned wind, the ground itself quaking beneath her feet at her will, the congealing bubble of water in her palm, and the flash of lightning and crack of thunder, small in scope but no less majestic.

"*Every Magi learns to use all five elements,*" Shallum told her in a never-forgotten combat lesson. "*The servants of the Dark One often use only a single element, but you must be ready to defend against an enemy that could use any of them.*" He smiled at her. "*Each element can be neutralized by another, but it is always easier to defend than attack...when done properly.*"

And so the training had begun. Arraya had already known how to conjure each of the elements and manipulate them to her will, so it became a sort of game, the apprentice varying her choices to try to penetrate the master's defenses.

"*Most Magi choose fire when it is time to strike,*" Shallum had told her during a break in their training. "*So, too, do many of the Dark One's minions.*"

"*Why, master?*" she had asked.

"*Of each of the elements, fire is the most destructive. Water and wind may unbalance your foe, earth may sweep him from his feet, and lightning may shock him. But fire burns, and fire hurts. It inflicts pain that disrupts your foe's concentration, his own ability to use magic. Against a mortal, fire will be most disruptive to his ability to wield a weapon.*

"*Above all, you must be prepared to defend against fire.*"

And so Arraya had tried. As Shallum now launched attacks against her, she tried to quench the fire with water, tried to smother it with earth. Each time, it burned through her defenses and scorched her — just enough for her to acknowledge she had lost.

"You must do better," Shallum had warned her. "Your foes will attack you without reserve. Feel the true magic! Do not think, do!"

As her confidence waned, so too did her ability. As Shallum's disappointment grew, so too did Arraya's inability to protect herself. "Counter!" Shallum had called. "Counter, counter, counter!"

In a flash of insight, Arraya had an idea – or perhaps a memory. She remembered, as a child, watching a wild fire sweep across dry grass during one of the drought years, the fire whipped into waves of flame by heavy winds.

As Shallum launched a final gout of flame at her, Arraya conjured the strongest burst of wind she could manage. The fire stopped between them, held at bay by the apprentice's will. Shallum had smiled at her. "Well done. I wondered how long you would try to destroy the fire. Protecting yourself does not mean an attack must be utterly destroyed; it only needs to be deflected." He winked. "I hoped you'd figure it out before your face was entirely burned."

"You knew many things," Shallum continued as Arraya's mind clicked back to the present moment. "You thought you understood everything, but there was so much you were wrong about." He frowned. "Now is not the time to initiate you into the secrets of the Magi, but believe me when I tell you this: the Council of Magi do not control your fate. Only you do."

He rose with his now-empty bowl in hand. "Come, apprentice. The Council will be meeting soon."

***

The Council's meeting place was in the eastern tower, at the very peak. Arraya had only climbed the long winding staircase once in her lifetime; as a small child, she had been brought before the twelve Magi to determine whether she would be trained.

Now, as she climbed the same staircase in dim light and with cold drafts breathing on her neck, she could only think one thing: *it's so much smaller than I remembered.*

She had to laugh at herself as she continued the climb, staying close to Shallum. *Of course it's smaller than I remembered. What was I, four winters old when I climbed this last time? Everything would have been much, much bigger since I was so small.*

The bit of cheer the remembrance had brought dissipated as she continued the long climb. *There's way too much time to think about this. Why would Master Shallum bring me to the Council now? I doubt it's because he thinks I'm ready to become a full Magi. But he said the Council didn't control my fate anymore. Was that true, or was he lying to me? If he chooses to end my apprenticeship, would he have to bring me before the Council to do it?*

The apprentice stumbled on the steps. Shallum didn't slow or turn, and Arraya straightened and hurried to catch up. *Quit thinking so much, Arraya,* she told herself. *Thinking won't change a thing about what's happening. Be prepared, but live in the moment.*

Live in the moment.

The Council door stood open with two apprentices standing at the entry, looking out. Shallum brushed between them without a word, but Arraya stopped to join them. *Apprentices don't belong in meetings of the Council*, she remembered.

Shallum looked back at her and frowned. "Apprentice, join me."

Arraya inclined her head and hurried into the chamber. She couldn't miss the gazes of the two apprentices, though, and could read their question on their expressions: *Why is she being called into the Council?*

The doors boomed shut behind Arraya, and she fought not to jump. Concentrating solely on Shallum, she hurried to join him, then stood behind him as he seated himself in one of the twelve chairs ringing the Council chamber.

"So the circle closes," one of the Magi intoned.

"The circle closes," the other eleven repeated.

Arraya stood straight, her mouth shut but eyes wide as she snuck looks around the room.

The chamber itself was far from ornate. Its single decoration was a very large circular rug, perhaps ten yards across, dyed in deep reds and purples. Twelve chairs rested on the outside edge of the rug, plain-looking but each carved from a single log, with no seams or joints of any kind. The openings in the wall for light were covered not with wax paper, but with actual glass. Torches were mounted in sconces around the room, but were unlit – the dawn sun provided all the light the chamber needed.

"Why have you summoned the Council to meeting, Shallum?" the youngest of the Magi asked, a man Arraya estimated to be sixty years old.

If he's the youngest at sixty, how long will I be here before I'm a Magi? she asked herself. *My training will apparently take a lot longer than I thought.*

"I have called this meeting of the Wise to discuss the Imposter-King," Shallum replied steadily, "and the destiny of Letale."

Hushed words were exchanged around the circle of Magi. "Do you have some new insight into the Mists?"

Shallum bowed his head. "With your permission, fellow Magi," he said humbly.

"Speak," an old crone of a woman rasped. "This is why you summoned us, is it not? Bring us to the heart of the matter, and quickly."

Arraya's teacher bowed his head again. "The Imposter-King's seat upon the throne is secure only because there is no heir to the true King left alive," Shallum said slowly. "Without another heir, the Imposter-King's rule is secure because there is no one left for the people and the nobility to rally under."

"You speak what we all know," a grey-haired Magi in dark-stained robes waved his hand impatiently.

"With the death of the last heir twelve years ago," Shallum continued to ramble, undeterred, "we, too, have had no focus. We are considered outlaws and a danger to the Imposter-King. Our power is hidden far away, ineffective without a rightful ruler to support."

The rest of the Magi began to lean forward in their chairs. Arraya found herself hanging on every word from Shallum's lips. *What is he getting at? Is he going to propose the Magi seize power?*

"Each of us understands these things," Shallum said placidly. "But in my meditations, I have seen a solution. I have *Seen* a solution."

"A vision," the old crone murmured. "A gift from Aither."

"I have seen a vision," Shallum confirmed. "An heir still lives in the city of Jepitsa, undiscovered by our foe and hidden from us...until now."

That seized attention around the room, and the murmurs became louder. *An heir?* Arraya thought blankly. *After eleven years, there's suddenly another heir?*

"Who is this heir?" one of the Magi asked, a man whose pate had been hairless as long as Arraya could remember.

"I know not his name," Shallum admitted. "I have seen only his likeness: a dark-haired boy of perhaps sixteen winters. He wore the clothes and presence of a commoner, not a noble."

"An heir hidden at birth," the crone breathed. "Perhaps the last true King understood the danger and hid away an heir, should the worst come to pass. And now it has."

"What do you chart as the Council's path?" the youngest of the Magi inquired.

"I propose nothing for the Council," Shallum replied calmly, "only myself." He waited for the murmurs to subside before adding, "I intend to travel to Jepitsa and find the heir, and return him safely here."

"A bold plan," the bald Magi commented. "It is dangerous for a Magi to travel to the heart of the Imposter-King's territory. There may be servants of the Dark One lying in ambush, or even those who follow the Imposter-King in good faith. We are his enemies, of course."

"That is why I choose only to hazard myself," Shallum said with another incline of his head. "I would not wish to put another in danger. I alone will travel the paths to Jepitsa and risk our enemies. With this Council's blessing, of course," he added.

"And your apprentice?" the crone asked. "Will she travel with you as well?"

"No," Shallum replied with an adamant shake of his head. "She shall remain here to train."

Murmurs again filled the air, longer this time. *Master Shallum going to Jepitsa? If he dies there, I may never have a master again.* A lump formed in her throat, inexplicably wedged there. *If he goes alone and fails, I may never become a Magi.*

"Master," she whispered in his ear. "Please, let me go with you."

He shook his head slowly. "Arraya," he murmured sadly, "you are my apprentice, and you have within you the seeds of greatness and wisdom. You still have much to learn, however, and I will not risk your safety in Jepitsa. It must be me alone."

"Master…"

He shook his head, and she straightened. *I've seen that look too many times. He will not allow me to go.*

"This Council bestows its blessing upon you," the crone said. "May the Aither watch over you and guide you."

Shallum bowed his head and rose to his feet. "Then with your blessing, I depart."

Without further word, the Magi strode from the chamber. Arraya froze for a moment, then hurried in his wake, her mind desperately searching for a way to attach herself to his mission. *I can't let him go alone. If he goes alone and fails, I have no future here.*

III

THE SUN WAS JUST PEEKING over the horizon when Ben, Corin, and Zeke finally set foot inside Riverfront. Ben was grateful to be back among the familiar rows of rundown shacks, the open fire pits, and even the hum of mosquitoes. To Ben's ear, the buzzing pests sounded sweeter than any music he had heard in a long time.

Riverfront had been a nickname Corin had come up with for the poor houses, but it had stuck and even spread. The little "city" consisted of several rows of rickety shacks, with open windows and walls of weathered wood, built along the bank of the mighty Key River. In the spring, flood waters would approach Riverfront but never quite seemed to reach high enough to wash away the houses.

All of the inhabitants of the slum lived with a constant, low-level fear that Riverfront would be burned to the ground. There always seemed to be distant talk from the nobility of purging the rundown shantytown of its inhabitants and buildings alike, but that talk never progressed into action. Ben speculated that the nobility left it in place because it effectively kept all of the "undesirables" in one place, sequestered from more proper society.

That, and it's not like anyone else wants the land we're using, Ben thought. Riverfront was always humid and filled with mosquitoes – the pests seemed to thrive in the wet conditions. While the spring waters never quite reached the shanties, it was never far away, either. Ben doubted nobility would want to live in such danger.

No matter what the nobility thinks of it, though, it's home, Ben thought with a small smile. *It's dirty and muddy and overrun with bloodsuckers, but it's home.*

Corin hid a yawn with the back of her hand. "I'm going to get some sleep," she declared. "That was a long night."

"Me, too," Zeke agreed. "Going to come to the house, too?" he asked Ben.

Ben shook his head. "I'll head that way in a little while, but first I want to clean up and maybe go to the Market."

"Don't forget the book for Alan," Corin warned. "He would be *very* upset if we forgot it."

Ben pulled the book from under his shirt. In spite of the night's escapades, including several forays into the cold creek water, the book's leather covering had ensured its survival. "I've got it right here," he ensured. "I'll keep it with me until I can give it to Alan."

"Good," Corin said in sleepy satisfaction.

Ben parted ways with his friends, heading down to a quiet, secluded little hollow on the river. Stopping only to stash his knife, the book, and his own bag of purloined valuables under a bush, he walked straight into the cool river waters without stopping to remove his clothes.

The water refreshed him. The mad events of the night seemed to ebb away as he scrubbed the mud out of his clothes and hair. *Definitely not going to go with Alan's plan next time*, he decided. *Next time, I plan it from the beginning, and make sure we have a way out before we go in. No more improvising.* He ducked his head under the surface, felt his hair tugged by the currents. He emerged again a moment later, enjoying the water cascading down his back.

Ben waded out of the river again and sat down on the bank to watch the dawn. The sun filled the morning skies with reds and oranges as the stars retreated before its advance. Ben laid back on the grass as the sun's rays soaked into him and his wet clothes. As the morning amber sky faded into blues, he sat patiently as the sun dried him out.

It was a double-edged sword, though, and he felt himself growing ever-sleepier in the warm sunshine. It took all his resolve to stand up rather than lay back and allow sleep to take him. His eyelids seemed to be lead-lined as he stopped at the bush to recover his stashed goods from the night's heist. After securing the book back under his shirt and his bag and dagger on his belt, he headed back into Riverfront.

The shantytown had sprung to life while he was bathing. Smoke from cooking fires rose in thin black tendrils; kids ran amok, playing and hollering and screaming. The older members of Riverfront – almost none older than twenty-five – watched the children in amusement, or undertook the dozens of tasks necessary for everyday life.

Ben headed straight for the Market. *Maybe the Market is why they let Riverfront stand,* he pondered. *After all, even the nobility wants things they can't have.*

The Market, as it was ubiquitously known, had much in common with other markets across all of the country. The staples for everyday living could be found there: bread, meat, wild berries, leather, wool, spun cloth, and even occasionally completely sewn garments. Items that were restricted inside Jepitsa proper could also be found, if one knew where to look and who to ask: knives, swords, bows, quivers of arrows, and armor. In darkened corners and booths, there was a quiet but brisk exchange of goods that had been liberated from the wealthy.

It was for those items that the nobility would sometimes appear, dressed in homespun robes or cloaks and attempting to maintain anonymity. The residents of Riverfront knew better. The nobility were betrayed by their clean fingernails, their well-groomed beards, their soft hands. Yet both the regulars and the nobles pretended otherwise – the visits by the wealthy often brought gold into Riverfront, and no one was willing to sacrifice that for the personal satisfaction of exposing the nobility to the masses.

Ben's objective was one such booth: Janet Eyesworth, usually called Plain Jane, was among the best fences he knew and would offer him good, though not the best, prices. *Of course, Plain Jane won't try to rob me on the backside,* he knew. *The nobles joke that there's no honor among thieves, but there are some of us who do play fair. Well,* he amended, *fair to each other, anyway.*

The young thief moved past several stalls belonging to fences he'd dealt with previously – "Fats" Orson, nicknamed for his girth; "Feathers" Roy, who was almost never seen without a tail feather in his hat; and the Terrible Twins, Bo and Lana, two siblings who were completely opposite in temperament but equally cutthroat in bargaining.

Finally he reached Plain Jane's stall and was surprised to find it closed up. *She's always open,* Ben thought warily. *Why would she be closed up in the morning when there's the most people around?* He walked around to the back of the stall and found the door. He reached up to knock, but thought better of it and instead leaned in, pressing his ear to the rough wood. *This better be worth the slivers I'll have to ask Corin or Zeke to dig out later,* he thought.

For a long moment, he heard nothing. Hesitantly, he reached up and covered his other ear to block out the noises of the market around him.

"Yes, I have it," Plain Jane was saying in a very low voice. "But I can't give it to you for two hundred."

"That was the contract we negotiated," a man's voice answered her. "Are you trying to back out of a deal with me now, Janet?"

Plain Jane was silent, and for several long moments all Ben could hear was the thudding of his own heartbeat in his ears. Finally, she said, "It cost me two-ten to acquire. I'm not going to pay you ten coin to take it off my hands."

The man chuckled. "That's your problem, not mine. I somehow doubt you're going to find someone else who will make use of it."

"Two-fifty," Plain Jane stated. "It's still a bargain at that price."

"Two hundred, as we already agreed upon," the man said flatly. "After all, I'm sure the Royal Guard would love to hear where this particular item can be found."

"You're a bastard," Plain Jane replied.

"Do we have a deal?"

"No." A chair creaked, and Ben guessed the fence had stood up. "Turn me in and you'll never get your precious item."

The man laughed. "Fine, Janet. Have it your way." Another creaking of wood followed the words.

Ben glanced around, looking for a place to hide. *This conversation's about to be over.* He glanced up, considering the possibility of quickly climbing to the roof of the short wooden booth, but rejected it just as quickly – he would no doubt make a racket that would quickly expose him.

He settled instead for a quick jog down to the other side of the booth beside Plain Jane's storefront. He stepped around the corner and leaned against the wall. Ben crossed his arms and waited. *Someone is definitely trying to get the better of Plain Jane. Wonder what she's got that's worth two hundred coin? That's a lot of gold for one object, no matter what it is.*

His speculation was interrupted by the whine of rusty hinges, followed by the slam of a wooden door. Ben waited, counting to ten in long, slow breaths. *I'd love to know who was trying to force her into a deal, but that's not important right now. If that was some angry noble, the last thing I want to do is draw attention from him.* He patted his inside pocket. *Especially with what I'm carrying right now.*

Finally, Ben straightened and turned the corner. As he'd expected, there was no one in sight behind the long row of wooden stalls. *Perfect. Whoever he was is long gone.* It took only a moment to reach Plain Jane's door. He stopped and knocked.

"C'min," the fence called.

Ben pushed the door open. Plain Jane was sitting in a chair at the front counter of the booth, the room lit by an open skylight. "Ben!" she called in delight.

Plain Jane had earned her nickname honestly. Her mousy brown hair was pulled back into a simple, shoulder-length ponytail. Her cheekbones were neither high nor striking. Her eyes were a flat blue. Her dress was floor-length, brown, and rough – Ben always thought it looked like burlap. But the dull appearance camouflaged her shrewd deal making and sharp business sense.

"So what have you brought me today?"

Ben smiled and withdrew his small bag of loot he'd carried out of the Rittin estate. "First things first," he said casually as he unbuttoned the bag and spilled the contents out onto the countertop for Plain Jane to examine.

"Oh," she murmured as several gems scattered across the rough-hewn surface. "Oh, my." She looked up at him. "You've been very bad."

"Or rather, very good," Ben said with a very slight smile.

Plain Jane picked up several of the gems one by one, turning them over in her hands to view each angle. With each one, she finished by holding it up to the skylight to check its clarity and brilliance. She was silent through it all, aside from "ooohs" and "aaaahs" and the occasional "hmm."

Ben waited patiently for the fence to finish her inspection. *Let her take her time. If I push her, I'll probably get less than if she has time to view them all carefully and consider it. She won't rush, so I won't, either.* He dreamed what he would do with the extra gold. *Maybe I'll buy myself a new knife. Swords aren't practical – they're too big and they can't be concealed. Armor would just slow me down. Maybe, if there's enough, I could get Zeke a new bow and Corin a new knife, too.*

His attention came back to the fence as she put the last gem down. "I normally don't ask this, but I have to know – where did you acquire these gems?"

Ben frowned. "You have never needed to know before," he said slowly. "Why now?"

52

Plain Jane's smile was faint. "They're the most impressive pieces of glass I've seen in a long time, Ben."

The thief's heart sunk. "Glass?" he repeated dumbly.

The woman nodded. "All but two of them are glass," she said. "Decoys, I'd guess, to hide the truly valuable gemstones." Plain Jane picked up two of the stones – one green-tinted, one red-tinted. "These two are genuine." She looked up sharply at him. "But to give you an offer, I have to know where these came from."

"Why?" he asked.

"Because they *are* impressive, and the owner went to the effort of attempting to camouflage them. That usually means he'll be looking for them, and unless they've traveled some distance, there's a good chance some buyers from the Guard will be here looking for them as well."

Ben grimaced. Plain Jane's explanation made perfect sense. While the Jepitsa nobles tolerated Riverfront and the Market, they had not hesitated to arrest fences who'd been found in possession of goods liberated from their wealthy owners in the city proper. *Of course*, Ben chided himself. *Lord Rittin will have someone here before long.*

"Lord Rittin," he admitted reluctantly.

Plain Jane nodded. "I should have guessed that," she said shortly. "There's only a few nobles in Jepitsa that would have that kind of wealth, and you don't usually travel outside the area." She studied the sunlight through one of the sparkling gems again. "I can give you fifteen for the pair."

"Fifteen!" Ben gaped at her. "That's robbery!"

"No," Plain Jane said smoothly, "what *you* did is robbery. But I'm going to have to sell these to Cowardly Wade, and he'll give me twenty-five for them." She shook her head. "He's the only one who travels far enough to make sure Rittin doesn't find them."

Ben sighed. "Fine, I'll take it." He hesitated. "I have something else, too," he said slowly. "I'm not looking to sell it, but I want to know what it is."

Plain Jane was already counting out Ben's fifteen gold coins, a tenth of what the thief had hoped to walk away with in his pocket. "What is it?" she asked distractedly.

Ben withdrew the book from his pocket and unwrapped its leather binding, then set it down on the counter beside the fake gemstones. Plain Jane set down a stack of coins on the counter and then picked up the book. She turned it over slowly in her hands as Ben pocketed his gold.

"Lord Rittin had this, too?" she asked.

Ben nodded. "What is it?"

"Trouble," she said slowly. "But believe me, you don't want to be caught with this book."

"Jane," he asked again. "What...?"

"It's the builder's book," she said. "For Key Castle."

"The what?" Ben asked. "What's that?"

"It's the castle in the center of Jepitsa, Ben. The biggest, most heavily guarded fortress in the entire country."

"I know what Key Castle is," Ben said in exasperation. "What's a builder's book?"

"Ah." Plain Jane smirked – she had known all along what he was asking. "A builder's book is the personal notes, plans, and records of the chief architect and designer for a structure. In this case, it has pretty much every stone in Key Castle mapped out – every passage, every well, every room, every door."

Why would Alan want all that information about Key Castle? The answer was obvious. *He's planning on stealing something from the King himself? He's going to get us all killed!*

Ben reached for the book, but Plain Jane held it back for a moment. "I'm serious, Ben. You should burn this and pretend you never found it."

"Can't do that," Ben grunted.

"Ben, if you get caught with this, you'll be hung within the hour. This book is three hundred years old and has every secret of Key Castle's construction. It's worth the life of every soul in Riverfront." Plain Jane's voice was serious, but so low it was hard to hear. "Please, Ben. Burn it."

She finally yielded the book. Ben carefully wrapped it in its leather bindings again and slid it under his shirt.

"I'm sorry," he said at last. "But this one wasn't for me."

Plain Jane met his eyes steadily. "It was for Alan, wasn't it?" When Ben didn't answer, she shook her head. "He's going to get you and Zeke and that pretty girl you're always bringing around all killed. He's trouble, Ben."

"You've been telling me that for two years," Ben retorted irritably. "It'll be fine."

"Ben, please…" she tried again.

He turned and walked away without saying goodbye.

The sun was well up in the sky when Ben stepped out into the bright open air. He quickly circled Plain Jane's booth once to ensure no one was following him, then headed into the market proper with a pocketful of coin.

I might have protested a bit, Ben reflected, *but I did pretty well with those two gems. It's not the fortune I thought it was, but this will keep me going for a long time.*

His next stop was at Feather's booth. Roy always had a stock of top-grade blades and bows under the counter. He haggled with the emaciated man for nearly twenty minutes before laying a gold coin on the counter in exchange for two newly-forged, never-sharpened daggers. In spite of his best effort, though, he came away without a bow – Feather's insistence on *six gold coin* for a single bow was more than Ben could part with.

As he walked away, he glanced back enviously at the ebony weapon, even as Feather stashed it under his counter again. He pushed it out of his mind, though – if he spent all his wealth that quickly, he'd soon be penniless and hungry again.

He traded another gold coin for a roasted chicken and a handful of silver at another booth. He walked slowly through the broad alleyway of the market, then, tearing off strips of cooked and seasoned meat with his fingers and enjoying himself. He casually glanced through other goods for sale: fabrics from burlap to silk, slightly overripe fruits from well beyond Jepitsa, fresh milk and cheese, tools ranging from hammers to axes to saws. Ben was quick enough to see other goods hidden away as well: gemstones, swords, steel arrowheads, and other contraband.

Ben's next stop, though, was his favorite in the entire market, and had been as long as he could remember: Bo's little booth, where he had sculpted water.

Sculpted water was the nickname for the beautiful artwork. Ben was tempted, as always, to dump out all the gold he was carrying in exchange for one of the carved boards – but even with his proceeds from the heist at Lord Rittin's manor, he didn't have enough. Still, he had to stop and watch as Bo laid out one of the boards in the sunshine.

The merchant retreated into his stall to retrieve a cup of water. With a smile in Ben's direction, and with more than a few people watching, he slowly dribbled water from the pewter cup onto the seemingly-flat wooden board.

As if by magic, the water began to slowly push across the board. Under Bo's careful guidance, the image took shape – a shimmering image of a horse rearing up, its hooves extended as though to defend or strike a predator. The sun's rays were caught by the watery horse, seeming to set it ablaze with brilliant light and fire.

Sculpted water boards, Ben knew, were difficult to carve and extremely expensive. The best of the boards were carved so subtly and carefully that the naked eye could not perceive the image were the board dry; only the slow drip of water would reveal it. However, only royalty could indulge the gold it cost to have such a masterpiece. Ben could still remember, as a small child, watching one such board shimmer in the sunlight, capturing his imagination.

Ben only had a few minutes to watch and admire the artwork; almost immediately after Bo put the sculpted water on display, a tall man in a long leather coat produced a bag of gold and began haggling with the merchant. When they had finished, the man picked up the board and dumped the water off, patted it dry with a rag, and tucked it under his jacket.

The thief sighed. *Someday, I'll have one of those*, he promised himself. *If nothing else, I'll have sculpted water.*

With the display of sculpted water gone, Ben continued his easy walk down the Market.

Ben always felt the need to stop at the largest booth in the Market, and he had no reason not to today. The booth was almost twice the size of Plain Jane's stall, and not just because it was wider or longer. The booth was *taller* as well to accommodate the merchant within.

Corpakle stood a solid handspan higher than any other man in the Market. He was a wall of solid muscle, with cords of strength that seemed to undulate under his skin when he moved. He often worked bare chested, wearing only a pair of breeches and boots even while selling his wares from the booth.

His wares were always interesting.

The massive man was a blacksmith of the highest order – when he so chose, he could forge a sword or dagger that would put Feather's goods to shame. According to rumors Ben had heard, the King himself wore a sword that Corpakle had forged in this very booth. Ben had held one of his daggers once and once only – Alan carried it as his personal weapon, and most prized possession.

However, Corpakle never had weapons on display. Ben wasn't sure why he never seemed to have any to sell. The only time Ben had dared ask the massive blacksmith about it, he had earned a glare that he still saw in his nightmares.

Instead of weapons, the man always had a variety of gadgets for sale. They were finely-crafted, finely-honed tools. Ben usually had no idea what they were for, but they often disappeared into the city proper, paid for by Jepitsa gold.

"Good morning, Pak!" Ben called as he stepped up to the booth, picking up a small hand tool of some sort.

The giant man grunted a wordless greeting.

Ben turned the tool over in his hands. One end sported a rotating handle, which turned an interior blade of some sort; the other end was a coarse mesh. "What's this for, Pak?" he asked the man. Ben knew the man enjoyed talking about his wares, all of which Corpakle crafted himself in the big booth. There was no fire burning in the forge today, but other tools of a blacksmith's trade were arranged neatly on wall hooks – hammers, tongs, and dozens of tools that Ben couldn't identify.

"Grinding meat," Pak said, easy and slow. "Take a tough cut of meat from an old animal and grind it through; it comes out the other side tender and ready to cook."

"Huh," Ben mused, setting it down. "Are all these tools for cooking?" he asked, waving vaguely at the steel tools lining the front of the booth.

"No," Pak said. "There are tools for all professions here – drills for boring holes through wood, stone, or metal, grinders for reducing coarse materials to fine ones, or wheat and corn to flour, a drill and seeder for planting garden rows more quickly than can be done by hand…"

The big man went on at length, but Ben tuned him out after a bit. In some ways he found it more exciting to imagine the uses of such exotic devices than to know the mundane truth of the tools. They were all built with absolute precision: rotating parts that meshed perfectly to allow them to turn smoothly in his hand a hundred times without any sign of wear, or any friction he could feel in his hands. In his mind, they were devices with magical imbuement, relying on invisible power and becoming instruments of war.

Not that magic is a good thing. He couldn't suppress his shudder. Only a few people in all the world could use magic in its raw form – the Magi. Everyone in Riverfront had heard the stories of the Magi and their attempts to overthrow the King. Very little was officially known about the Magi, but rumors were whispered in back alleys and taverns and around the campfire at night: stories of the dark forces the Magi harnessed, tales of the corrupting influence of magic, and fables warning of the risks and consequences of dealing with powers beyond what mortals should dabble in, all under the shadow of the Dark One, the Aither.

Ben realized then that Corpakle had stopped talking. He shook himself out of revere, glanced up at the man and lamely asked, "What were you saying?"

The big man chuckled and shook his head. "And people accuse me of being short-minded."

"It's not like you're a *real* giant," Ben retorted.

Corpakle rolled his eyes. "I wish you'd use the correct term. I am indeed a Rephaim. Please stop suggesting otherwise."

"I've seen Rephaim before," Ben said. "You're a big human, that's all. Rephaim are twice as big as you are!"

The big man sighed. "How many times must we cover this same ground, Ben? I was born a midget for my race. It's one of the reasons I'm here and not in Cosmane with my people, as I would be a liability for them there."

"Everyone knows giants are dumb, too," Ben said, now just needling the big man for the fun of it. *Once I have him started, it's easy to just keep him going.*

"Do you feel the need to insult me at every turn?" Corpakle asked with a hint of irritation. "We have discussed this as well. My people are not 'dumb' or foolish or inferior; we are close to each other in intelligence."

Ben tried to hide his grimace. *Pushed too far.* "I'm sorry," he said placatingly. "I just like to tease you, Pak. You're so easy to get going."

The big man almost instantly became introspective. "I forgive you. I should not indulge my temper so – it is feeds the stereotype of the Rephaim as large, dumb, short-tempered people incapable of higher thought."

The young man hid his smile. *I don't know why Pak is so convinced he's a giant, but it makes for a fun game. Seriously, why does he think anyone believes giants are capable of building gadgets and tools like these?*

"So, Ben," Corpakle asked conversationally, "what does Alan have you doing now?"

"Not stealing from you, of course," Ben teased. "I'm just the official scout; the team will knock your booth over later."

Corpakle chuckled loudly, a pleasant booming sound. "Alan is smarter than that, young thief," he said after his guffaws quieted. "He only tried it once."

"Wait," Ben stopped, holding up a hand. "Alan tried to steal from you once?"

"And only once," Corpakle confirmed. "He tried to slip into my booth under the cover of darkness one night, and I caught him red-handed. After he returned all my goods, and gave me everything else he had in his carry pouch, I allowed him to retain a single blade from my stock as a reminder not to ever try such a foolish act again."

That must have been how he got that dagger, Ben guessed. "I didn't know that."

"Few do," Corpakle said. "He does not brag about his failures." His expression became pensive. "Ben, you have a good heart. I know you are a thief by necessity – you spend your gold freely to support your friends, rather than hoard it for your own personal gain. You should reconsider what you are doing now, following him in that life." The big man hesitated before offering, "I would gladly take you on as an apprentice here, where you could earn an honest living."

Ben shook his head. "Not interested, but thanks for the offer." He grinned at Corpakle. "When I'm old and grey and can't keep up with the game anymore, I'll probably take you up on it."

Corpakle just shook his head as Ben turned his back and walked out into the sunshine.

By the time he had reached the end of the market, the small chicken was almost entirely gone. He stopped only long enough to pick the last of the tender meat from its bones before tossing the carcass to a dog lying near Cowardly Wade's booth. The dog's eyes snapped open and it leapt up to catch the chicken, then immediately sunk back down, gnawing at the bones.

Smiling and whistling a tune, Ben strode jauntily away from the Market towards his home.

Like many of the citizens of Riverfront, Ben shared a shack. The small one room structure sheltered not only himself, but Zeke and two others, Rowan and Brom, both of whom were several years his senior. The four of them were often gone – after all, there was nothing tying them to Riverfront except their friendships – so the shack seldom had more than one or two occupants.

Ben let himself in through the rickety door and found only Zeke asleep on a pile of blankets in the corner. Ben considered following suit, but changed his mind, snagged a blanket, and walked back outside. The sun warmed his skin, and he decided instead to sleep outside to enjoy the heat. He clambered up the side of an old empty barrel and pulled himself up onto the top of the squat, flat-roofed structure.

He spread the blanket out on the roof and then laid down and closed his eyes.

This isn't such a bad life, he decided. *I mean, sure, the guards would have my head if they knew all the things I've stolen over the years. Alan isn't much of a leader. Riverfront isn't the cleanest place in Jepitsa. But Zeke is a good friend, and as long as there are gullible fools like Lord Rittin around, I'll always have plenty to eat. And then there's Corin...*

He smiled as he basked lazily in the sun's warm rays. *Someday I'll score it big, and take her away from here and we'll live like royalty. I was close on this last heist, and if Rittin hadn't left those decoys I'd already be gone from here. Someday soon, though...then neither of us would have to steal ever again. We could be happy and free.*

He felt his weariness wash over him again, but this time he let it take him. *There's no danger here, nothing I have to do until tonight when the Brigands meet. I can just rest.*

IV

THE APPRENTICE OF THE MAGI stood in her greatcoat, arms crossed. "Master, please, let me go with you," she pleaded yet again.

The master shook his head as he lifted a battered leather saddle from its hook. "Arraya, you understand why I cannot take you."

"With all respect, Master Shallum, no, *I don't*," she contradicted. "There's no reason I can't go with you."

The master strode to the chestnut horse waiting patiently. He dropped a padded blanket over the gelding's back, straightened it, then tossed the saddle on with a grunt. "Do I need to go over all these reasons again?"

Arraya's grip on her own arms tightened. "If you are to convince me that I should stay here, yes, you do need to repeat yourself."

The magi flashed a smile over his shoulder at the girl. "You are stubborn and impudent for an apprentice," he commented. "Most Magi don't reach your heights until they are threescore winters or more."

"Master," she said in exasperation.

"Fine, fine," Shallum sighed as he loosened the saddle's cinches, allowing them to fall to the horse's sides. "First, it will be easier for me to enter and leave Jepitsa by myself."

"I could be your daughter," Arraya answered. "No one would expect a man with a daughter to be a member of the Council of Magi. It would make your disguise far more convincing."

The master ignored her as he reached under the chestnut's belly to draw the band across, snugging the saddle in place. "I can also move faster by myself than I can with someone else tagging along behind me."

"I'm your apprentice, and I move fast," Arraya countered. "With the True Magic, I can keep up with anyone. You've commented yourself that I'm far quicker than any other apprentice you've trained!"

"Third," the master continued, "I don't know what I will find. It may take time to scout out and find the King-to-Be. Days, perhaps weeks will be required if he is guarded by someone competent enough to keep him out of the sight of the Imposter-King."

"If I come along," Arraya replied, her voice rising in irritation, "we can cover the ground in half the time. It would be far more efficient and expose you to the dangers of Jepitsa for less time."

"Fourth, Jepitsa is dangerous to our kind," Master Shallum said as he tightened the saddle's back cinch. "Even though it's been twelve years since the last attempt to overthrow the Imposter-King, the guards still seek us out. To be caught in the capital city is a death sentence, or perhaps even worse."

"Worse?" Arraya asked skeptically.

The Magi nodded as he picked up a set of saddlebags, already packed with dried meat and bread, and tossed it across the horse's back behind the saddle. He started tying it in place as he spoke. "An enemy of the Imposter-King, caught in his seat of power? Execution would be swift and simple, and charity is not to be found in his heart. More likely he would use you for his own purposes – enslave you, perhaps, or sell you off."

Arraya shuddered at the thought.

"No, it's better for me to go alone and leave you here in safety." He finished with the saddlebags and returned the stable's small tack room, picking out a leather bridle with a silver bit. "Please, apprentice, understand that I ask you to stay not only for your sake, but for my own. Do you think I would be able to search effectively and with a clear mind, should I know you were in mortal danger with me?"

"Master..." Arraya started.

"Please, Arraya, understand. You are a talented apprentice, but I cannot put your neck in the noose alongside my own. I am willing to risk my own being to find the King-to-Be, but I will not risk yours unless it is utterly necessary."

"I've been training for this my whole life," Arraya protested, her voice sounding weak even to her own ear. "You've taught me the arts yourself. I am capable of helping you find the King-to-Be, and with my help your chances of success are much greater."

Shallum shook his head as he slipped the bit in the horse's mouth, then pulled the bridle over his ears. "No. You are a capable and wonderful student, and I am proud of you, but this is not your time."

"Master," Arraya tried, "have you not told me that the Magi's life is one of service? We sacrifice everything a mortal would value to achieve the power – a power we use in service, not for our own gain. Don't ask me to turn aside from service now!"

The master walked around the horse to its right side, lengthening the stirrup there. "Service, apprentice? How can you serve if you are dead?"

"You've also told me the Magi are willing to sacrifice their lives for their causes and their charges," Arraya said bluntly. "You recognize it and follow that path even with your decisions right now, choosing to ride into Jepitsa, the den of the enemy, without help or assistance. Why do you deny me the same chance to serve?"

"You are not yet a Magi," Shallum rebuked her. "Your time has not yet come. You are determined and disciplined for an apprentice, but until you have reached your full powers it would be foolish for you to risk yourself."

"If I die now in pursuit of the King-to-Be, then I will have saved the Council of Magi the additional years it would have taken for me to be fully trained before I was struck down," she said morbidly.

Shallum moved around to the left side of the horse and began to adjust the stirrup there as well. "Are you still my apprentice, Arraya?" he asked. "Or will you forsake even that to follow me?"

"I am always your apprentice," Arraya answered, dipping her head.

"Then as my apprentice, you need to follow my instructions," Shallum ordered, his tone as inflexible as the mountain itself. "Do you agree?"

"Yes, master," Arraya agreed, not successful at hiding her frustration.

"As an apprentice, you still have much to learn," the master continued. "Do you agree?"

"Yes, master," the apprentice repeated, her voice now contrite.

"Then stay here and learn," he said. "There is much you need to understand before you become a true Magi. There is also much undiscovered."

The later statement caught her off guard. "Undiscovered, master?"

Shallum nodded as he straightened from the stirrup. "Tell me, apprentice: how could someone conceal the King-to-Be from our sight?" he asked. "The visions of the Magi are strong and accurate, and yet someone has deceived us for many winters."

Arraya opened her mouth to speak and then stopped, realizing she had no answer.

Shallum swung himself up on the horse, gathered his reins, and looked down at her. "Understand, apprentice," he said slowly and quietly, "there is no one I would rather have at my side when I ride through the gates of Jepitsa. But you must complete your training before you are ready to risk yourself to the hazard. Your time will come, but it is not now."

The flame-haired girl found she had little else to say. "Goodbye, Master Shallum," she whispered.

"Goodbye, dear Arraya. I will rejoin you here soon."

The apprentice found she could do little else but cross her arms in the voluminous sleeves of the greatcoat and watch as Master Shallum rode off at a slow trot, out under the still-brightening skies of the cold morning, off toward whatever fate had in store for him.

***

Arraya spent the remainder of her morning in the library.

Like the other structures in the hidden redoubt of the Magi, it was a cold building primarily constructed of stone. She suspected it was originally intended to be a great hall of sorts, a place for mustering the troops or celebrating in the wake of a great victory. Stripped of all its furnishings, it would have been a large, empty chamber fitting for hundreds of warriors to meet.

The Magi, however, had repurposed it. A large, rounded fire pit took up the center of the entire structure, five strides across for the apprentice. It was kept filled and burning at all times of the day, one of only two places that could always be counted upon to be warm.

From that central ring bookshelves flared out in straight lines like the spokes of a wheel. The shelves were stacked tightly with dusty tomes from the last hundred years. Any time during the day there would be a half dozen apprentices wandering the shelves, peeking through carefully preserved pages to find knowledge or, far more elusive, *wisdom*.

A second level had been constructed by the Magi and their allies, consisting entirely of wooden planks and supports. Accessible via a ladder, the second floor had an even larger hole over the fire pit, the planks far enough back to prevent a potential fire danger.

The second floor was more open; instead of bookcases stretching as high as Arraya could reach, the racks barely reached her waist. Instead of housing thousands of books, these racks cradled dozens of scrolls – the teachings of the Order of the Magi.

Apprentices were far more often found on the second level than on the cold stone of the first. In part, it was because the scrolls of the Magi were typically seen as more important to the Scions attempting to become Magi themselves; mostly, though, the second level was more popular because it was warmer due to the rising heat from the fire ring.

Arraya was on the second level sitting near the open edge, but instead of reading through a scroll she was perusing a book from the first level.

The apprentice was mildly annoyed that she couldn't set aside her concern for her master well enough to concentrate on the text. *A Magi should be able to focus wholly on the task before her, setting aside the petty, unfocused concerns and worries she may otherwise have.* She had heard Master Shallum tell her those words on several occasions, and she had usually risen to the challenge; now, though, she couldn't seem to shake her unease.

She set down the book beside her and laid back on the wooden floor, soaking up the warmth. *I can't imagine a greater luxury than warmth,* she thought to herself as she closed her eyes. *The people who live outside Cosmane have no idea how good they have it.*

The thump of another body sitting down forced Arraya to open her eyes. *Who is it?*

The almost pure white hair answered her unspoken question. "Jacinta," the apprentice said.

The other girl smiled at her. "Ho, Arraya," she said cheerfully. "Enjoying the warmth?"

"When you live where there's snow year round," Arraya replied with a small smile, "you take the heat when you can find it."

Jacinta nodded, then looked down and picked up the book Arraya had been browsing. "Master Shallum has you reading about the orcs?"

"I was trying to," Arraya said with a shrug. "That book is drier than Cosmane is cold."

The white-haired apprentice offered a sympathetic smile. "Mistress Esther had me reading about the orc clans a month ago. Now she has me reading about the Erixans."

Arraya nodded. "I actually read a book on them a few months ago on the side – a tome called *Secrets of Thunder* by a court adviser to King Hesekah. Lots of speculation about a guild of, depending on who you believe, either secret guardians or assassins."

"Mistress Esther told me *Secrets of Thunder* was nothing but gossip," Jacinta said, making a face. "I had to read *The Island-Nation* instead."

"Is it as bad as Master Shallum suggested?" Arraya asked with a shudder.

"Probably worse." Jacinta said, crossing her legs and leaning in before lowering her voice to a conspiratorial whisper, "So, where's Master Shallum?"

Arraya kept a straight face. *If the other apprentices don't know, it's not my place to tell them.* It was another truism her master had taught her repeatedly. *Knowledge is concentrated power; the more it is spread, the less potent it will be in your hands. Secrets must remain among few or they become as stagnant as standing water, of no use to anyone.*

"The way I hear it," Jacinta continued, her voice still low and quiet, "you and Master Shallum met with the full Council, and then he took a horse from the stables and vanished. Somehow I doubt he went to visit the salamanders."

Arraya snorted at that. "What, are you saying you don't like the salamanders?"

"I *do* like them," Jacinta protested, "but it has nothing to do with this."

The apprentice shrugged. "I won't pretend I understood everything that happened in the Council meeting," she said honestly, "but whatever they sent him to do is important. I probably shouldn't speculate on it."

"So boring," Jacinta sighed. "How long will he be gone?"

Arraya shrugged again. "A few days, a few weeks? I don't know."

"Well, Tawana and I were talking about going to visit the salamanders," the white-haired apprentice began.

"Your masters are going to let you run off for a few days?" Arraya asked skeptically.

"We were going to go for just a day on our next Resting-Day," Jacinta said.

"Isn't it a day either way?" Arraya asked.

"Tawana found a shortcut. If we left the night before, we could be there by morning, spend most of the day there, and be back by dark again." She smiled. "It would be good for you to get out of here, Scrollworm," she teased.

Arraya growled at the reference to her reputation, even among an order of scholars, as an apprentice more eager to read than to go out on adventures like her fellow students.

"You don't *have* to go," Jacinta said placatingly. "Just thought you might want to get out of here for a while."

Arraya sighed. "Maybe I should." She picked up the book again. "I'll think about it."

The other girl rose to her feet gracefully. "We'd love to have you along," she said before departing.

***

The apprentice stopped reading only long enough to eat a small lunch, then spent the rest of the day back in the library curled up with her assigned book. She slowly worked her way through it, but she fully expected she wouldn't remember any of it the next morning. Finally, she gave up on it and walked back to her chambers, feeling utterly exhausted in spite of her lack of activity for the day.

Arraya wrapped herself in a heavy quilt as she paced across her small room, her head still spinning with the day's events. "Another heir," she breathed. "How did we miss him for so long?" She shook her head at herself. "Twelve years since the last heir died at the hands of the Imposter-King, and the Council of the Magi missed all signs until now?" She wrestled with the question. "How could those of us with the True Power have failed to see it for so long?"

"Because we only see what the Aither allows us to see," a voice answered her.

Arraya spun towards the doorway, then immediately dropped into a deep, respectful bow. "Mistress Esther," she said in reverence.

The grey-haired Magi smiled from the doorway. "Apprentice Arraya," she greeted the young woman.

"I'm sorry if I show disrespect, mistress," Arraya said quietly. "I don't mean to question the wisdom of the Council."

"Ah, but you did, apprentice," the Magi said as she glided across the floor to where Arraya knelt on the cold stone floor. "You wonder how a bunch of old Magi could be so blind as to miss something that must be obvious."

Arraya swallowed hard. *Busted.* Her thoughts finally seemed to untangle with the swiftness of a hare. *Think, Arraya, and get yourself out of this. Quickly.* "Mistress, I only wondered how such a thing could be hidden from the eyes of the Council. If an heir exists, shouldn't the Council have been able to see him, divine his existence, before now?"

Esther smiled. "Apprentice, there are many who would deceive us or hide knowledge from us. The Dark One, Erebus, and his minions know that we are the greatest servants of the Light one, the Aither, to still walk this world, and thus the greatest threat to their plans and purposes." Her tone was solemn. "The Imposter-King who sits upon the throne knows, too, that we will act quickly to end his rule should there be another with legitimate right to rule. He perverts the natural order, calling darkness the light and light the darkness."

"But how could the Imposter-King blind the Council?" Arraya asked.

"I know you are young, child, having seen only fifteen winters, but your Master clearly should better educate his pupil." Esther shook her head. "Tell me, apprentice, what do you know of the nature of mortals?"

Arraya frowned at the question. "Mistress, I don't understand how that follows what we have already spoken of."

"Answer my question, and you will understand."

The apprentice's thoughts raced back to her hard earned knowledge. *What is she looking for?* At last, Arraya spoke with slow care. "The mortals who walk this world are creatures of good and evil. They kill, rape, steal, lie – all for personal gain. They sacrifice others to elevate themselves. But some of them are good – the lesser of them often reveal charity and love towards each other, sacrificing their own well-being for another's, or giving to charity."

"But they are the lesser," Esther confirmed. "Those who do not seek their own elevation."

Arraya nodded. "Those with power seldom if ever seek anything but their own elevation, and even acts of charity are calculated to further heighten themselves."

Esther sighed. "Shallum has neglected your education, apprentice."

"Mistress?" Arraya asked, taken aback. *How did I answer incorrectly?*

"Tell me, child," the old Magi asked softly, "What makes a mortal greater or lesser?"

"The power they wield," Arraya explained carefully. "The greatest of the mortals are those who wield power – rule over their fellow mortals, raise armies, command kingdoms. The least of the mortals are those who do nothing but serve others, and have no freedom, no power over themselves."

Esther shook her head. "Greatness has nothing to do with power, apprentice. I will need to speak with Shallum about your instruction."

Arraya's heart sank as visions of her future floated before her eyes: endless hours poring over old tomes, mindless physical labor of splitting firewood and hauling water to provide her "time to think," as Shallum described it, and endless small tasks like cooking, sweeping, and weeding the extensive gardens around the Magi's Cosmane fortress. *Wonderful. Oh, so wonderful. I'll never become a full Magi at this rate.*

"So, apprentice," the Magi interrupted her, "tell me – how could the Imposter-King have blinded us?"

"He couldn't have," Arraya said dully.

"Perhaps, perhaps not. If he was responsible, how could he have done such a thing?"

Arraya turned the question over in her mind. *The Imposter-King has no way of touching the True Power, of manipulating its flows. Only the followers of the Dark One could manage such things. But that would mean...* Her jaw dropped open in shock. "The Imposter-King colluded with the Dark One?" she asked, the words sounding surreal in her own ears.

Esther dropped her head in a bow. "Now, apprentice, you begin to see the possibilities."

"But why would he have colluded with the Dark One to do such a thing, rather than destroying the heir outright?" Arraya shook her head. "He's shown no interest in letting potential rivals live before. Every one of the royal family he found he has destroyed before."

"Perhaps he knew only of the existence, and not the location," Esther said gravely. "Perhaps this heir was removed from the High Castle at birth and hidden away from all who might know, to protect the royal bloodline should the worst happen. Such things have happened before, and will no doubt happen again."

"If this heir was so hidden, how could the Imposter-King have known?"

"Child, stop and think," Esther said in exasperation. She rapped Arraya's head lightly with the tip of her wooden staff. "There are many ways such a thing could come to pass. The details of it are not important to us now – the past will not lead us to the future."

The apprentice rubbed the new bruise silently as she pondered over the words. "Mistress," she said carefully, "is it possible for *Aither* to have hidden the heir from us?"

Esther's eyes locked onto Arraya. "Why would the Light One hide hope and knowledge from us?" she asked curtly. "Why would our own Master and Lord keep the heir concealed?"

Arraya swallowed hard before answering, knowing her words would likely bring another rap. "To prevent us from doing something stupid," she whispered as she closed her eyes.

The expected strike did not arrive. Arraya slowly opened her eyes to see the Magi studying her in surprise. "An interesting answer, apprentice," she said at last. "Perhaps your education has not been wasted."

"Then you think…"

"No," Esther shook her head. "But sometimes the moon shows in truth what the sun belies."

So there's a chance I'm right, Arraya pondered. *I don't think Master Shallum ever suggested that.*

"For now, apprentice," the Magi said, "do not trouble yourself with this. The Council will bring the heir into our ranks, and prepare him to sit upon the throne. Your master will see to that."

Arraya nodded, keeping her mouth shut for fear of ruining any progress she'd made in impressing the Magi. *So stick to your studies, keep working hard, and maybe someday you'll be a full Magi. Long after the Imposter-King has been dethroned, of course, but Magi live a long, long time. My turn will come.*

Esther seemed to notice for the first time that Arraya was wrapped in a heavy quilt. "Are you cold, child?"

Arraya nodded slowly. "Yes, mistress."

"Long ago, before the Imposter-King, our seat of power was in Jepitsa itself," Esther said softly. Her tone was solemn, but tinged with sadness. "It is warm there,

with many fruits that we cannot find here in Cosmane."
She sighed. "Now we hide here in the ice and snow,
concealed from the Imposter-King and his armies."

"Why not confront him directly?" Arraya asked quietly.

The Magi's staff rapped her atop the head again, and
her tone was harsh. "Child, you already know the reason
for that. We Magi do not, cannot rule. We can only advise
and follow and help, not lead. To do otherwise is the
province of the Dark One and his followers."

The apprentice rubbed her increasingly sore head.
"Yes, mistress."

"With this new heir, perhaps, we will see the end of this
frozen fortress," Esther said, her voice solemn again, "and
we shall return to Jepitsa to bring light and life and justice
back to Letale." She shook her head, and her voice was
friendly rather than authoritative when she looked the
apprentice in the eyes again. "Why don't you crawl into
bed, young one, and stay warm? It is late, and morning will
come soon enough."

"Yes, mistress," Arraya agreed. She bowed her head
again, then rose and crossed to her bed and its heaps of
blankets as the Magi turned to the door.

"Mistress?" she asked. Esther stopped at the doorway,
turning silently to wait for the apprentice's question. "Why
did Master Shallum choose me as an apprentice?"

"Has he not told you?" Esther asked in return.

I hate it when she does that, Arraya thought. *Can't answer
my question, just ask more questions in return.* "No," Arraya
admitted.

"Then it is not my place to tell you," Esther said. "Goodnight, apprentice." Before Arraya could ask anything more, the Magi slipped out and closed the door behind her.

The apprentice sighed as she sat down on the bed. *I don't really want to sleep*, she told herself. *There's so many things to think about and do.*

Master Shallum is gone and will be for some time. A trip to Jepitsa, even taken in haste with the endurance of a Magi, will take a week in one direction, and another seven days to return. If he comes with the heir in tow, it will likely take ten days or more for his return journey.

Everything's changing, she told herself. *The Council of Magi has a chance to break the hold of the Imposter-King over all Letale. My training advances. Master Shallum has left me here, alone, for the first time I can ever remember. What do I even do with time outside of training?*

That thought brought her pause, but the answer came to her in the silence of her own thoughts. *Study, of course. It's a chance to read more books, and perhaps I can even persuade Mistress Esther to allow me to study the ancient scrolls of the Magi. There is always more to learn, and I am a long way from mastership of the True Power.*

She pondered that. *But what is mastership? Is it just being able to fully master the True Magic, or is it mastery of knowledge? Master Shallum has told me more than once that the magic is only a small part of the power of a magi. He knows so much, but he's hinted that the knowledge doesn't necessarily come from the magic. Maybe I need to start studying about people and history outside the order of the Magi.*

She pondered that for a long time – long enough that sleep caught up with her and stole her away while her thoughts were elsewhere.

Her dreams were fractured things, her private terrors of abandonment and failure intermixed with hopes and dreams of acceptance into the Council of Magi. It was a familiar collage – the patterns of it had haunted her for the decade since she had begun her training. Of course, as a child, her dreams had been far more hopeful – visions of defeating the servants of the Dark One, advising the rightful King on the throne in Jepitsa, of leading the Council of Magi itself.

As she grew older and her training intensified, she had found she had limits – boundaries to her own capabilities that terrified her. Under Master Shallum's harsh but careful training, she had found she could stretch her limits and accomplish feats she had previously found impossible. But the limits privately haunted her, and her dreams of success slowly transformed into nightmares of failure.

And occasionally, those dreams were punctuated by the sharp, vivid images she had eventually learned were visions of the future.

The hard, cold, damp stones of a dungeon surrounded her. Around her were faces – faces unfamiliar to her, but some part of her recognized them. A boy, about her own age, his hair a dark tangle around his face and his garb dark and rough. A thief, *her vision-self thought.* A boy acting only in his own interest. He has no idea what he could be, *should* be.

Beside the thief was a girl, similarly garbed and dark-haired, clearly his ally. She clearly could be beautiful, even under the dirt and grime and grease, but her terror robbed her of her beauty. She was a cornered animal, seeking only escape.

The apprentice gathered the magic to herself, preparing to act. Act how? *she asked herself.* What am I doing?

More faces, then — a blur of images as the walls of the dungeon blurred away. A blonde-haired girl, her face stone as she fought, more thieves garbed like the two she had seen in the dungeon. The clink of gold coins sounded in her ear, then the booming of nearby thunder. Fire and smoke blinded her, and the coppery smell of blood and the rank odor of burned flesh tried to choke her. The apprentice's vision-self coughed, gathered more of the magic to herself, preparing for...what?

The vision began to fade away, and the apprentice was content to let it. The blurring images made no sense and gave her no context, providing her no way to interpret the scenes before her.

An instant before the vision could vanish away completely, she was back in the dungeon again, and Master Shallum stood before her. His expression was a mixture of pride and regret, confidence and fear.

And pain.

Fire crashed over him like a wave upon a shore. Her master screamed in pain as the fire licked at his flesh, singeing away his hair, sending him tumbling to his knees. He screamed again, but the sound of his voice dwindled as the hellish inferno raged around him, trapping him within walls of fire.

The apprentice's vision-self tried to turn to see his attacker, but before she could see him, her vision faded entirely.

"Master!" she screamed, clinging to the vision with every ounce of tenacity she could pour out, but it wasn't enough. Darkness clouded everything, and even the sound of the Magi's scream vanished.

Though her hearing was deafened and her vision blinded, she could still smell the sickening, sweet scent of burnt flesh.

Arraya sat straight up in her bed, throwing off her blankets. She gasped for breath, gulping the air greedily and then snorting it out, trying to clear her nose of the phantom smells from the vision. She coughed and choked and stumbled out of her bed, trying to shake off the terror sucking at her very soul.

She fell to her hands and knees and that, more than anything, began to restore her sense of reality. As the cold from the stones seeped into her palms, the fear began to subside, and the apprentice began to sort out the conflicting images.

Who was that boy, and the girl with him? Those thieves? And...Master Shallum...

The fleeting image of her master trapped in the flames, burning like tinder, smashed into her and left her gasping for breath.

"Master Shallum," she murmured aloud. *No, it was just a dream. Wasn't it?*

Arraya forced herself to acknowledge the truth – self-deception had no place in the heart of a Magi, not even an apprentice. *It wasn't a dream. It was a vision.*

Master Shallum dies. She swallowed. *In a dungeon. And given that I have seen it* now, *when I still have time to act, well...then it was probably in the dungeon of the castle in Jepitsa. He's riding into a trap, and he doesn't even know it.*

The apprentice retraced her memory of the vision. *There must be a servant of the Dark One working for the Imposter-King,* she decided. *It would take someone of incredible power to defeat him, and even then, it must have been by surprise.*

There's only one thing I can do. She swallowed as she forced herself to stop and review her memories and conclusions, but she was forced inevitably to an inescapable action. *I must go to the Council, so they send me to Jepitsa to find Master Shallum before this can come to pass.*

V

A COLD BREEZE DRIFTING ACROSS Ben's face snapped him awake. He shivered, snuggled deeper under his blanket as he struggled with the sudden awakening. *That's cold!* he thought sleepily as he tried to remember where he was and what he was doing.

He looked around, wondering why he wasn't in his bed. Slowly comprehension returned. *That's right, I went to sleep on the roof of the house, because it was sunny and warm. I'd been up all night and then spent my morning at the Market. Did I eat a chicken?*

The memory of the roasted bird made his mouth water and his stomach rumble. *What time is it? When did I last eat?*

Slowly he realized that night had already fallen. "Oh," he said aloud. "Oh. I slept through the whole day."

He rubbed at his eyes, wiping away sleep sand. *I had something to do tonight. What was it?*

Oh, right. The Brigands.

He looked to the western horizon and could see no trace of fading sunlight. "Great," he mumbled aloud as he threw off the blanket. "I'm late."

He hopped down from the flat-topped building, his blanket flapping like a cape in the wind. Already late, he decided to duck into the building rather than rush to the meeting of the Brigands.

The little hovel was empty; his roommates were all gone. It wasn't uncommon; many of the inhabitants of Riverfront chose to spend their waking hours at night rather than in the daylight. Ben was typically among them.

The teenage thief returned his blanket to his bed. After reluctantly shrugging on a light jacket against the cool night air, he rummaged around for food. He came up with a handful of strips of jerky, dried and salted meat that most of Riverfront subsided on. Fruits and vegetables required either long distances of travel, labor-intensive work to produce, or plenty of gold. Meat, on the other hand, was easy to find when a thief didn't care about the law declaring all living game animals property of the king himself.

The jerky calmed the rumbling in his stomach. Reluctantly, he replaced the remaining jerky where he found it. Then he recovered the builder's book, secured his dagger in its sheath, and headed out into the cold night air to meet with the Brigands.

The Brigands met, as they always did, on a tiny island out in the river itself. Fortunately, the river itself was shallow in one place, allowing even the youngest members of the thieves' group to cross over without serious danger.

Ben stopped at the river's edge and looked out at the dark island. A number of large trees towered up from the bit of dry land, and heavy brush covered the ground. *If there was somewhere else to be, I'd be there*, he told himself. He checked the book again to ensure it was secure in its pouch. *Too bad I can't just sell this to make a profit. I hope Alan has a good plan for this.*

The thief looked down at the cold water rushing past. He looked down further at his warm, dry feet in their shoes, and then back at the water. *I'm already late, what's a few more minutes?* he decided. Ben sat down on the riverbank and pulled his shoes off. Tying the laces together, he hung them around his neck, then hitched up his trouser legs and crossed the river.

"Oh, that's cold," he mumbled, wincing with each step. As soon as he was across and on the island's bank, he dropped back down to pull his shoes. He spent a moment lacing them up, then climbed back to his feet and started hunting for the trail in the brush.

It took less than two minutes for Ben to find the hole. He followed the barely visible path through the brush and up onto higher ground on the island.

The wind ruffling leaves would have unsettled him, but he had walked the path more times than he could count. Experience aside, his dagger was a familiar weight. *Even if someone is stupid enough to try to attack someone with no money, I could fight them off,* he thought smugly to himself.

It took several minutes of slow walking, and two backtracks, to find his destination: the squat stone tower at the center of the island.

Ben had no idea how the fortification had been built. There were no stones like it on the island, and it had been in shambles from the first time he had set foot within the walls. It stood barely higher than any of the shacks the denizens of Riverfront called home, but was large enough on the inside to hold a hundred people.

"Stop," a cool voice ordered from somewhere above him in the darkness.

Alan posted guards, Ben thought admiringly. *Just in case someone came poking around.* His heart thudded in his ears as he carried the observation to its conclusion. *He never did that before, though. He really does have something big in mind this time. I'd bet it has something to do with this book, too.*

"Who hails this fortress?" the voice asked.

Ben looked up through the darkness and thought he saw the outline of a young man, a longbow drawn with an arrow notched and pointed down at him. *Or maybe you're imagining it,* he told himself. *I mean, Alan wouldn't have anyone killed. It's not his style.*

"It's me, Ben," the thief said. "I've come for the meeting of the Brigands."

Silence ensued for several moments, before the archer said, "Proceed." As Ben stepped forward, the guard added, "Next time be on time."

"I'll remember," Ben muttered under his breath as he walked forward and entered the stone tower.

He brushed aside the blanket hung over the tower door, and his eyes, adjusted for the darkness, were assaulted by brilliant torch light. The blazing oil-soaked sticks lined the walls, illuminating the chamber nearly as bright as day.

As was usual for a meeting of the Brigands, a table pushed against the wall was loaded with food – a roasted pig, apples, pheasants, loaves of bread, and bottles of mead. The sight of so much food was enough to send Ben's stomach rumbling again, insisting that a handful of jerky really wasn't enough sustenance for the night.

At the "front" of the room – and it was only such because a large wooden chair had been elevated above the room on a dais of crates – Alan sat quietly conversing with a few of the most talented thieves, including both Zeke and Corin. Sitting in uneven rows, nearly the entire complement of the Brigands, numbering over forty thieves, conversed in loud and boisterous tones, clearly bragging about successes and conquests, while others bemoaned their failures and bad luck. *Guess I wasn't as late as I thought*, he told himself. *I may have been the last Brigand in, but they hadn't started yet.*

Ben immediately headed for the table of food, pocketing an apple and tearing off a leg of pheasant to chew on. With his free hand he snagged a bottle of mead, a sweet drink that would leave him relaxed and warm. With his food in hand, he studied the room again. *I suppose*

I should go up front near Corin and Zeke and Alan, but I'd rather not be in front, he thought. *Don't like the attention.* He glanced at the table, then slid down to seat himself on the floor. *This should work fine, though.*

Alan looked straight at him, but Ben couldn't read his expression from across the room. *I'm not going up there,* he told himself. *I don't want to drag out the business with this book until after the meeting is over.*

Ben watched as Alan looked over his shoulder significantly at Zeke, who picked up a long, carved staff nearly as tall as he was, and pounded the end of it on a stone three times. The loud *crack-crack-crack* echoed through the dilapidated tower. By the time the third crack had echoed into silence, all conversation had ceased and the Brigands were all watching the front of the room.

Alan slowly stood up and took the proffered staff from Zeke's hand. "This meeting of the Brigands is now in order!" he shouted to the room. "We will proceed with reports." His eyes roved up and down the seated rows of thieves, all of them so young.

"Treasury!" he demanded.

A dark-skinned girl, whose heritage called back to the deserts of Rapien but who had never set foot outside Jepitsa, stood up with a battered piece of parchment in hand. With great flourish she unrolled it, holding it aloft for all to see. Her voice was proud when she spoke – she was one of the few Brigands who could read.

"The treasury has a hundred and eighteen silver coins," she announced. "Including the new income from the pickpockets, and the payout from the other jobs we pulled in the past month."

Low murmurs ran through the gathered crowd at the announcement, and Ben's voice joined them seemingly of its own volition. *One hundred and eighteen coin is a huge amount,* he told himself. *That would be enough to leave here and become a noble in some far away land. Of course, it's not like any of us would run off with all the money and leave all the rest of us destitute.*

A sharp *crack* from the staff on the stone silenced the room again. "What were the ins and outs?" Alan demanded.

"Two hundred and twelve coins were paid out to the Jepitsa Royal Guard to keep silent about the Market," the girl reported faithfully. "Seventy-five coins were used to purchase new bows and quivers of arrows for our guards. Eighty-one coins were used to buy nails and wood for fixing shacks in Riverfront. Twenty coins were used to buy mortar for repairs to the tower."

Ben remained as silent as the rest of the Brigands as she continued her report on expenses. *Weapons and fortifications? It's like we're building an army,* he thought, a little amused. *It's not like we can fight the guards, or that the tower would hold up if the King's army decided to take it.*

"Income," the treasurer said, bringing Ben's attention back to her report. "Eighty-four coins from the pickpocket team at the Market. Twenty coins for payment for our completion of the Sabak job. Thirty-six coins for payment for completion of…"

Ben's mind wandered again. *I wonder if this is what the king's court is like?* he pondered. *Do they have constant reports on completed jobs and money? Or do they just sit around all day eating peaches and roast pig and drinking wine from great big jeweled goblets?*

The *crack* of the staff on the stone brought his attention back to the moment. The dark-skinned girl was just seating herself, her report complete. Alan was looking around the room, clearly deciding on who should report next. "Pickpockets!" he called at last. "Where is the pickpocket report?"

A filthy, blonde-haired boy, no older than ten, stood up to represent the pickpockets. Around him were clustered the other pickpockets – mostly children younger than himself, deemed too small and too unreliable to bring along for major heists. They often worked in pairs or teams, with one acting as a distraction with the others waiting ready to take advantage of opportunities to relieve a mark of his valuables or money. Quite often, the dirtiest and poorest-looking one would sit in the Riverfront Market and beg for money; when someone stopped to take pity on him, another would quickly lift a purse or wallet and disappear into the crowd with the valuables.

Ben understood their tactics and purpose well; he had been a pickpocket himself when Alan had recruited him into the Brigands. It was there he had befriended Zeke and the two had grown close.

"We had a bad month," the boy said. "We lifted one hundred and fifty-nine silver coins in the market…"

His report was interrupted by the loud *crack* yet again. "The treasury only received eighty-four," Alan interrupted, rising. "Where is the rest of the money?" His tone darkened. "Are you trying to rob the other people in this family? Holding some back for yourself, are you?"

"No, no, no, sir!" the boy protested. "Nothing like that!" He swallowed noisily, audible even from Ben's low and distant vantage point. "Ivy was caught with her hand in a noble woman's purse, and she dragged her into the city and demanded she be thrown in prison by the royal guards! We used some of our money to get her back!"

Alan slowly seated himself, his expression unhappy. "Where is Ivy?" he asked.

A nine-year-old brunette girl rose to her feet to stand beside the boy. "I'm here."

"How were you caught?" Alan asked.

"I tried for too many coins," Ivy explained, her eyes downcast. "My hand wasn't big enough, and when I pulled it out I dropped a coin that landed on her foot. She caught me right away."

"How was Ivy rescued?" Alan asked.

"We bribed a guard to let her go," the boy said as Ivy seated herself on the ground again. "He wouldn't take less than seventy-five. At first he wanted three hundred!"

"I'm glad you were able to get Ivy back," Alan said with a smile. "We look after our own." He looked across the audience, seemingly looking squarely in the eyes of each Brigand in turn. "We are all here because the outside world has abandoned us to fate. We are a family, and more than that – families are bound together by chance and by blood, but we are a family by *choice*. We have *chosen* to become a family, so it is all the more important to look after each other."

Smiles lit up faces around the tower, and Ben couldn't help but smile himself. *Some of us were cast out by our own blood,* he told himself. *That makes us choosing to be family even more special.*

Alan turned now to look at another thief, a boy named Jorax. "Report on the Schack job?" he asked.

Jorax stood up, his expression irritated. "We already told you about..."

The *crack* of the staff on the rock silenced Jorax. "The jobs we do are for the benefit of all the Brigands," Alan said coldly. "All our jobs need to be reported to everyone. It's only fair that each and every one of your fellow Brigands knows about your successes and failures." He paused for a moment before adding, "We are a family, and we must be honest with each other. We also must rely on each other."

Jorax looked contrite as he quietly began to speak again. "We were hired for a shill job, to frame Count Koman's right-hand man, Schack, of a crime to get him out of the way."

"How do you stage the frame-up?" Alan asked.

"We worked with Cowardly Wade," Jorax explained. "We offered him forty percent of our take to lift a silver ring from one of his customers, Lady Eleanor of Rapien."

"Forty percent?" Alan asked with a lifted eyebrow. "Cowardly Wade would have done it for twenty-five."

Jorax shook his head. "He was too afraid of Lady Eleanor's escorts – there were two of them, warriors from Rapien that looked even scarier than the best of the Royal Guard. He said he wanted fifty, and I talked him down to forty."

Alan clearly was unhappy with the answer, but waved it off. "Please, continue."

"We found Schack at Plain Jane's stall and slipped the ring in his pouch. When Lady Eleanor started an uproar because her ring had gone missing, the guards started searching for it. He pulled out some silver to pay Plain Jane, but he pulled the ring out with his money and Jane saw it. She started shouting for the guards, and he tried to drop the ring, but everyone was already trying to get away from him." Jorax smiled a little. "No one wanted to be too close to those Rapien warriors. They looked like they would have cut him up right there if the Jepitsa guard hadn't gotten to him first."

Alan nodded. "Excellent. And the pay?"

"Our take was sixty silver coins. I already gave it all to the treasury."

"Very good!" Alan complimented him. "You've done well for your family!" The leader of the Brigands stood up, pointing his staff at Jorax. "Everyone look! *This* is how we act. We are the best thieves in all the land, and we can take care of each other because of it!" He smacked the staff on the ground again before seating himself. "Very well done."

"Thank you," Jorax mumbled, sitting down again on the cold stones.

Ben frowned. *Jax should be ecstatic after that*, he thought. *He did a great job and got recognized for it. Why is he upset?*

"Kinea!" Alan thundered. "How did your delivery go?"

Ben tuned out as the girl stood up to report on a delivery run. *Delivering goods isn't really our specialty, but when it's something hot, you can't exactly ask the Imperial courier service to hand it off, can you?* He chuckled to himself at the thought. *Yeah, they'd love to deliver stolen goods for us. I don't see how anything could go wrong with* that.

Alan asked for more reports as the meeting rolled along: a carriage heist involving a noble from Cosmane, a burglary job inside Jepitsa itself, and even a paid job to forge numbers in some shopkeeper's books to get him in trouble with the King. Ben listened to it all, soaking in the details. *It's amazing, the things the Brigands can do. I bet we make more of a difference in Jepitsa than the King's court!* He smiled at that. *They're probably more feared than we are, though. We take from the rich; they* are *the rich, so they take from the poor.*

The meeting lasted perhaps another hour before Alan rose to his feet and brought the staff down hard on a rock again, with a loud *crack-crack-crack*. "You have done well, Brigands!" he shouted. "I will have new assignments for you tomorrow — new jobs, new marks, new tasks. Dismissed!" he thundered, with another *crack* of the staff. "And may the shadows hide you!"

The Brigands began rising to their feet and scattering, often with a handful of food from the table. A few were slow to move, having grown sleepy during the meeting; far more were gone in a few heartbeats, their bodies used to resting during the day and acting at night.

Ben waited until the crowd had cleared before he rose to his feet and moved to the front of the room to join Corin, Zeke, Alan, and a few others.

"Do you have it?" Alan asked him as he approached.

Ben pulled the book from his pouch and tossed it casually to Alan, now seated again on his elevated chair. "As requested, the builder's book for Key Castle."

Alan caught it and immediately began to unwrap its cover, eager to look within at its contents. He was pulling the cover open when he finally comprehended Ben's words. He looked up, his jaw dropping. He gaped at Ben for a moment before finally forcing words out. "You know."

Ben nodded. "I do." He glanced around at the group. "This book has all the details on the construction of Key Castle. Materials lists, labor lists, sketches of the layout, *everything*."

Silence hung over the group as Alan and Ben stared at each other. *Sorry, Alan,* Ben wanted to say. *I didn't mean to go behind your back, but you wouldn't tell me and I had to know what I was stealing for you. I know it's not what you wanted, but* you're *the one always talking about how honest we need to be with each other, and how we shouldn't have secrets.*

"If that's true," Corin said slowly, breaking the silence, "that book could be our death warrant. If the King finds out we have that information, the Royal Guard would burn down Riverfront and kill us all to get it back."

"*If* he knew," Zeke interjected. "He doesn't know. He couldn't know."

"So, it has to be worth some serious coin," Corin said eagerly. "There has to be a lot of enemies of the King who would love to get their hands on this."

"If we sold it, certainly," Alan said, finally breaking his own silence and looking away from Ben. "But you're assuming that's the best way to make a profit from this book."

"What else would we do with it?" asked one of the other two boys. He was a year younger than Ben, but stood a good head higher and was far heavier. He wore his nickname, Bruiser, proudly, and he wasn't hesitant to use his muscle to get his way. "Use it for kindling?"

Corin glared at him. "You're all brawn and no brain," she said. "No, Alan didn't have us steal this from Lord Rittin just so he could sell it, did you, Alan?"

Ben nodded. He'd been pondering the possibilities of the builder's book ever since Plain Jane had identified its contents and origin. "No, I'd bet you have a heist planned, don't you? You're planning on us knocking over the King's own castle."

"That's insane," Zeke said. "We'd never get away with it. Are you serious? That's the craziest thing I've ever heard of. How would we get in, through the front door?"

"That's what the book is for," Ben explained. "To find another way into the castle, some way that no one knows about. Otherwise it would be a death sentence to walk in there."

"So what is it?" Bruiser asked. "What are we going to steal?"

Alan shot a glare at Ben before turning to meet each thief's gaze in turn. "This has to be utterly secret," he said, his voice barely above a whisper. "But this is the heist of legends."

He's angry with me because I could have messed up the plan, Ben thought glumly. *My need to know could've screwed it all up and made this impossible. We're lucky it's just us here right now.*

"Well?" Corin asked. "What is it?"

"I need each of you to trust me," Alan said, ignoring Corin's question. "But this theft could change everything. It could bring more silver to Riverfront than we've ever even dreamed about. This job alone could pay out more than what a whole year of our regular work brings in."

The thieves were leaning in now, eager to hear the details. "Tell us," Bruiser demanded.

"Patience," Alan said, holding up his hand. "First, I need you to swear an oath to me."

"An oath?" Zeke asked skeptically.

"An oath," Alan repeated. "An oath of allegiance. An oath of loyalty. Swear that you'll follow my orders for this job. Swear it!"

"I swear," the gathered thieves repeated.

"Swear to me you'll never speak of this job to anyone!" Alan demanded. "Swear that you'll carry the secret of this theft to your grave!"

"I swear!" the thieves all said as one, Ben included. *This has to be something huge. Something that no one else would even dare try for.*

And then Alan told them. The target for the job was so astounding, so *impossible*, that merely comprehending it was enough to set Ben back on his heels. He looked from face to face as he struggled with the implications of the theft. He saw amazement on Zeke's face, disbelief on Bruiser's, and pure determination painted Corin's expression. He wished for a moment he had a mirror to see his own face, to see if it reflected the shock, the amazement, the disbelief, the fear he felt as he repeated Alan's words to himself.

"We are going to steal the crown."

VI

THE COUNCIL OF MAGI WAS far more intimidating to Arraya when she stood in the center of their chamber alone, bereft of the presence of her master.

They were an old and wizened bunch, all grey hair and wrinkles and balding pates. None of them were under sixty winters old, the apprentice estimated. The Council of the Magi may have been regarded once as the wisest collection of scholars in the world, but Arraya couldn't help but think, *Maybe they know so much because they've been around so long they've just seen everything.*

She made sure no trace of the humor she found in the thought made it to her face.

"The apprentice approaches without the master," one of the Council Magi said, the old woman Arraya thought of as a crone. "Has she forgotten her place?"

"Nay," a male voice said from behind her, "she comes with visions of her own. She seeks action, a course to pursue."

"Yet she comes directly to us, rather than waiting for her master to return," a third voice said.

Arraya closed her eyes. *I feel like they can see right through me. How do they know all this?*

"We know because we are the Magi," Mistress Esther said aloud. "Your thoughts are open to us, like a book whose pages are torn out and scattered upon the ground. You have no secrets here."

The apprentice gulped and remained silent.

"Tell us, apprentice," the old crone said, "what visions have you seen? What truth has the Aither allowed you to glimpse?"

"I saw Master Shallum," Arraya said quietly. "Burned alive in a dungeon in Jepitsa."

"Burned, you say?" asked a Magi whose head stubbornly retained its last few hairs. "The Imposter-King chose to burn him at the stake?"

"No, master." She drew a deep breath in to clarify. "It was fire summoned by magic, directed at him to destroy him."

Murmurs began to flutter around the room, indistinct and tenuous. "What else did you see?" the same man asked her.

Arraya closed her eyes and brought the images back to the forefront of her mind. "Two thieves, terrified for their lives but not in shackles," she said slowly. "And..."

"Is there anything else you remember about these thieves?" another voice interrupted, its cadence betraying the speaker as a son of Rapien. "Any details?"

"A boy and a girl, about my age," Arraya answered, a bit confused by the interest. "And...I remember thinking that the boy could be so much more than what he was. No, not that he could be – it was that he *should* be more."

More murmurs. Arraya turned the vision-pictures over in her head.

"Could this thief be the heir?" a voice asked.

The apprentice hadn't considered the possibility, but now, she did. "It would fit," she said slowly. "It would fit very well, actually. That would be why he was held in the dungeon. If he were the heir, and the Imposter-King needed to keep him alive for some reason..." She frowned. "But I don't know why I thought he was a thief. He or the girl."

"Visions are gifts from the Aither," the crone rasped. "Each thought, each scent, each sight, each sound of such a vision are truer than the reality around you. If you believed him a thief *during the vision*, he surely is what you claim. If you only drew that conclusion afterward, when reflecting upon what you have been gifted with, it may be untrue. Your logic, your reason, your knowledge cannot match revealed truth."

Arraya nodded, her eyes still closed.

"Was there anything else?" another Magi asked.

The apprentice shook her head. "It was so fast, and the images were too swift for me to comprehend," she said quietly. "I only know it was my master, and the thieves, and my master's death."

"It is possible the Imposter-King has drawn the Dark One's minions to himself," a completely bald Magi mused. "They would be natural allies against us."

"The Imposter-King has shown himself far too clever to allow such treacherous things too close," the Rapien Magi replied. "To be a servant of the Dark One is to lay claim to power and to seek it; service to a king, even an imposter, would be beneath them."

"Rune Sages, perhaps," the crone chimed in. "Perhaps even the orc-kin, a new weapon to use against us."

"The orcs have shown no interest in joining the Imposter-King before," another voice commented dubiously. "Even the most powerful of their Seers would be no match for Master Shallum."

"If it were a true and fair duel, of course not," the Rapien Magi agreed. "But the apprentice has given no indication that it was such a contest."

"So what are we going to *do*?" Arraya asked, a touch of impatience creeping into her voice. "All of this is well and good, but Master Shallum's life will end if we don't act!"

"You are so certain, apprentice," the crone said. "Visions are truth, but they are not immutable. Perhaps in acting we shall bring it to pass, or cause an even worse fate to befall the Magi. We must consider all possibilities before choosing a course of action."

"That will take *forever*," Arraya said, a bit of whine in her tone in spite of her best efforts. "The longer we take, the further Master Shallum rides into a trap!"

"Apprentice," Mistress Esther said with a touch of rebuke, "mind your place. Before you were even born, the Magi were advising kings on the path their rule would take. To act in haste is to act without forethought."

"A lot of good your forethought did when the Imposter-King took over," Arraya retorted.

As one, each of the Magi extended their staves down. As one, they crashed against the stone floor, a deafening boom that echoed in the apprentice's ears. She looked from face to face, seeing irritation and outright anger on their faces. *About that forethought*, she winced. *I need to work on that before speaking. A lot.*

"Yes, you do," Mistress Esther agreed quietly.

Arraya swallowed hard. "I'm sorry, Masters," she said contritely, dropping to her knees in subservience. "I spoke out of turn."

"I am unconvinced you did," the Rapien Magi disagreed. "Sometimes haste is necessary."

The apprentice was staring too hard at the floor to catch the meaning of his words.

"Indeed," the crone said. "It is too easy to wrap hesitation in the cloak of planning, to delay action by providing pleasing reasons. Master Shallum is neither the youngest nor oldest of us, and while he may ride into disaster, we spend our time debating action and inaction."

Arraya dared to look up. "Masters?" she squeaked.

Mistress Esther rose to her feet. "We are in agreement, then?"

Murmured assents were her reply. Mistress Esther stepped forward, standing across from Arraya. "Rise, apprentice," she said firmly.

The flame-haired girl rose unsteadily to her feet, her eyes still fixed firmly downward.

"Apprentice Arraya," she announced, "we thank you for bringing us this information. We have considered it, and we believe action must be undertaken. Therefore, you will ride out and pursue your master, overtake him before he should reach Jepitsa, and warn him of the danger ahead."

Arraya ran the instructions through her head, then squeaked, "Just me?"

"A capable apprentice should find no trouble with such a simple task," Mistress Esther intoned. "Master Shallum has spoken highly of you in the past, and we the Council have no reason to believe more assistance is necessary."

"I haven't left the mountains since I was a child," Arraya breathed. The thought of leaving the fortress behind and riding out on her own to find Master Shallum sent a shiver down her back.

"Then perhaps it is time," Mistress Esther said simply. "Go. Choose a horse from the stables here and pursue your master. Bring him back safely."

"What about the heir?" Arraya asked. She glanced down, saw her hands were shaking, and folded them across her chest to try to keep them still.

"If the heir has survived this long, he is likely in no immediate danger," another Magi declared. "He will surely wait until we can safely arrive at Jepitsa and recover him."

Arraya swallowed. "Alright," she managed. "I'll go."

The Magi nodded as one, and then stared at her silently. The apprentice stood rooted in place, looking blankly from face to face, before she blushed. *Oh. Guess that means I need to leave.* She turned and started to the door.

"Apprentice," Mistress Esther called before she could reach the portal.

Arraya turned and bowed her head again. "Mistress?"

"It is the custom of Magi to carry with them a proper stave," Mistress Esther said, stepping across the stone floor to stand before her. "It has no power in itself, but it is a symbol – and a reminder – of who and what we are. In these walls, there is no need for such trinkets, but the world stretches out before you." The old woman held out her staff to Arraya. "It is most fitting as well for a Magi to carve her own stave, but time is short."

The apprentice took it. As she wrapped her hands around it and lowered its end to the floor, she felt for the briefest of moments a surge of certainty, power, and knowledge. Above those, however, was a sense of *calm.* She could find Master Shallum. This was her path, laid out before her since the Aither himself authored it. It was her destiny.

"Thank you, mistress," she said, bowing her head as the calm collapsed again into uncertain fear.

Silence met her, and she turned uncomfortably and walked out. The massive Council chamber doors boomed shut behind her when she had stepped through.

Now, to find Master Shallum.

***

The skies were dark and the air bit shrewdly at her as the apprentice stepped out of the secure tower that had been her home for so many years. She did not look back as she walked through the cold toward the stables. *Don't look back*, she told herself. *You'll be back. You can't afford to be distracted now. Focus on finding Master Shallum, and then worry about returning home. You'll be fine.*

The stables was one of the few wooden structures standing in the massive stone fortress. A door hung from a rail, and she pushed it aside with no small effort, opening just enough gap to slip through. As soon as she was inside, she slid the door shut again.

The stable was warmer than she expected. A single stone fireplace provided heat on the far end of the building – far too little to truly warm the entire stable – but the presence of many horses helped raise the temperature to something far more comfortable than the outside cold.

The familiar smells of the stable invaded her senses – the distinct smell of hair, the unpleasant but omnipresent odor of manure, the comforting scent of well-cared-for leather. She stopped for a moment just to enjoy. *If I weren't a Magi, I would love to just work with horses,* she thought. *I can't imagine a life simpler and more pleasant than that.* Reluctantly, though, she forced her thoughts back to the moment and the reason she was in the stable.

Arraya would have been content choosing her own horse, saddling up, and riding out in pursuit of her master, but she knew better than to cross the stable master, an Elven woman with a razor sharp tongue and a short temper.

The elf was sitting cross-legged in front of the fire, a saddle laying on the floor in front of her. A can of polish stood open nearby, revealing her task to the approaching apprentice.

"Miss Isilwen," Arraya greeted her gravely.

The elf did not look up from her task. "Apprentice."

Arraya hesitated. *If I were a master, she would be on her feet already asking what she could do for me,* she thought with dismay. *So how do I approach this?*

Straight forward, she decided.

"I need a horse."

The elf laughed. "Of course you do, apprentice. For what reason, and how long, and by whose authority?" she asked crossly.

"To pursue Master Shallum," Arraya answered. "I do not know how long it will be. I act under the authority of the Council."

Isilwen rose to her feet and turned, all in a single smooth motion. "By the Council's authority, you say?" she asked with a raised eyebrow.

Arraya nodded. "Yes. The Council has given me instruction to bring my master back before disaster can overtake him." *It's true,* she told herself. *Even if it didn't quite happen like that.*

"Come, then," the stable master said. "There is little time to lose, then."

The elf walked so quickly back up the rows of stalls that Arraya could hardly keep up.

The elf stopped just as quickly as she had started walking, swinging wide a stable door. She clicked her tongue several times, a rapid-fire sound, and a red roan mare stepped out. "Gee," she ordered, and the horse turned and walked along the stalls. Isilwen swung the door shut and followed after.

Arraya shook her head. *It's amazing that she can do that without the True Magic, or any magic at all,* she observed distantly. *Just amazing.*

Isilwen walked the mare down the aisle without touching the horse, finally calling, "Whoa," when she reached a rack of tack. Quickly, efficiently, the stable master swung a saddle over the back of the horse, tightened it down, then followed suit with a bridle, slipping the bit in the mare's mouth and the straps over her ears so quickly Arraya almost missed the smooth motion.

"I expect you to return my mare in perfect condition," the elf said sternly. "If you return her lame, we will have a very long discussion on the care of horses."

Arraya nodded meekly before climbing up into the saddle. "Yes, ma'am," she said.

Isilwen turned and walked away. The apprentice kicked her horse forward and headed for the stable entrance.

***

Maybe setting off in a snowstorm wasn't the best idea, Arraya decided.

The road was hard to see through the blowing white haze of snow. It was impossible to tell the time of day accurately, but the apprentice knew that dawn had passed as the haze had become brighter in the last hour.

Her horse apparently had better perception than her, though, as the loyal animal kept pushing forward along the road. *Unless she's trying to return us home*, Arraya considered. *Horses are known to return home if they're lost.*

Her master had taught her the basics of "talking" to animals, though Arraya knew very well that such speech wasn't possible. Animals had varying degrees of intelligence, but speech at the level of humans or Scions was simply not possible. Still, she centered herself and calmed her thoughts, then reached out and starting pulling in magic.

The first breath of power warmed her against the cutting cold of the wind. As she continued to gather the magic, she felt as though she were standing out in the sun on a warm summer day, enjoying the heat. While she relished in the sensation, comfort wasn't her intent – she shaped the magic in her mind and breathed it back out, closing her eyes as she gripped the horse tightly with her legs.

Arraya kept her own thoughts and emotions under tight wraps, allowing the sensations of the horse's mind to enter her own. The red roan was in good spirits but unhappy with the blowing snow; determination kept her plodding forward. She knew the road intimately, even buried under the ever-deepening snow drifts, and she was bound and determined to carry her rider to her destination, even though it carried the horse away from the stables step by step.

Arraya allowed the spell to dissipate, and her mind was wholly her own. The storm was starting to lessen, now, though it was still leaving behind a white powdery mess. The obstruction pulled at her heart, threatening to sink it in a sea of despair. *I've lost a lot of ground to Master Shallum,* she thought glumly. *He left before the storm had blown in, and I'm moving a lot slower than he is because I had to fight my way through it.*

Still, horse and rider continued to plod on through the snow. By noon the storm had quit entirely, though clouds lurked on the distant horizon like predators preparing to pounce. Mindful of her horse's limitations, she stopped twice for breaks, allowing the animal to breathe and regain its strength.

On the second of those stops, she used a careful bit of fire magic to melt away the snow. The red roan was delighted to graze on dry grass. Arraya herself gathered snow in a tin cup and used the fire to melt it down as well.

I can eat snow directly if I need to, but it's much better to save my energy like this. Eating snow directly will chill me much faster.

As a Magi, though, I can always create heat. She smiled as she studied her tin cup, half full of water. *That's the advantage of being a Magi, I guess – I have access to power and resources that humans don't. Not even the Imposter-King, with all his tricks, can conjure lightning or hurl fire.*

After her horse had grazed twenty minutes, she pulled herself atop the animal again and started down the road again. The brief break had raised the red roan's spirits – she didn't even need her spell to notice. The mare had a prance to her step again, an eagerness to continue the chase through the cold day.

Arraya herself was eager to catch up to Shallum, and she continued to push on as quickly as she could. As they descended down out of the mountains, the snow began to recede. High on the mountain, it had reached the red roan's belly; down low, nearly out of the ranges of Cosmane, it was hardly ankle-deep.

She became more wary of her surroundings as she continued her journey, however; she began to see signs of other life among the leafless trees. The tracks of wolves and bears littered the edges of the road in places, even with the recent snowstorm; some trees had been chopped down recently, leaving behind stumps sticking up through the snow.

People made her more nervous than the thought of predators. *The Magi secluded themselves in the Cosmane fortress for more than one reason. Yes, the Imposter-King wants all of us with the Gift dead and gone, but there is resentment among the peasants for our failures. After all, the Magi failed to stop the Imposter-King from rising to power in the first place.*

Still, there's hardly anything to identify me as a Magi's apprentice. The rough-spun cloak over her head and shoulders could be sewn in a hundred villages across all of Letale. She wore no Magi's robe underneath it, having replaced her comfortable and warm robes for colder, scratchier trousers and blouse. Her leather boots could likewise be worn by any craftsman or outdoorsman across the entire kingdom. *I'm as anonymous as can be*, she thought to herself.

The snow had been reduced to a dusting on the ground – almost more memory than reality – as the sun began to set. She decided to stop and make camp for the night before she lost the light entirely. *If I have to use magic to conjure light to make my camp, it doesn't matter what I'm wearing – anyone with an ounce of brains will know I'm a Magi. Well, an apprentice, anyways*, she amended.

After observing carefully to ensure no one was around, she melted off a large portion of ground with a careful blast of fire. The red roan snorted its approval at the open space and, after Arraya had stripped off her packs, demonstrated by laying down on the open – if somewhat damp – earth.

Arraya spent her last few precious minutes of daylight gathering dry branches from the trees. *With my fire, I can light anything short of it being submerged in water, but there's no reason to make it more difficult than it needs to be.* She swallowed.

Especially with the limits of my power. I'm not a true Magi, and it would be very bad of me to have spent my strength on building a fire only to get attacked by bandits or wild animals.

She arranged the wood in a rough pyramid, as Shallum had once told her worked well. Darkness had already fallen, and she hesitated as she reached for her power. *If anyone is standing out in the darkness watching, they'll see me for sure.* She considered. *Then again, if they're any distance away, they won't be able to tell what I'm doing.*

With a whispered word and a release of her will, fire leapt from her fingertips to the piled wood. In moments, the flames climbed to the peak of the pile. The apprentice smiled. *You taught me well, Master.* Her smile faded. *I only hope I can reach you in time so you can* continue *to teach me well.*

She settled in beside the fire, basking in the warmth. Her eyes grew heavy as she relaxed in the warmth, and she knew she would fall asleep if she wasn't careful. Instead of succumbing, she began to draw subtly upon her magic, using its power to refresh her as though she had slept for hours. Arraya steadily grew more alert as the magic seemed to tingle its way through her very bones, providing strength.

There was always a cost to such uses of the power, of course. Her physical body had limits that she was not capable of exceeding. Drawing on the magic now would allow her to continue to stay awake and alert, but eventually she would have to pay the price.

With the True Magic, I could make myself immune to pain or as strong as a giant. That wouldn't really be smart, though, because my body will still suffer the consequences of it and I may not even feel it until it's too late.

The apprentice continued to stare at the fire, turning over the options in her mind. *I'm not going to make up any more ground on Master Shallum tonight*, she reluctantly concluded. *And I doubt there's anyone around to put me in danger. I have no valuables to protect. If I use the true magic now to push myself, I'm doing it for no real gain in my goal. I could stay awake and alert all night, but it won't help me catch Master Shallum.*

Forced to an inevitable conclusion, she relaxed the spell she had woven around herself. The power seemed to drip back out of her, from her fingertips and toes and her eyes and ears. As it did, she felt the weariness rise back up to fill in the holes the power had left. At last, Arraya allowed herself to fall asleep before the warm fire.

***

Faint rays of sunlight were beginning to crack the stranglehold of dark in the eastern skies. When the apprentice awoke, the fire was long out and cold had stolen over her again. She drew upon the magic for warmth by reflex, and it seemed to settle around her like an impossibly comfortable quilt.

She considered stirring the fire back to life – with her magic, it would be little enough effort. *It doesn't matter, though. I'll be leaving here soon enough, and taking care of the fire may delay me and set me back from finding Master Shallum.*

Arraya shook her head and caught the mare, saddled her up again, and found a stick of jerky to chew upon.

By the time Arraya was ready to break camp, enough light had scattered across the sky to make the trail visible. She mounted up and cued her steed forward. *I catch Master Shallum today*, she told herself. *He didn't have a very large head start, and I'm sure I'm pushing forward harder than he is.* The horse trotted along easily in the cold, crisp morning air, and the apprentice found herself enjoying the ride, even with the uncomfortable urgency underneath it all pushing her along.

Patience, she told herself. *You can't run this horse into the ground. Be patient and you'll catch up.*

Abruptly, the horse reared up on her hind legs with a startled cry. Arraya, caught off-guard, found herself falling before she could act. *Oh*, was all she managed before she smacked into the dirt of the trail.

The red roan snorted and whinnied again. "What is it?" Arraya asked aloud as she started to rise to her feet.

Pain flashed through her head as something hard smashed into her temple. She tried to weave a spell, summon her power, but she couldn't seem to push past the pain. The world darkened, and she knew no more.

VII

THE INSANITY OF A PLAN to *steal the royal crown* kept Ben questioning his own mind. *Have I gone crazy, or are we really plotting to steal the royal crown from inside the biggest, best-protected castle in the entire country?*

The small band of Brigands were seated atop the crumbling stone tower where they had met the night before. The table that had previously hosted the roasted pig and fruits now was covered with sheets of parchment, some sketched upon, some not. Small pots of ink and quills were scattered about, leaving dark blotches to show their passing.

"Remember, we're only after one of the crowns," Alan reminded the conspirators. "They are virtually identical in every way, so the value is the same, but we don't want to steal the King's crown."

"Because he would notice," Zeke chimed in.

"Exactly. The queen's crown is unused and sits in the heart of Key Castle," Alan continued. "If we do this right, a team will get in, steal the crown, and get out, all without being detected. The theft shouldn't even be noticed for days or weeks, until someone goes looking for the crown for some reason. If we would nab the King's crown, he'll notice almost immediately, and they'll come looking for it."

Heads nodded around the table in agreement. "They would burn Riverfront to the ground," Corin murmured. "They'd almost certainly know it was us that took it – I mean, is there anyone else who would even *try* doing that?"

"No one sane," Ben muttered. "I mean, just for thinking about this, we should probably all be locked up somewhere. We've done a lot of thefts, and we're the best at it, but going into a castle patrolled by the Royal Guard to steal *the crown*?"

"*A* crown, not *the* crown," Alan corrected. "The King's crown is too big a chance. We want the Queen's crown."

"How are we even going to fence it?" Corin asked. "I mean, this is going to be harder to sell than anything else we've ever taken. *Ever*. It's not like it can't be identified, and if we melt it down, it's hardly going to be worth anything."

Alan smiled. "I already have a buyer lined up. He's aware of just how hot the crown will be, and he wants it anyway – for a fair price, too. He said he'd send a courier to pick it up from Riverfront."

Corin frowned. "You're sure he knows exactly what he's going to be getting?"

"Yes," Alan assured her. "He approached me by courier to offer a king's ransom for the crown, but left the details entirely up to me. Believe me, he wants exactly what we're getting for him, and he's paying every bit of gold it's worth."

"This is still absolutely bonkers," Ben said. "It's a *castle*. How do we even get in?"

"That's what we're working on," Alan reminded him, his tone harsh. "Questioning our sanity isn't going to help us get into the castle, now, is it?"

"It would if they decided to lock us up there," Zeke joked. "Then at least we'd be inside."

Bruiser snorted. "And then what, break out by brute force? Even if you managed to escape, they'd be looking for you."

"I was joking," Zeke muttered. "I didn't actually think it was a good way to get in."

"So, then the question remains: how do we get in?" Alan asked as he spread sheets of parchment out, each painstakingly traced with ink lines. "I copied all the plans I could find out of the builder's book, because I didn't want to rip the pages out. After all, when we've got the crown, we'll probably want to sell the book, anyway."

The thieves fell silent as they studied over the floor plans. "Not a lot of ways in," Zeke commented.

"That's sort of the point," Ben retorted, giving voice to his frustration. *This is crazy. How could we possibly do this?*

"Where do we figure the crown's being stored?" Corin asked.

"Here," Alan said, tracing over a small room with his finger. "It's centrally located, underground, and hard to get to."

"Only a single hallway that leads to it," Ben muttered as he looked over the diagram. "You can't tell me they won't have guards in front of it."

"Of course they will," Alan replied calmly. "The King and the Royal Guard aren't stupid. There's a reason I told you this would be a legendary heist."

"So," Zeke spoke up, "even if we can get inside the castle without being detected, we still have to talk our way past some guards to get into the most secure room in the castle?"

"There's no way this could work," Bruiser interjected. "The only way we'd get in there is by fighting, and as soon as we started knockin' heads together, the entire Royal Guard is going to be all over us. This can't be done."

"Ye of little faith," Alan said mildly.

Bruiser's best friend, a boy that mirrored his size but not his temperament, spoke up. "So what tricks do you have to get us in there?" he asked.

"Thank you, Timid, for showing some faith," Alan said haughtily. "At least *someone* still respects me." He reached around the table, drawing together the sketches of different parts of the castle. "Remember, every sketch you're looking at only really shows one flat picture. The trick is how all those pieces go together."

The thieves exchanged looks. Alan sighed. "Here, I'll spell it out."

He started with a single sheet of parchment. "Here are the drain tunnels under the castle," he explained. "They were built to carry away garbage and sewage."

"How big are they?" Bruiser asked uneasily.

He's afraid of tight spaces, Ben recalled. *He doesn't do well on jobs that make him crawl in.*

"Large enough to walk through," Alan said. "But they're locked off by gates, and they've collapsed in at least two places. It's not possible to get in from the outside. Timid scouted it for me."

The boy just nodded.

"Over those tunnels," Alan continued as he picked up another page of parchment, placing it on top, "are the dungeons. It's a miserable, cold, wet, hole-in-the-ground. They throw people in and forget about them. Right now, there's no one in there."

"How do you know?" Ben asked.

"Bribed a guard," Bruiser answered.

"You bribed a guard to see if anyone was in the dungeon?" Corin asked in disbelief.

"I told him I was looking for my big brother," Bruiser said smugly. "Bribed the guard for that information, and he told me there was no one there."

"After he took your money," Alan grumbled.

"After he took my money," Bruiser confirmed.

"Over the dungeons are several rooms," Alan continued, adding another sheet of parchment. "Including the room where the crown is locked up. There's some other vaults that aren't as secure, the guard barracks, and the entrance into the dungeon."

"Sounds like we'd be walking straight into prison," Ben said.

"Patience," Alan chided him. "The next level up is the ground level. Mostly guard barracks, the kitchens, the armory, the stables." He laid the parchment down on top of the pile. "You can see the castle walls and the barracks built into them, and the keep in the middle. Pretty much everything is under the keep."

"Pretty much?" Corin repeated. "What's not?"

Alan ignored the question as he laid down the last parchment. "The upper level of the keep, where the King's quarters are, his great hall, the castle's towers, and everything else is."

"So how are we going to do this?" Ben asked.

Alan shook his head as he picked up the stack of parchment. He discarded the sketch of the sewers, and then the sketches of everything above the ground level, leaving only the dungeon, the vaults, and the first level. He carefully straightened them, then held them up over his head. The sun shone through, allowing the thieves to see all the sketched lines from each parchment.

Corin was the first to see it. "The dungeon is right below the vault, isn't it? That's our escape route."

"Actually, it's our entry route," Alan corrected. "The builder's book has all the information on the material they used to build the vault. It wouldn't take more than an hour of work to break through into the vault to get the crown."

Ben shook his head. "This is crazy. We're going to break into the castle, let ourselves into *the dungeon*, and then work down there for an hour without drawing anyone's attention? Won't we be making enough noise to bring the whole Royal Guard down on us if we're trying to hammer through stone? And besides, how are we going to get into the dungeon in the first place? I mean, we could get arrested and thrown in there, but that would make it a bit harder to get back out."

Nervous chuckles met his protest, but Alan just smiled. "To get in and out, we're going to need to steal a few things first, before we ever go in."

"What sort of things?" Ben asked warily.

"A small number of items enchanted with magic properties," Alan said.

The chuckles turned to nervous murmurs.

Magic isn't something you mess around with, Ben thought. *It's dangerous to everyone. If you're not careful, you go crazy, or it twists you all around into something else. Even the old Magi were careful about how they used it, and they were a bunch of Aither-worshippers.*

"What sort of magic items?" Corin asked tightly, concern etched in her expression. "I don't want to mess with any Magi or Rune Sage's stuff. If something goes wrong, we could find ourselves dead or turned into mice or lizards or something."

"We'll need only a few things," Alan promised. "Some of them aren't even enchanted."

"What are they?" Zeke asked.

"We'll need three sets of the Royal Guard's armor to wear," he said, ticking off each item on his fingers. "We'll also need a tool capable of silently breaking the stone. And we'll need a tool to get us inside the castle in the first place."

"And you already know where all these things are?" Ben asked in disbelief.

"Of course," Alan answered smoothly. "If I didn't, this would be impossible. It is merely difficult."

Stares met his pronouncement, but he just smiled at them for several moments. "Assignments, then," he relented at last. "Corin and Ben, you're first. Everyone else, out."

"Why?" Zeke asked, a little irritation in his voice.

"This job has to happen under absolute strict secrecy," Alan explained. "Which means we're breaking up into teams for these jobs, and no one can know what the others are doing. That way, if one team gets caught, it won't endanger the rest of us."

Zeke reluctantly rose to his feet and departed, along with Bruiser and Timid.

When all three thieves had vanished down into the tower, Alan leaned forward in his chair. "Your job is to get us our means of infiltrating the castle."

"Which are?" Corin asked.

"On a ship at the Jepitsa docks," Alan answered. "It's a trading vessel from the northern continent."

"So what are we taking?" Ben asked eagerly. *This may be crazy, but it'll be the most exciting job we ever pull. There's no way I'm going to get left out of this.*

Instead of answering immediately, Alan produced a fresh sheet of parchment and began quickly sketching out the castle. The drawing was rough and quick, crudely lining out the four massive stone walls and the seven towers ringing the keep. Then he turned to the surrounding terrain, shading in the rise and fall of the gently sloping terrain, as well as blocks to represent the homes built nearby, all belonging to members of the royal court.

"On the east side of the castle," Alan explained, "the ground is a bit higher, and on that spot, Lady Irilyn has her mansion. From the roof, the wall of the castle is only a bit higher – maybe as much as I am tall."

Ben studied the drawing with interest. "So that's our entry point."

Alan nodded, but Corin asked, "If it's that easy to get in there, why would the king let the house stand there?"

"If Jepitsa ever fell under siege and someone tried to take the castle, the king would just order all the close houses to be burned to the ground," Alan explained. "With dry thatched roofs, a few burning arrows would start a fire that no one could put out in time."

"But we're not laying siege, we're just breaking in," Ben reasoned.

"Exactly."

"So how do we get in?" Corin asked.

"One of the beggars at the docks told me that the captain of the trading ship was trying to sell a new machine of war to the Royal Guard," Alan explained. "It was supposed to throw a hook up a castle wall to allow someone to climb over."

"That's stupid," Ben protested. "If you use just one, you can only get a few people up at a time, and it takes a long time to climb a rope straight up. Any guards even half-awake would either cut the rope or kill the attackers as they came up one at a time."

"Which is why the Royal Guard declined to buy it," Alan said with a smile. "But again, we're not attacking the castle."

"We'll still have the same problem, though," Corin commented. "It'll take us a long time to climb up that rope, and I can't imagine a patrolling guard wouldn't see it. How often do they walk the walls?"

"Every five minutes or so," Alan said. "They're not very steady. Sometimes it's more often, but most times it's less."

"That's still too frequent for us to climb up without someone noticing," Corin grumbled.

"Yes," Alan agreed, then tapped on the sketch of Lady Irilyn's house. "That's why we're not going to climb. We'll set the device up there, shoot a rope over to the castle wall, and then cross the rope to the castle wall. It should take less than two minutes."

"How are we going to cross the rope?" Ben asked dubiously.

"None of us are performers, so we won't try to walk it," Alan said. "We'll have to do it the hard way, hand-over-hand until we're across."

"How big is this thing?" Corin asked.

"The beggar told me one man carried it out and demonstrated it, so it can't be too big." Alan shrugged. "I haven't seen it for myself, and we'll have to try it out here with the tower, but I don't see any reason why it won't work." He looked from Corin to Ben, then back to Corin. "Any other questions?"

"How long until the ship sails out of Jepitsa?" Ben asked.

"I don't know," Alan answered honestly. "But they've been in port here for almost a week, so it won't be too much longer. Besides, the river won't stay deep enough much longer for that ship to move, so I'd bet you have to either try for it tonight or tomorrow night. I wouldn't count on it being here much longer."

Ben nodded and looked over at Corin. "Looks like we're partners for this, huh?"

The dark-haired girl gave him a smoldering smile that set Ben's heart to thumping. *Has she always looked like that?* he wondered.

"Partners," she said simply.

Alan took the parchment, folded it up, and slid it into his pocket. "Send in Bruiser and Timid," he said dismissively.

Ben and Corin took the hint, rising to their feet and heading down the stairs into the tower. Below, Bruiser, Timid, and Zeke were sitting on the floor conversing in low tones.

"This is absolutely crazy," Corin murmured.

"I thought I was the only one who felt that way," Ben replied. He nodded at Bruiser and Timid as he passed. "Alan wants to see you two."

"On the up side, if we screw up our job, the theft won't happen," Corin offered. "Without our loot, there's no way to get inside."

"I doubt he'd just let it go," Ben said. "I bet he has a backup plan in case we do fail."

"Think so?" Corin asked.

Ben nodded. "Alan keeps calling this a huge score, the biggest thing that's ever happened to Riverfront. There's no way he doesn't have a second plan in case something would go wrong with the first. We're way past talking about silver coins here – he's probably getting us paid in solid gold bars."

"So, what do you want to do now?" Corin asked. "We're not going to get any more information out of Alan right now."

Ben nodded. "We should go case the ship. Lot easier to do it in daylight when we can actually see."

"Good idea," Corin agreed as they walked out the base of the broken tower.

Ben fell back to thinking as they crossed the river and started walking along the riverbank toward the docks, a good twenty minutes away on foot. *Corin seemed more than happy to be my partner on this job. Maybe she actually is interested in me. I mean, I know she likes me and all, but maybe she actually likes me.* He did his best to keep a hopeful smile from stretching his lips. *Maybe when this is all over, I should spark her.* That thought was immediately followed by, *Or maybe we're already sparking through this whole job, and I don't even know it yet. That sounds about right.* He sighed. *Is it this difficult for the rich people, too? Probably not. I mean, they don't have to worry about being caught by the guards and thrown in a dungeon, and they've all got their nice neat homes and meals and all that other stuff.*

"Ben?" Corin asked quietly, interrupting his thoughts. "What do you think will happen to us if we steal the crown?"

"Alan already has a buyer lined up, so we'll get rid of it right away and be all the richer for it," Ben answered automatically. "Why?"

"Well, let's say it all goes off right," Corin said slowly. "Let's say we steal the crown and we get out and we get the pay. What happens to us then?"

Ben shrugged. "Then we probably don't have to worry about stealing for a long time," he answered.

"But then what? Do we stay in Riverfront? Do we still live like thieves and help the Brigands, even though we don't need to anymore?" Corin persisted. "Do we buy some fancy house inside Jepitsa and live like nobles?"

He opened his mouth to answer, then closed it as he considered her question more carefully. It was an honest, and painful, idea to consider. *If we still live like thieves, we'll all eventually be caught and thrown in jail*, he knew. *But if we use all the payout to buy a house in Jepitsa and live like the king, the guards will* know *something changed. There's no way they wouldn't figure out that we had to have gotten the money from somewhere.*

Corin's voice seemed tiny. "Even if we succeed, we're going to have to leave, aren't we?" she whispered. "There won't be any staying here if we pull it off. Otherwise, we'll eventually be caught, or maybe even Riverfront will pay for it." She blew out a sigh. "Admit it, Ben. If we get out with the crown, everything is going to change. Everything will *have* to change."

Ben refused to agree. "There has to be something else we can do," he said instead. "I mean, Alan has to have thought about this, too, right? He must have some plan for all of us. Otherwise *he* would have to leave, too."

"Are you sure he's not planning on leaving?" Corin asked.

Ben shook his head. "Why would he leave? He calls the Brigands his family."

"Yeah," Corin said flatly. "Family."

She sounds a bit bitter about that. Ben observed. *Like she doesn't believe it.*

"Do you remember your family?" Corin asked abruptly. "Your *real* family, not the Brigands."

Ben shrugged a little uncomfortably. "Not really. I think I was five winters when they were killed in the last attempt to overthrow the king."

"What do you remember?" the girl asked.

The memories were faded and few, and Ben hadn't spent much time keeping them fresh. "They were peasants, I think. They lived only a little ways from Key Castle. When the Magi came with their puppet-king, they set fire to all the houses close to the castle to try to force the king out. I remember the fear, and not really being sure what was happening..." his voice trailed off. *I remember them cut down*, he added silently. *I remember someone running them through with swords, and trying to get Mama to wake up. I remember someone picking me up and carrying me out of that hell.* Aloud, he said, "Besides that, there's only a few things."

"Tell me," Corin said.

"I remember the smell of wood," Ben continued reluctantly. "The house always smelled like fresh-cut wood. I even remember my hands being sticky with sap a few times." He shrugged. "It's so long ago that I'm not sure what's real, and what I made up afterwards."

"They were carpenters, then?" she asked.

"I guess so," Ben hedged. "I mean, I don't really remember. It would make sense, though." He glanced over at her. "What about you? Do you remember your family?"

Silence met his question. The two walked along the riverbank, but it didn't feel companionable. *I suppose I shouldn't have asked*, Ben thought glumly. *She must not have wanted to talk about her own family. She just seems so bitter about the Brigands. It's like she doesn't trust Alan.* That thought registered with cold clarity. *What if she's right? I mean, it's not like she's the first one to suggest that Alan isn't trustworthy. Maybe we really do need to get away from him.*

"I remember my parents," Corin said, her voice so low Ben could barely hear her. The sudden intrusion of her voice snapped his line of thought and brought his attention back squarely on her. "They threw me out into the street the day before the rebel army stormed Jepitsa. I was crying in the gutter when the rebels stormed the castle and broke down the gates."

"Why would they throw you out?" Ben asked, the words out before he could think better of it. *Stupid, stupid, stupid,* he scolded himself. *I'm sure that's exactly what she wanted to hear. Why don't you just ask her if she thinks her parents hated her? It's just as blunt and probably would have the same answer.*

Surprisingly, Corin just shrugged. "I don't know," she said honestly. "We had food, so it's not like we were starving and they couldn't afford me anymore." Her eyes were distant when she added, "Maybe they just didn't want me anymore. Maybe they were trying to protect me."

"Protect you? Protect you how?" he asked skeptically. "You were so much better off in the gutter than in their home," he added, then winced. *Wow, that was stupid, too. Maybe even dumber than the first time.*

"They tossed me out just before the traitors arrived," Corin said softly. "Maybe that's what they were protecting me from. If they were loyalists, maybe they were afraid I'd be taken or killed if I stayed with them."

Ben didn't respond, choosing instead to remain silent for fear of saying something even worse. Corin seemed to be lost in her own memories as they continued to walk toward the Jepitsa docks and their target.

Stick to the job, he told himself. *Worry about Corin later. Find your mark and make your plans to steal what you need. Keep your head on straight, Ben.*

The docks were huge, easily large enough to handle six or eight ships at a time, by Ben's estimation. As the two thieves approached, Ben picked out four different ships in dock with several more waiting nearby in the river. Yet another ship was pulled all the way up into a drydock, with carpenters nailing fresh-cut new planks into place and pulling old, barnacle-covered, cracked boards away.

"Which ship is it?" Corin asked quietly, breaking her silence.

Ben shrugged. "Alan told you as much as he told me," he responded honestly. "We'll have to scout them all out, I guess, and find our mark."

VIII

ARRAYA'S TEMPLES THROBBED AS THE world began to brighten. She tried to bring her hands up to rub at the offending pain, but she couldn't seem to muster the strength. Her hands and feet gave her no sensation at all, and as her senses sharpened, she realized her nose and cheeks were numb from cold.

What happened? she wondered as she tried to pry her eyelids open. The additional light stabbed at her eyes and she squeezed them shut again for a moment before forcing them open. Bright, if somewhat distant, fire light assaulted her again, but she refused to be cowed. Slowly, she managed to focus her gaze and began to take in her surroundings.

As she tried to make sense of the landscape, her tumbling memories slowed, then locked into something approaching comprehension. *I was riding down the* mountain, trying to catch up with Master Shallum before he could walk into a trap at Jepitsa. No, I was out of the mountains. I was in the forest, and then there was a sharp pain and I fell from my horse. Then nothing.

The apprentice continued to push through the jumbled images, trying to push her way to a conclusion. I was struck in the head, and now I lie thirty strides from a campfire. I must have been ambushed by highwaymen.

With that conclusion fixed in her mind, she tested her hands again. I'm bound with my hands behind me, she concluded. A similar quick flex revealed her ankles were tied just as tightly. Well done, apprentice, she congratulated herself. Your attempt to rescue your master from certain doom has put you in the hands of criminals. No doubt they are prepared to end your life.

That thought niggled at her as clarity finally returned to her vision, allowing her to take in her surroundings. Why am I still alive and bound, rather than dead in a ditch?

Arraya didn't move anything but her eyes as she studied the campsite. A dozen or more bandits were clustered close to the bonfire, dressed in rags and scraps of armor. Definitely bandits, not the army of the Imposter-King, she decided. Armed well enough, though, with swords and bows alike. And in my current state, I wouldn't be able to fight back.

She focused her gaze more tightly on the highwaymen. It was a struggle to make out the details, but she finally concluded, They're Tillik bandits. What are they doing here, *on the edge of Cosmane? We're very close to Werbri, and a long ways from the swamps of Telka.*

The apprentice could only look around at her surroundings for a few moments before a sense of helplessness threatened to overwhelm her. Arraya closed her eyes and worked to keep the feeling locked away, trying to focus instead on an escape plan.

With my hands bound, my options are limited, she concluded tightly. *I can't conjure up fire to burn my way out of these bonds. They're too snug for me to wiggle loose. I can't addle their minds, either.* She swallowed. *So remain patient and alert, and wait for an opportunity to escape. Patience, patience, patience, and you'll find a way out.*

She spent several minutes just concentrating on breathing. The apprentice felt her heart rate slow as she calmed her mind. *Patience,* she decided more firmly. *You're a Magi, Arraya. You have been trained well by Master Shallum. Keep your wits about you and you will survive even this.*

Her introspection was interrupted by a swift kick to her gut. Arraya's breath left her in a flash, leaving her gasping. Her eyes opened of their own accord, in time to see the retracting boot of a Tillik bandit.

The highwayman bent down over her. The unwashed reek pouring off the Tillik was almost enough to gag the apprentice in spite of her discipline. She managed to turn her head enough to look up into an unblinking, yellowed reptilian eye. Mostly, though, she concentrated on trying to catch her breath.

"Good," the Tillik hissed, "you're awake. It is time for you to eat, captive."

He gripped her long red hair with a scaly claw and pulled her up to a sitting position. Arraya barely managed to strangle her scream to a pained groan, drawing on every bit of the discipline Shallum had instilled in her during her long, intense training. The apprentice glowered at the Tillik as she shook her head, trying to push away the pain. *When my hands are free, I'll burn you from the inside out*, she thought nastily. *Just a bit of fire conjured inside that lizard skin and you'll regret having laid a hand on me!*

The Tillik stepped away from her toward another bound figure, a captive Arraya hadn't even noticed previously. She took advantage of the moment to size up the Tillik bandit.

Like others of his race, the lizard-man stood about as tall as a human man. His skin was grey and scaled, not unlike that of his smaller, four-legged cousins. This particular Tillik favored his right leg, she noted – either a fresh injury or an old wound that never healed correctly. His long tail dragged in the dirt behind him with the limpness of an older member of his race. His stubby snout was lined with a mix of whole and broken teeth, capable of effortlessly ripping away flesh from their prey.

What are the lizards doing here? she wondered again. *And what are they going to do with me?*

The Tillik jerked the other captive up to sitting, the blonde-haired girl in a mirror pose of Arraya's own awkward, bound position. The girl growled at the Tillik, sounding more angry than pained from the rough handling.

"Quiet, or I'll remove your tongue," the Tillik threatened. "The boy will be along with your gruel in a few minutes." The bandit kicked the blonde-haired girl in the kidney, drawing a pained gasp from her before he stalked off again.

Arraya watched the girl sit with heaving shoulders for a few moments, her face hidden behind a curtain of hair. Her tunic was white wool, though the left sleeve was brown and a different material. Her hair was a tangled, dirty mess, which shook as the girl attempted to control herself. Finally, the girl looked up enough to see the apprentice. Her blue eyes seemed to stare straight through Arraya's and into her soul.

The apprentice, however, was not one to be unsettled by an intense gaze.

"Ho," Arraya greeted quietly.

The other prisoner nodded in acknowledgement. "Ho," she replied.

"Who are these thieves?" Arraya asked without preamble.

The girl studied her for a long moment before replying, "You are an odd one."

"That is not an answer," the apprentice stated flatly.

"You sit bound in the wilderness, beset upon by the inimical, and you remain collected," the girl continued as though Arraya hadn't spoken. "You are dressed as a peasant, perhaps a girl from a mill or farm. Yet I can't imagine a flame-haired girl from such a profession would manage this serenity. So, I ask myself an important question: who could this stranger be?" She snorted in derision. "I can only imagine a few types of people who would be so fearless in this situation. I doubt any of them would be my ally, particularly if they are allied with these scaleskins."

Arraya stared at the blond girl, unraveling everything the other captive had said. *Wait…what she said…does she think I'm an ally of these Tillik bandits? Of course. They're trying to get something out of her, and she thinks they're using me to do it.*

"Answer me one simple question, and I'll do my best to prove to you I'm not allied with the Tillik," Arraya said.

The girl's eyes narrowed, clearly looking for the trap. "Ask," she said at last.

"Who do the Tilliks think you are?" Arraya asked simply.

The girl studied Arraya for several heartbeats before slowly answering. "They believe I'm a noble from Rapien, traveling to Jepitsa to attend the king's court. They intend to ransom me back to the Rapien court for gold."

"If I can tell you then who you truly are, will you believe I am not an ally of these highwaymen?" Arraya asked.

"I promise nothing," the girl replied. "But I will consider what I hear."

Arraya studied the captive with a critical eye, re-evaluating her initial snap-judgment of the girl. *Yes, it has to be*, she decided. *It's the only thing that makes sense.*

"You are not of Rapien," Arraya said, her voice low. "The sun darkens their skin and their hair. Your skin and hair alike are too light to be a citizen of Rapien, let alone a noble. Rapien is also to the west. Were you truly voyaging from Rapien to Jepitsa, you would have no reason to be this far south. Your features mark you as born of Cosmane, here in the south."

The girl snorted. "Is that all the reason I'm supposed to believe you?" she spat, venom dripping in her words. "Because you think I'm from the area we're sitting in?"

"I never said you were of Cosmane," Arraya reproved gently. "Only that your blood is of this area. No, you are from Erixi, the island-city in the east."

The girl's mouth fell open in shock for a moment before she snapped it shut. "Is that the best you have? Wild guessed and speculation?"

The apprentice smiled. "Come, now. While Erixans are dark-haired, they have adopted from both Cosmane and Rapien in the past. Your shirt betrays your origins, even if the Tilliks do not recognize it."

"What are you talking about?" the girl snapped, but her voice lacked its previous heat. "My shirt?"

"Of course. The left sleeve is not wool, but leather, to protect your arm from the danger of your preferred weapon." Arraya locked eyes with the captive girl. "You're a shootist from Erixi. An assassin."

Before the captive could speak, a Tillik stepped out of the shadows, his arms cradling a large iron pot. "Gruel," he stated, his voice not nearly as flat or harsh as his predecessor.

Both Arraya and the other captive were silent as the Tillik captor poured out bowls of thin gruel. "My name is Seewulz J'Ram," he said conversationally as he worked. "What are your names?"

Neither girl spoke. The Tillik sighed as he lifted one of the bowls. "This is why I hate taking ransoms," he grumbled. "There's no one as hostile as a noble held against her will. It's not worth the effort."

He approached the blond girl first. Arraya watched carefully. *He's younger than the others, maybe even just a boy*, she observed as she studied his brighter, more supple skin. *Inexperienced. If someone is going to make a mistake and give me an opportunity, it will be him.* She flexed her wrists a little, trying to work feeling into her hands. *If he unbinds me to eat, I can call up wind and fire and these Tilliks won't have a chance.*

The young Tillik knelt beside the other captive and lifted the bowl to her lips. He gently tipped it back, forcing her to drink it or spit it out. Her hands remained firmly bound behind her back, giving her no chance to fight back.

The girl swallowed the broth without protest or comment, never meeting his eyes or giving any further cooperation than the simple act of eating required.

Arraya blew out a quick sigh. *So much for that idea. I'll just have to bide my time.*

The Tillik stood with the bowl, leaving the Erixan with gruel dripping from her lips. He returned to the pot and exchanged the emptied container for a filled one, this time approaching Arraya.

As he lifted the bowl, she decided to try a different tact. "My name is Arraya," she said quietly.

The Tillik hesitated, clearly floundering with his next action. "Ho, Arraya," he greeted her.

"What is in the bowl, Seewulz?" the apprentice asked him. *Anything to get him to slow down and make a mistake. Anything to give me an opportunity.*

"Barley broth," the Tillik said. "Seewulz is my clan name; J'Ram is my given name."

"Your family name is first?" Arraya asked. *Maybe I can develop a rapport with him. If he feels some connection with me, he may be willing to act against the rest of these bandits.* She swallowed. *Yes, it's not likely, but work with what you have, Arraya.*

The Tillik bobbed his head in confirmation. "Yes. It makes far more sense than a given name first. Other Tillik will wish to know me by my clan first, and my own identity second."

Arraya opened her mouth to ask another question, and found it filled with warm gruel instead. She hastily swallowed, trying to keep herself from choking.

"Now, you must eat," J'Ram said solemnly as she tried to keep swallowing the thin fluid. "It would hardly do for a captive to come to harm in my care. A human harmed or dead is hardly of use to us for ransom, and my *ilduce* would be unhappy should we lose potential profit."

Arraya was finally granted reprieve as the bowl emptied. "What is *ilduce?*" she asked, wheezing for breath. "Is that your father?"

"In your tongue, it would be 'chieftain' or 'leader,' I think," the Tillik said. "I follow his commands, as do all Tilliks of this band."

"Of this band?" Arraya asked. "This isn't your clan?"

J'Ram shook his head. "I do not follow the path of my clan," he said quietly. Then he looked up at her as though startled, his golden eyes wide. "I speak too much," he said at last, rising to his booted feet and dusting off his clothes. "Sleep now, Arraya. Do not try to escape, or the *ilduce* will be unhappy."

The lizard-man stopped long enough to collect the mostly-empty pot and disappeared into the darkness again.

Arraya pondered the encounter. *So, there may be some dissension in the ranks,* she observed. *This isn't his family, just a few highwaymen, so he likely won't be very loyal to them. And from what he's said about his* ilduce, *I would guess he fears him more than loves him. Now all I have to do is find something to offer him that shows him turning on the other bandits and setting me free would be the most valuable thing to do.*

Yeah, right. I'm sure that'll work out perfectly for me.

She looked up from her musings to see the other captive staring at her again, icy blue eyes just as intense as before. "Yes?" Arraya asked.

"Who are you?" the girl asked.

Arraya shook her head. "Not until you give me your name. If you want me to trust you, you must trust me first."

The girl cocked an eyebrow at her. "Shouldn't it flow both ways?" she asked.

"It will, once you establish trust." Arraya leaned forward, trying to find a more comfortable sitting position. "I took the first step by showing you that I was not working with these highwaymen. It's your turn."

The girl gnawed her lip. "Fine." She remained silent, and Arraya thought the impasse would remain, but the Erixan surprised her. "My name is Naomi," she offered reluctantly.

"You really are an Erixan, then," Arraya stated, not asked.

Naomi nodded. "Yes, I am." Her expression darkened. "I was sure my shirt was obscure enough that no one would identify me by it."

"It is," Arraya assured her. "I doubt more than a hundred people on the whole continent could have identified you."

"Then how did you manage it?" the Erixan countered. "And what's your name? Who are you?"

The flame-haired girl stopped herself from answering. *Okay, wait,* she told herself. *There are more lives than your own at stake. Master Shallum, on the way to Jepitsa, is still in danger. All the Magi still hidden in Cosmane could be compromised, not to mention the apprentices. If I say the wrong thing, or the wrong person hears me, my words could be a death sentence for dozens of people.*

It was all solid logic, of course. But her heart contradicted her head. *You've already took a step of trust towards this girl. She could be a valuable ally in escaping these bandits. Two of us would have a much better chance of surviving than one alone.*

Naomi continued to stare at her with that unsettling, unblinking gaze. "Well? What, are you a spy from one of the kingdoms on the northern continent? Maybe you're a courier for the King himself? Or an assassin from one of the southern tribes, or..." her eyes clouded with suspicion, "*you* are from Rapien, which is why you knew I *wasn't*."

Arraya watched as her hopes for an alliance with the Erixan began to evaporate. *Take the chance!* "My name is Arraya," the apprentice said. "And no, I'm not from the northern continent, I don't work for the Imposter-King, and I'm not from Rapien, either."

"Then who are you?" Naomi asked, her voice openly suspicious again. "Maybe you *are* working for the Tilliks."

"No." Arraya took a deep breath. *If I do this, I'm betraying the survival of the Magi. The knowledge of their – our – survival will no longer be secret.* "I'm an apprentice of the Magi," she said, her reluctance every bit the equal of the Erixan's.

Naomi's eyes widened from suspicious slits to shocked saucers. "A Magi?"

Arraya nodded slowly. "Yes. I'm still an apprentice, but yes, I'm a Magi."

Naomi snorted. "You must either be crazy or think I'm stupid."

That wasn't what the apprentice had expected, and it rocked her back. "What?" she asked cleverly. *Great, that helped win her over.*

"Yes, a Magi would just sit here bound hand and foot while bandits try to figure out how to make money off her," Naomi said derisively. "She wouldn't, I don't know, conjure up fire and burn away the ropes, or maybe just call lightning down to strike the bandits dead. Nope, she'll just sit and act helpless like a farm girl."

Arraya wasn't sure how to respond, and she stared with jaw dropped while Naomi continued.

"Okay, I'm going to assume crazy rather than thinking I'm that stupid. You can't *possibly* think I'm that stupid." Naomi frowned at Arraya. "Definitely crazy. That would explain why you were riding by yourself with no weapons and no escort in bandit country. If you're crazy enough to think you're a Magi, you probably really did think you could using magic to protect yourself."

"I..." Arraya started.

"So tell me, crazy girl," Naomi continued, "why don't you just use magic to untie these knots so we can both walk away?"

"It's one of the rules!" Arraya protested.

"Rules? What rules?" Naomi demanded. "Is this just some insane game that you're playing?"

Arraya shook her head. "Nothing like that. But there's rules to being a Magi."

"Oh? And these rules say you have to stay tied up if someone binds you?" the Erixan grumbled. "Why did they have to put the crazy girl with me?"

Arraya's temper flared. "Enough with calling me crazy," she growled.

"The bracelet fits, so it sure looks like it's yours," Naomi snapped back.

This is not *going as planned*, Arraya thought darkly. *Definitely not as planned. She's lucky I* can't *draw on the magic right now.* She took a long, deep breath and blew out her irritation with it. Several more such breaths left her mind calmed and back in control. "What do you know about the Magi?" she asked, her voice soft.

Naomi raised an eyebrow at Arraya's mood change, but didn't comment. Instead, she answered, "The Magi are freaks – the only people who can use magic raw, without runes or anything to control it. They used to advise the king, but there was a falling out twenty years ago when the throne changed hands."

Arraya chose not to dispute Naomi's characterization of the succession war from two decades prior – a war completed before either of them had been born. "Magi aren't much different than normal people, physically," Arraya explained, "except we're born with the gift. Yes, we can manipulate and feel magic without any of the crude tools the Rune Sages use. There's restrictions on how we can use it, though."

"Restrictions?" Naomi frowned. "What do you mean, restrictions?"

"If we don't follow the rules, we lose our power," she said. "And then we're no different than any human."

"So, one of the rules is that you can't use your magic to escape something like this?" Naomi guessed, bringing the conversation back around to where they had started. "And if you did, you'd lose your ability?"

Arraya shook her head. "Close, but not quite. Using magic will never cause us to *lose* the magic; it's other things that do." She shrugged. "There's a reason no Magi has ever assumed the throne, for example – if he tried to rule, the True Magic would abandon him."

"So why can't you burn off these ropes?" Naomi asked.

The apprentice hesitated. *I'm telling her too much, even if she doesn't completely believe me. Of course, in for an ounce, in for a pound.* "My magic doesn't work if I'm bound," she said reluctantly. "I can't touch it, can't summon it, can't do anything with it unless the ropes are cut off."

"You really are crazy," Naomi said flatly.

"It's true!" Arraya protested, a bit hurt by the repeated accusation. "My master taught me it was to ensure that even a rogue Magi could be restrained, if needed. We can be captured and held like any other being, if necessary. We're not above the laws that everyone else must abide by."

"Crazy," Naomi muttered. "Absolutely crazy."

The two girls sat in silence as the fire burned down. Arraya struggled with the numbness in her hands, aching for the rope to be released. Without the magic to draw upon, she found herself colder as the hours passed. It had been so long since harsh temperatures had truly concerned her that she had nearly forgotten the sensation and the *pain* as frigid air sank its talons into her.

Drowsiness slowly settled on her shoulders with the weight of a mountain. She worried the cold would kill her in her sleep, but without her powers she had no real way to fight it off, and helplessly dozed off in her stupor.

Ropes bound the apprentice hand and foot, and the blizzard whirling around her blinded her. She tried to draw on her powers for strength and warmth, to destroy the rope and keep herself warm, but the magic would not answer her summons.

"Even the Magi have limits," her master said, unseen but heard in the blinding white of the snowstorm. "We wield great power – perhaps more than any other being to walk this world – but it comes with costs and rules."

The wall of white seemed to part, and her master stepped through it. "It is easy, as a Magi, to become convinced of your own invincibility. You can tap into the most primeval of energy and bend the world to your wishes. You can crack mountains and part rivers to walk on dry land, summon storms or banish clouds from the sky."

The apprentice wondered in her cold haze if the falling snow was natural, or if her master had summoned it for this lesson.

"Yet if you are bound, your powers are nothing. I understand what you are thinking, even now, little one: what if I can free a hand, or free even a finger? At what point does my power return?"

He knelt in the ankle-deep snow around her. "It is not the bindings that matter – it matters not if it is rope or chain or twine. It is the symbol *of capture that deprives you of your power. You are a prisoner, a slave, and as such you have no* right *to wield the true magic."*

The apprentice found her voice. "What if I escape?"

"You're not listening, apprentice," the master said. "You try to find an escape from a defeat already inflicted upon you. You are trying to evade the consequences of your failure. Before you can use the magic again, you must accept the defeat. Then you must earn *the return of your power."*

"Earn it? How?" the apprentice asked in her confusion. "By escaping?"

"By being worthy to use it." The master paced a slow circle around the bound apprentice. "Exercise of power requires free will. If you are beholden to another's will, whether by shackles or by sworn servitude, you cannot use the power. Only if your mind is free and your soul is your own, will the magic embrace you."

"What other rules are there with our power, then? What will cause me to lose it?"

"They are few in number, but important. To break any of these rules will be to give up the true magic forever. There is no negotiation, no warnings — there is, or isn't. Cross the line and the magic will no longer be yours, and you will be a mere mortal forever. Do you understand this, apprentice?"

"I do," the apprentice said.

"First, the path of power is a solitary trail. If you are to be a Magi, there is no room in your life to love or be married. Our power is too vast, too dangerous, to allow our personal feelings purchase. A mistake could be disastrous for everyone. Thus,

your power will ebb should you choose to pursue the path of love."

"No husband, no children?" the apprentice asked.

"Does that sway you from the path of the Magi?" the master countered. "Perhaps it is time for your training to end, if you do not think you can make the sacrifices necessary."

"I can," the apprentice declared. "I can do what is necessary."

"Second," the master continued, "the path of power is a trail of service. With our great power, the temptation to rule will always exist. Our magics could be used to enthrall populations, raise armies, and utterly destroy our foes. Because of this, you can never sit upon a throne or take power over another. Should you choose to become a queen, your power will abandon you, and you will be merely human."

"Third," the master finished, "the path of power is restraint. Just as you cannot love, and cannot rule as distant royalty, you can never infringe upon another's ability to choose. No one can force you to give up your gifts – only you can make that choice. In turn you cannot force another to give up their own decisions."

"Do you mean I can't act at all?" the apprentice asked in confusion. "For surely anything I do will cause changes and remove choices from others' options."

"That is the nature of living, apprentice," the master reproved her gently. "What you cannot do is infringe directly upon another's free will. You cannot twist his mind nor enslave his soul. Just as your powers can only be taken from you by your decisions, so too is the ability for others to choose *sacrosanct. The ability to choose is what differentiates us and our brethren races from the beasts that roam the land. If you deny another the right to choose, so too shall your power be denied to you."*

The ropes fell away from the apprentice's wrists and ankles. In an instant, the power flowed back into her chilled limbs, and she could sense the magic all around her. The briefest twist of her will seemed to warm the very air, driving back the biting cold. "Is losing the power permanent?" she asked.

"If you break any of those three rules, yes," the master said. "Hold those above all other commands. If the Council of the Magi or the King himself commands you to break one of the three rules, you should not listen."

Arraya blinked herself awake as a Tillik stirred the dying embers of the fire. The small warmth felt good against the numbness that seemed to spread throughout her body. She immediately closed her eyes to a squint, watching the Tillik as she tried to clear the fog from her mind. *Wait for an opportunity*, she told herself. *Maybe they'll untie you to ensure your hands aren't damaged. All you need is a chance.*

She recognized the figure stirring the fire as the younger lizard-man, J'Ram. She laid as still as possible. *If someone is likely to make a mistake, it'll be the young one. He's less experienced than the others.*

The apprentice was painfully aware, for a brief moment, that the description would fit her as well. She was heir to an ancient tradition and an unrivaled power, but her inattentiveness and inexperience had directly led to her current predicament. She had no doubt Master Shallum would have ridden through the ambush unscathed.

The flames were starting to grow as J'Ram piled more dried timber on the coals. The warmth began to grow, and Arraya had to fight the sense of contentment and drowsiness that followed it. *Don't give in and fall asleep. You can't afford to miss your chance.*

Another Tillik figure stepped into Arraya's field of vision – the older Tillik, the *ilduce*.

"J'Ram!" he called gruffly. "Quit wasting your time with that fire. These thinskins don't need to be pampered."

The younger Tillik dropped his head in subservience. "Yes, *ilduce*."

"I need you to prepare these two before the sun is up. We'll be breaking camp and moving further west," the *ilduce* ordered. "Can't afford to run afoul of any patrols. Jepitsa is extending its reach further all the time."

"I shall feed them and ensure they are ready to march by dawn," J'Ram confirmed.

The *ilduce* laughed. "They will not be joining us."

The younger Tillik rocked back on his heels. "I'm to...kill them?" he ventured.

Arraya's heart fell. *If he does that, he'll never unbind me. I'll be dead without the chance to protect myself.* She silently strained against the bonds, but they were well-knotted. Similarly she reached for her power, but the magic refused to answer her summons.

"Was your father this foolish, too?" the *ilduce* spat. "No. The courts of Rapien claim they know nothing of the first captive, and the second is no more than a peasant. Killing two young thinskins would be a waste when there is still value." Arraya swore she could see the *ilduce*'s eyes glitter with malice in the firelight. "A slave caravan from Prona will be passing this way as soon as the sun is up. Mark these two with brands, chain them as befitting slaves, and we'll sell them shortly after dawn. Then they're the Pronan's problem."

IX

THE DOCKS WERE TOO BRIGHT for Ben to feel entirely comfortable as he and Corin laid on their bellies behind a low bush, watching.

Nightfall had offered some small amount of concealment, but it had also brought with it the light of the moon. The docks and the ships were bathed in dim, pale light – bringing enough illumination to make the thieves' job much harder. Both he and Corin had expected an overcast sky, with the clouds working in their favor to obscure the light, but right before sundown the clouds had dissipated. Now, Ben felt exposed even under the comforting familiar darkness.

"This is going to get interesting," Corin muttered. "Do we need to rethink our approach?"

Ben nodded. "I'm don't think our first plan is going to work real well."

The first plan had been to sneak down onto the docks between guard patrols and simply walk right up onto the ship they had identified as the merchant vessel. The patrols were opposing circuits, with each guard meeting his counterpart twice during a patrol. Ben and Corin had watched and timed the circuits, finding they had plenty of time to slip between the guards, but they had counted on darkness to prevent the guards from seeing past the light cast by their torches.

"So, second plan," Corin said. "How do you feel about that right now?"

Ben grimaced. "That's going to be *cold*," he complained.

"You're a big Brigand," Corin joked quietly. "You can handle it."

"You first," Ben offered. Corin's hesitation brought a smile to his face. "Admit it, you don't want to go swimming through the river right now, either."

"I just don't like swimming at night," the girl said dismissively. "Too easy for something to go wrong."

"Got a better idea?" Ben asked.

"That's the problem. I don't."

"Me, neither," he admitted, studying the docks further. *We might be able to slip past the guards*, he told himself. *Those torches are bright, which means they can't see very far in the dark. If we're careful, we might be able to get between them.*

"We're going to have to swim," Corin said at last. "We can't risk trying to get between the patrols."

"Circle around and swim to the dock?" Ben asked.

Corin nodded. "Climb onto the dock and climb one of the ropes right up to the ship," she agreed. "That should get us on board without anyone getting a good look at us."

"You hope."

"I hope," Corin repeated.

Retreating further down the riverbank took only a few minutes; while the bright moonlight made a straight attempt too risky, neither Ben nor Corin were concerned about exposure to far-away observers. When they had retreated a few hundred paces up the river, Corin led the way into the cool water of the river.

Ben grimaced as he slid in behind her. "I don't like swimming in clothes," he grumbled.

"Me, neither," Corin said teasingly.

"That wasn't what I...oh, never mind," Ben growled. *Was she teasing me?* he wondered to himself. *Or is she actually interested in me?*

"I vote against swimming," Corin whispered to him, though there was clearly no one around to overhear. "Let's just stay close to the shore and walk as close as we can. If we swim, we'll be tired by the time we get there."

"Sounds good," Ben agreed.

Submerged neck-deep in the river, the two thieves slowly walked back to the docks, fighting against the current the entire way. The river wasn't swift at all, but the inexorable pull of the water seemed to sap Ben's strength. In the concealment provided by the water, he felt much better about his chances of escaping detection, but it slowed him immensely. He guessed it took about three times as long to walk back up the river then it had to walk down the shore.

When they had nearly reached the harbor and the docks, Corin finally slipped away from the bank and plunged into deeper water. Ben followed her unhesitantly. The water seemed almost warm after the pair had been submerged in it long enough, though Ben wasn't sure if it was really the temperature of the water, or just how cold his body really was.

The two paddled out into the river, trying to minimize their splashing as they swam toward the ships. *If we make too much noise, someone will come investigate*, Ben knew. *And in the water like this, it'd be even harder to get away. We're not going to be able to outrun the guards like this.*

As they neared the first ship, Ben began to feel warmer. *Swimming is good for me*, he thought. *Keeps the cold away.*

They reached the first ship and swam just past it, to the long wooden dock running alongside it. Corin ducked under the surface of the water for a moment, then surfaced below the dock, completely concealed from anyone looking down at the water. She gestured for Ben to follow, and he did, though he smacked his head against the dock when he surfaced.

"Quiet," Corin hissed as Ben rubbed his head. "That's a good way to get us caught."

"If I do it again, I'll be knocked out and it'll be the least of my worries," Ben said stiffly. "Thanks for caring."

"I care," Corin said. "I care about not getting caught."

"Just what I thought."

"Okay, so our target ship is the next one in, right?" she asked.

Ben nodded. "That's the only one in dock that looks like it could handle ocean travel. Everything else is too small and too light. If this ship really came from the northern continent, that would be it."

"Swim or walk?" Corin asked.

Ben looked across at the ship, then up at the dock above them. "Swim," he decided. "If we walk, there's a worse chance a ship watchman or a guard will spot us. If we swim, we're near-concealed for the entire way, and we can just pop up on the dock and walk onto the ship. Less chance of getting caught."

Corin nodded in agreement. "Just wanted to make sure we were on the same page," she said.

The two thieves slipped out from under the dock and started swimming for the next ship. As he paddled along, Ben kept looking for the light of torches. *All it takes is one guard to stop and take a leak, and this whole thing will be for nothing*, he knew.

But their luck held, and they reached the next dock without incident.

Corin was silent as she found the wooden ladder nailed to the dock. The wood was half-rotted from its extended submersion in the river, but it held her weight as she slowly climbed. The girl was careful to move slowly, trying to minimize the sound.

Ben winced at every stray drop of water splashing back into the river. *It sounds like an army marching in,* he thought. *Even though the guards probably can't hear it.* He knew all his own senses were on high alert, watching and waiting for any sign of detection. It was the familiar rush of a theft, walking straight into a target knowing full well the job could go sour in a heartbeat and doom him to years clapped in chains and rotting in a dungeon somewhere.

Corin slid stomach-down onto the dock, keeping her profile low. When her feet had vanished over the edge, Ben followed suit, starting his own ascent.

He was halfway out of the water and lifting his left foot to step up when the rung under his right foot broke. He very nearly plunged back into the river, and the *crack* of the breaking wood echoed like thunder in his ears. He nearly fell, but held himself up by the strength of his arms alone. Immediately he froze, listening for any sound of detection.

Sweet silence was all he could hear, aside from his own and Corin's very faint breathing. He hung like that for seconds, or minutes, or hours – he couldn't tell with the sound of his own heart pounding in his ears. When no one rushed to investigate, when no guards came storming up the dock, he finally swung his left foot onto the rung and continued his ascent.

He belly-crawled over the edge, slowly pulling himself along until he lay even with Corin on the rough planks of the dock.

"That was kinda loud," Corin whispered. "What happened?"

"Rung broke," was Ben's succinct reply.

The two laid side-by-side for some time, watching for any sign of the guards, or any ship watchman on the lookout for intruders. When they saw a single guard appear from the east and disappear to the west, followed a few moments later by a guard from the west heading east, they began to count in whispers. When they had both reached a hundred, they began to crawl toward the gangplank leading up to the ship.

The merchant vessel was silent and still as a watery tomb when they had reached that milestone. As they had planned, Corin and Ben both rose to a crouch, waited a half-dozen heartbeats for any shouts of alarm, then sprinted up the plank, sacrificing stealth for speed for that span.

Immediately after reaching the deck, Corin dropped flat, laying prone in the shadow cast by the railing. Ben followed and realized, only as he was dropping, that she hadn't left enough room for him behind her. He wound up laying half on top of her, an awkward bundle in the concealment of the shadows.

"Sorry," he whispered.

She shot him a gleaming smile through the darkness. "Who said that wasn't what I was trying to do?" she teased.

Ben shook his head. *If she's interested in me, she picks odd times to show it.*

Corin had just started to crawl forward when Ben heard footsteps approaching. He laid a warning hand on

Corin's leg and squeezed, bringing her immediately to a stop. They both froze, trying hard not to even breathe, as the footsteps grew louder.

Then there were three sailors walking up the gangplank from the dock. *If they see us,* Ben decided, *we'll go for the rail and dive for the river. It's not real deep, but that's the only way we're going to get away.*

The sailors were in good cheer, laughing and stumbling along. *Drunk,* Ben decided. *Have to enjoy the city life when it's to be had, right?*

Then the sailors were on the deck of the ship, so close Ben could smell the rum on their clothes, could reach out and touch their legs if he so chose. But it wasn't three sailors – it was four, with the fourth carried by two of his fellows.

Ben merely watched and waited, and imagined Corin was doing the same, as the four men meandered across the deck and then vanished below deck. The night grew still again in the wake of their passing.

"That was too close," Ben whispered. "If we would've been a minute or two slower, they would've seen us."

"They were so drunk we could've been standing up and they wouldn't have noticed," Corin retorted, a bit too loudly for Ben's comfort. "C'mon, let's do this. If I'm going to spend all night lying down, there are far more comfortable places to be than here."

Ben snorted and followed Corin as she rose into a crouch and hustled across the deck. Their movements still seemed obvious to him, their footsteps loud, their breathing harsh, but their luck had seemed to hold well so far. *Still, all it takes is one mistake*, he told himself. *Don't make that mistake.*

Corin found the hatch leading down into the belly of the ship. The captain's quarters were a very large cabin on the stern of the ship, while the crew quarters were immediately below and accessed by stairs. The cargo hold, however, had its own hatch toward the bow. The girl gently pulled the door up and let it pivot on its hinges before laying it back on the deck with nary a whisper to mark its opening. Without waiting for Ben, she slipped down into the dark hole.

Ben hesitated just long enough to take one more look around before following her down.

The stairwell was steep and slippery; Ben clung to the side of the stairs with his hands to keep his balance. He reached the deck half-blind and bumped into Corin, forcing her to stumble a step before she caught herself. Ben chastised himself and took a lateral step to his right, plunging himself into the utter darkness of the hold.

The hold wasn't completely dark, of course, but he was forced to wait until his eyes had adjusted. He could no longer hear Corin and assumed she was waiting as well.

Overhead, there were footsteps across the deck. "Hey," a voice slurred drunkenly, "who left the cargo hatch open? The captain would be mighty displeased if he saw."

"Best the captain not see, then," another voice answered. A moment later, the hatch slammed shut, and the faint illumination of the moon vanished.

The footsteps receded, and Ben reached out to find the ladder. Instead, he found Corin's hand, reaching out to him as well. "Corin?" he whispered.

"'M here," she replied, her voice a low murmur.

"Don't suppose you have a light?" he asked.

"I saw a torch right before the hatch closed. I don't have a way to light it, though."

"I have a flint and steel in my pocket," Ben said. "Can you get the torch?"

"I'll try."

Ben stayed standing, rooting his feet to the deck while Corin attempted to find the torch. It took several minutes, and twice he could hear her run into something, but at last she returned with the unlit torch.

She reached out and took his hand. "Here," she murmured, laying the torch in his hand. He took it and then crouched down on the deck, laying down the torch and pulling his flint and steel from his pocket.

The set was soaked from his swim, of course, but it didn't matter. He worked by touch; he carefully laid the torch down and positioned himself over it. A quick strike of steel on stone and sparks dropped onto the oil-soaked torch.

Fire rose up, and Ben dropped his fire-starting kit to lift the torch from the deck. "Don't want to burn the ship down," he muttered. "Hard to steal then."

He was blinded for a moment by the light as the torch blazed up, and he was forced to look away for a few moments to allow his eyes to adjust. A few heartbeats later, he could see Corin's face glowing golden in the light. More dimly around them were stacks of crates and barrels, clearly holding whatever goods the merchants had brought to Jepitsa.

"So, now the hunt begins," Corin said with a smile.

"We need to keep it quiet and careful," Ben warned.

"Why? The crew quarters are all in the back of the ship," Corin stated.

"Because they probably all tie together," Ben pointed out. "I mean, if something would go wrong, you'd want the crew to be able to get to the cargo hold, wouldn't you?"

Corin nodded reluctantly. "Makes sense."

"So, we don't go any further back in the ship than we need, and we keep it as quiet as possible," Ben said decisively. "Slow and careful."

"Let's start looking, then," Corin said. "Start with open crates first, right?"

"Right," Ben agreed. "If they were demonstrating these things to the Royal Guard, they might not have sealed them up yet."

"Guess we'll have to stick together," Corin said. "I don't see any more torches."

Ben peered around in the darkness, then nodded in agreement. "Together, then."

While Corin held the torch, he pulled open the nearest crate. When he had it mostly open, she pushed the torch forward to see the contents of the crate. It was half-filled with bolts of cloth, some which Ben identified immediately as wool but was puzzled at the rest.

"Silk, I think," Corin murmured as she ran her fingers over another bolt. "And cotton," she added, touching another.

"Not what we're looking for," Ben stated.

The girl nodded and reluctantly pulled back from the crate, her fingers lingering over the silk. "Too bad. I would love to get some clothes made of this. It's incredible."

Ben rolled his eyes and moved to the next crate. Its lid, too, was not tightly fastened, and a bit of wrestling allowed him to pull back the top. Corin peeked in and reported, "More cloth."

The next three crates were the same, but the fourth held something else entirely. "Sacks of something," Corin reported.

"Here," Ben said, offering his knife.

The girl took it and stabbed into a bag, then withdrew it to reveal a dark powder on the blade. She tasted it. "Sugar, I think," she said. "Tasted a little different than ours, but very sweet."

After several more crates, they came to a stack of barrels. "Do we bother?" Corin asked. "I mean, they're probably not shipping tools or weapons in barrels."

"No, but I'd still like to know what's in them," Ben said with a smile.

Corin returned his smile with a grin of her own.

The boy popped the next barrel open and frowned. "Molasses?" he guessed.

The girl dipped her finger in the thick liquid, tasted it, and nodded. "Molasses," she confirmed.

A dozen more barrels and sacks were far less exotic: jerky, salt pork, dry beans, three barrels of pickled vegetables, salt, herbs, and flour. When they found two barrels of rum, Ben had suggested trying to take them with when they found the tool Alan had sent them for, but Corin nixed the idea.

"I don't get it," Ben grumbled when they re-sealed the last barrel. "We've dug and dug and dug, but there's no machines here. There's stacks of valuable goods and lots of food, but nothing like what Alan described."

"We didn't get the wrong ship, did we?" Corin asked uncertainly.

Ben shook his head. "The other three ships in dock are all from Letale. Alan was absolutely certain this came from off-continent."

"Maybe he was wrong," Corin offered.

"Yeah, maybe." The thief frowned. "Tell me something, Corin. Where do all these things come from?"

"What do you mean?" she asked.

"The cargo. Where did it all come from?"

The girl frowned in turn, looking around at the crates of goods. "Well, some of the cloth is local, but silk comes from across the sea," she said slowly. "This molasses is better than any I've tasted, so it probably does too. Same with that weird sugar."

"That was what I thought, too," he said. "So why is it all locked up in here and not out on the dock or sold to the traders here at the harbor?"

Corin looked apprehensive. "I'm not sure." She shrugged after a moment. "It doesn't matter anyway. We need to find what we came for, and get out of here."

"Right," Ben said dryly, "but we have the small problem of *finding* it."

"Details," Corin joked with a dismissive wave of her hand. She sobered. "Any ideas?"

Ben nodded. "Well, it's not here with the goods, so maybe it's with the ship equipment."

"And where would that be?" the girl asked.

"Maybe down another deck? We're not at the bottom of the ship, and I haven't see any of the carpenter's equipment or anything. There has to be more on this ship."

"So, we just need to find a way down," Corin reasoned.

Ben led the way back to the narrow staircase and, as he began to step up, he glanced down and blushed. Silently, he pointed to the hatch sunk into the floor, clearly leading down into the ship.

Corin was nearly as red as he; instead of speaking, she handed him the torch. "Here," she said. When she had passed it across, she reached down and took hold of the ring embedded in the hatch and gave a powerful heave, tugging it up on its hinges.

Ben stepped down into the darkness, half-blind with the torch too close to his eyes. He could hear the water lapping against the hull and, from the gentle curve of the floor, guessed they were on the lowest part of the ship.

Corin descended behind him. He held the torch up and peered out into the hold, and began to pick out the details. "This is it," he said quietly.

Nearby was a workbench, with unsecured tools littering the surface: hammers, saws, nails, and implements he couldn't identify. Large coils of rope were piled haphazardly on the floor. Further away, he could see neat stacks of wood and iron rings – the components of barrels, probably broken down when emptied to save space and ready to put back together in a few hours' notice when needed again.

"Look here," Corin said softly.

Ben turned to follow her gaze. Small cells were laid out one next to another, clearly for holding prisoners or captives. They were all empty, fortunately. At first, Ben thought the cells had caught her attention, until he spotted something unusual at the far end of the hull, barely within reach of the torch light.

A heavy metal door inset into a wooden wall.

"What do you think's behind there?" Ben asked.

"Only one way to find out," Corin said.

The door was locked, of course, but the thieves were hardly surprised. Corin extracted her lock picks from her pocket and went to work while Ben turned and held up the torch, watching for any stray sailors.

While he listened to the lock jingle and clink under Corin's assault, he realized that standing guard was rather useless given his only weapon was a small dagger. *If some guard or sailor stumbles onto us with a sword, we're both dead,* he reflected. *Wonderful odds. And I'm going to stand here and watch anyways.*

"How's it going?" he murmured.

"Slow," was Corin's frustrated answer. "I haven't seen a lock like this before."

"Want to switch?"

"No," was her immediate answer, determination coloring her words. "It'll just take a...there!" With a distinct click, the lock yielded and the door swung open nearly silently on well-oiled hinges.

Ben stepped back as Corin opened the door. She reached up and took the torch from his hand and stepped into the room. Ben followed her in immediately, abandoning his watch. *No light, no point,* he decided.

Then he caught a glimpse of the room's contents and gasped. Corin looked around in stunned silence.

The walls were filled floor-to-ceiling with racks and racks of weapons. Straight-bladed swords, curved cutlasses, great swords, war axes, long bows, quivers filled with arrows, maces, warhammers, bladed pikes, and more weapons Ben couldn't even recognize. "Wow," he said at last.

"Yeah," Corin said. "Wow."

The two thieves stood in stunned silence for long moments, half-mesmerized by the armory. Finally, Corin stirred. "I think I see them."

"Huh?" Ben asked brilliantly, shaken out of his reverie. "See what?"

"That thing Alan sent us for," Corin said. She pointed at a rack on the far wall, opposite the door. "There."

Ben studied the rack and the six contraptions hanging from it. He slowly put the details together in his mind with the description of its capabilities. *That would be a hook to grab onto the wall*, he thought. *That part looks like it'll push the hook out, and there's a spool for the rope and a handle to pull it tight. Yes, that's got to be it.*

Corin handed him the torch again, then reached across and picked up one of the devices and slung it over her shoulder. "This is what we came for, so let's get out of here."

"Good plan," Ben agreed. He turned and stepped out of the armory, Corin right behind him.

The torchlight illuminated a dozen men standing stock-still, staring at the two thieves, all armed with swords or daggers.

Corin bumped into Ben. "Hey, why'd you stop?" she hissed. Then she peeked past his shoulder. "Oh. That's why."

X

ARRAYA COULDN'T HELP BUT STARE at the fire, and the dangers it held.

Across the blaze, she was dimly aware of the Erixan girl, Naomi, also staring at the fire. The apprentice had little doubt that her own dread was far greater than Naomi's paltry fear.

The object of her fear rested within the flames, barely visible but dangerous all the same. It glowed dully with absorbed heat. It was a brand, an iron shaped to sear her skin and identify her forever as a slave.

If they mark me as a slave, will I lose my powers forever? she wondered. *Master Shallum told me I would lose my power if I was enslaved to the will of another. A mark from that brand could mean the end of me as a Magi.*

She glanced across the flames at Naomi, reluctantly trying to break her thoughts away from the danger. *Maybe it's not fair for me to think she's losing less than me,* she told herself. *If she's clapped in these chains, she's as bound as I am and may never see freedom again.* She tugged at her bonds yet again – it was far more times than she could count – but they remained as firm as ever. *All I need is a moment unbound and I can escape.*

Of course, they're not going to give me the opportunity.

Fear continued to eat away at her confidence, and her courage wavered. *What will I do?* she asked herself. *What can I do? I'm a Magi, one of the few chosen of the Scions, and yet I've given up control of my own destiny through mistakes. If I lose my power, will it really be the fault of my captors, or is it justice for my mistakes? Master Shallum warned me over and over about the risks I face and the choices I must make to keep my power, but I stumbled into this anyway.*

The apprentice looked around for a long moment, checking for any Tilliks close enough to overhear. Satisfied that none were within earshot, she raised her voice. "Naomi."

The blonde Erixan raised her gaze and locked eyes with the apprentice. "What, crazy girl?" she asked with a veneer of disdain not quite masking the undercurrent of fear.

"I'm not crazy," Arraya replied, trying to keep her calm. *Don't rise to the insult,* she told herself. *It won't help you escape. She's as scared as you are, and she's trying not to show it.* "Have you gotten your hands loose?"

"If I had, I wouldn't still be sitting here," Naomi growled.

Arraya sagged. *So much for that hope.* She sighed. It would have been a long shot at best anyway. She tried to tug at her bonds yet again, but her wrists were sore and chafed from the constant attempts, and the pain made her hesitate. *No,* she told herself. *You can't let the pain conquer you. Under Master Shallum's instruction, you've hurt far worse than this. Are you going to let a little pain steal your destiny as a Magi?*

She knew it was more than a little conceited to believe that she would become one of the full Magi; almost all the apprentices would wash out, with only a tiny fraction ever coming into the full power of the Council members. At that moment, though, she didn't care about conceit; she cared about *escape,* and the conceit gave her the motivation to keep trying.

Unfortunately, motivation alone wouldn't cut her bonds.

She continued to struggle subtly against the ropes as the first rays of dawn scattered across the darkened skies. Invisibly, she strained against the unseen bonds that kept her from tapping into her power. The internal struggle was even more frustrating than the rope bonds; she could sense the True Magic just beyond her grasp, and felt as though she could reach out and grasp it, if only she could stretch her senses and her control a bit further. Yet no matter how hard she pushed and stretched and reached, no matter how focused her concentration, it remained elusive.

What do I do now? she wondered as she saw J'Ram, the young Tillik, walking toward the fire. *Once I've been branded as a slave, I may never touch my power again. This is it. It's now or never.*

Arraya had hoped the danger she was now in would allow her to finally connect with her power, but even as J'Ram stepped into the circle of firelight, she couldn't summon it.

The Tillik picked up the branding iron from the fire carefully, his clawed hands covered in heavy leather gloves. *I bet that whole metal shaft is hot*, Arraya distantly observed. The upright lizard held the entire iron up in the slowly brightening pre-dawn sky. The intricate pattern of iron glowed against the darkness, held well away from the Tillik's body on a long simple rod.

Slave, the apprentice interpreted the pattern. *Slave.*

The very word filled her with dread, fear, disappointment. As J'Ram stepped toward her, her imagination showed her the pain of the hot iron burning into her flesh, marking her forever.

The Tillik stepped behind her and pulled the back of her shirt up, exposing her skin to the cold air. She closed her eyes. *I will not flinch. Even if this steals my power, I will not dishonor the Magi with weakness now.*

Instead of the pain of a burning iron scorching her flesh, she was shocked when the bonds around her wrists loosened and then fell away entirely.

The Tillik stepped away from her wordlessly, then walked away from the apprentice and straight over to the Erixan. Arraya watched, dumbfounded, as J'Ram knelt down behind her and similarly cut away the ropes binding the blonde girl. The Tillik walked back to the fire and thrust the branding iron back into the flames.

Naomi watched the Tillik with wary eyes, but Arraya was too shocked to properly evaluate. *He just cut us loose. Both of us. We're free. We could jump him right now, or we could get up and run away.* Her thoughts raced with possibilities, but a larger part of her wanted to understand just why the young Tillik bandit had chosen to set two potentially valuable slaves free instead of branding them and clapping them in irons.

J'Ram walked away from the fire as though nothing had changed, disappearing into the darkness. Arraya carefully rubbed at her wrists, continuing to sit as though she were still tied up. *Wait until the opportune time*, she told herself as she started to untangle her thoughts from her shock at the turn of events. *Do not act until you are ready. Wait until the best opportunity presents itself.*

She looked across the fire and saw Naomi also discreetly rubbing her wrists, trying to restore her circulation and rid herself of the semi-painful tingles as feeling began to return to her hands. The girl met her eyes and nodded slightly. *Good*, Arraya thought. *She's still an ally. She's waiting, just like I am, until we have a moment. I can't trust her to not throw me back at the Tilliks if it will make her own escape possible, but she's the closest thing I have to a partner right now. She's the only one I can even remotely trust right now.*

Of course, the apprentice was wrong.

As she continued to rub at her wrists, she focused on her power. The faintest tingles of magic danced at the edge of her perceptions, now within her grasp.

She was six years old, standing in a dark room. A single candle provided what little light was to be had, and she was cold. The old tower of the Cosmane fortress was drafty, and every one of those drafts seemed to lick at her neck with tongues of ice.

The man who had taken her away from her parents sat across from her. "It is time for you to find your power," Master Shallum told her.

"My power?" Arraya asked in a quivering voice.

"Yes, your power," the big man said. "You are very special, little Arraya. Do you believe in magic?"

"Of course," the little girl replied indignantly. "The Deep Magic is what makes all the rules of the world."

"Yes, it does," Master Shallum said approvingly. "The Deep Magic is the foundation of the very world." He was silent for a long moment before relenting with an explanation. "The Deep Magic is the foundation, but it is untouchable by anyone but the Aither, who laid it down in the first place. He also created other magics for us to use. Even the Magi, the greatest of those who can use any form of magic, cannot use the Deep Magic, but we use the True Magic – the power nearest to the great Deep Magic."

"So what do I have to do?" the little red-headed girl asked.

Master Shallum smiled. "Look at the candle," he said. "Concentrate on the bright light it casts. Look at the brightness of the flame, and then at the wick of the candle, and then at the point where the two meet. Especially there."

"What is there?" the little girl asked.

"That is where the True Magic is," Master Shallum said. "It fills all the space around us, in between everything we can see."

The little girl focused, staring at the candle. "I feel weird," she declared at last. "Like all my skin fell asleep. It's tingling all over."

"Good," Master Shallum said. "You're drawing closer to the True Magic. Now, put out the candle. Don't blow it out, or use your hand. Make it stop with your mind."

The words were confusing to a six-year-old, and while she didn't understand most of what she was told, she did understand the task at hand: put out the candle without touching it.

As she stared at the flame, she focused on it with her imagination, seeing it wither and die as real as if it were happening. When the room actually plunged into darkness, she was so shocked she let out a strangled gasp.

"I can't see you, Master Shallum!" she cried.

"Calm, young one," his voice echoed out of the darkness. "Do not be afraid."

The darkness seemed to close in around her, choking her off. In a panic, she tried to find the candle, imagined it flaring to life again...

...And it was so. Light, far more brilliant than before, flooded the room as a flame half the length of her arm flared up from the candle.

Master Shallum laughed in delight, a cheerful booming sound that calmed the frightened girl. "Well done, Arraya!" he congratulated her. "Many can snuff out a candle, but you are the first apprentice I've taken who could relight it as well!" He smiled at her, the expression warming her in spite of the cold drafts. "Well done!"

Arraya was snapped out of her half-forgotten memories when the young Tillik, Seewulz J'Ram, stepped back into the firelight. He walked without hesitation to Naomi first, laying down several things next to her. When he walked to Arraya, in fact, he had only one thing left in his grip – the staff Mistress Esther had given her before she had left the Magi's fortress in the mountains.

"Take up your weapon," the Tillik said, low and quiet. "When a moment arrives, take it and flee. Don't let yourself be caught again. The next time, the *ilduce* will have you skinned alive before risking your escape again after this."

"What about you?" Arraya asked. "What will happen to you?"

J'Ram shrugged, an oddly human motion from the lizard-man. "I will stay where I am," he said simply.

"Hardly a fitting place for a traitor," the *ilduce* spat from the shadows.

Arraya turned her gaze in time to see the old limping lizard-man step into the firelight. "I didn't expect you to care for these thinskins," the leader of the highwaymen said. "How dare you betray us for these nothings!"

J'Ram did not deny the accusation. Rather, he dropped to his knees. "We are hunters, are we not?" he asked. "Hunters seek worthy prey and strike to kill. Hunters do not trap the helpless and sell them off like flesh merchants. We dishonor ourselves."

"Foolish," the *ilduce* spat. "You are young and could be forgiven, but your ill-thought actions harm us all. That is unforgivable." The dark eyes glittered with malice, and Arraya could not suppress her shudder. "You will suffer the same fate as these thinskins."

"You would sell me to the Pronan slavers?" J'Ram asked in shock.

"You are not worthy as a Tillik hunter; consider it a service, your final service to your clan."

J'Ram seemed to struggle for words. Arraya reached out mightily for her power, trying to draw in every bit of the True Magic she could summon. *All I need is enough strength to smash him down,* she thought darkly. *One good summon of fire and he's done.*

The tingles in her hands were painful, and she could more steadily touch the magic. Whether it was the pain or the time spent bound, however, the apprentice struggled to draw up enough magic to summon her fire. *If I can't strike in a moment or two, it won't make any difference!* she thought desperately as the *ilduce* stepped around the fire and advanced on young J'Ram.

Fortunately, both Tilliks froze at the sound of a strange series of clicks.

Naomi, the Erixan shootist, was on her feet with a long weapon in her arms. Her gaze was steadily peering down the long slender metal tube, its end pointed squarely at the *ilduce*. "You'll want to stop right there," the Erixan said dryly.

Arraya blew out a long sigh of relief.

"Not a Rapien at all," the *ilduce* spat. "Who are you?"

"I'm from Erixi," Naomi said calmly. "I'm sure you can put the rest together."

The *ilduce* eyed her warily. "You fill my ears with untruths," he accused.

"Step towards me and find out," Naomi replied coolly.

"I have no need," the *ilduce* said. "You think I came here to confront a traitor alone?"

Arraya whipped her head around to gaze out into the darkness. Dozens of reptilian eyes were just barely visible with tiny specks of reflected firelight. "Naomi," she said tightly, "we're surrounded."

The shootist's eyes never left her target, the *ilduce*. "You told me you're a Magi, right? Then conjure up some fire and get rid of them."

The idea was more than sound, but Arraya was still struggling to summon up her power. *How do I explain* that? she wondered. "About that," she mumbled.

"I knew you were crazy," Naomi said, still perfectly calm and poised. "I wasn't counting on you to get us out. So, here's what's going to happen," she continued, her object of address shifting the *ilduce*. "You're going to step away from my friend the redhead here, and you're going to leave J'Ram with us. You're going to walk over and rejoin your group."

"Or what?" the *ilduce* taunted. "You are going to throw your little toy at me? If you were really an Erixan shootist, you'd already have acted."

"Take a step toward me or my friends here," Naomi said in that perfect resolve, "and I'll add a new hole to your scaly head. Now, make your choice."

The *ilduce* snorted but backed away slowly, his clawed hands raised. The end of Naomi's weapon tracked him as he moved, the Erixan staying utterly focused on the leader of the highwaymen.

Unfortunately, that precluded attention on her own back.

Fortunately, Arraya had that part handled.

"Behind you!" she shouted as a Tillik leapt from the shadows, claws outstretched toward Naomi's exposed neck.

The shootist turned in a single smooth motion, dropping to a knee. A loud *BOOM!* shattered the early morning air, the very sound of the blast sending Arraya reeling and her ears ringing.

The Tillik highwaymen were just as surprised, but recovered faster than the apprentice. More of the lizard-men hurled themselves at the Erixan. More cracks like thunder echoed out, though they weren't near as deafening as the first, mostly because Arraya's ears were still ringing.

Five more Tilliks had dropped when the shootist suddenly lashed out, swinging her long weapon like a club to catch the next Tillik alongside the head with the wooden butt. The highwayman dropped with a strangled gasp and the crunch of crushed scales. Naomi dropped the long weapon and withdrew a much smaller, one-handed weapon from her belt. Its crack was even louder than the larger weapon's report, and another Tillik dropped.

Arraya could only watch in amazement as nine, ten, and then eleven of the lizard-men were sprawled out around them. The entire battle had maybe lasted half that many seconds, and now the survivors were backing off, forming a loose circle around the two girls and the young Tillik J'Ram.

Naomi stepped over to the apprentice, then knelt down beside her. "Can you walk?" she murmured.

Arraya nodded. "I can bloody well walk out of here."

"Good, because I've only got one shot left," Naomi whispered. "If they rush us again, I can't hold them off."

"That's it?" Arraya asked, a bit taken aback.

"I can reload, but if I try to do that now they'll perceive it as weakness and rush us," the shootist said. "C'mon, I'm getting you out of here." She glanced over at the cowering J'Ram, who seemed equally terrified of the *ilduce* and the Erixan. "You, too. I don't think staying here would be good for you."

Arraya rose to her feet, the tingling fading from her hands and feeling fully returning to her limbs. She watched the shootist collect her first weapon from the ground and sling it over her shoulder. *That was amazing*, she thought.

No wonder they're feared. And it's no wonder everyone's been trying to get their weapons.

"Now," Naomi announced loudly, "if you all will make some room, we'll part ways before I have to part more of you from your lives."

"No," the *ilduce* spat, limping forward from behind the ring of Tillik bandits. "You have insulted us, and you insult us even now. Your weapon is at its limits, is it not? That is why you seek parlay rather than continue to kill."

His words seemed to inspire instant confidence in the Tilliks. "So much for bluffing," Naomi muttered. "Here it comes."

"Instead of escape, or selling you into slavery, I think we'll take your skins ourselves," the *ilduce* declared. "Lay down your weapons now, and your deaths will be quick. Persist in your attacks, and your screams will last for many days."

The Tilliks began to advance, the circle tightening around the trio. Arraya recognized fear beneath Naomi's bravado.

Fortunately, there was a solution to that.

The apprentice watched the approaching Tilliks through half-lidded eyes. Just a bit of a smile crossed her lips as she let her bonds of control slip just enough.

Fire blazed up in a wall between the trio and the nearest group of Tilliks. The lizard-men stopped dead in their tracks, then hastily retreated from the flames. Another wall burst up from the ground, then another, then another, creating a fortress of fire around the two girls and the young Tillik.

"What is this?" the *ilduce* shouted. "What sorcery have you wrought?" The old lizard stared haughtily at Arraya. "This is *your* doing!"

"I am Arraya, daughter and apprentice of the Magi," she told him defiantly. "And you will *not* take us as slaves or trophies." Then she reached out with every bit of power she could muster and *pushed*.

The flames leapt into the skies, far brighter than the coming dawn. Then in a rush they spread outward in all four directions, spreading like a wildfire across the prairies driven by storm winds. Fleeing Tilliks screeched in terror as they fled, trying to escape the conjured fire.

Arraya was content to let them flee. *I know the Masters have killed with magic, but I don't want to kill anyone with* anything. Exhaustion began to drag at her from channeling so much power so quickly. *You overextended,* she told herself. *You tried to do too much too fast. It'll be okay this time because they're all running, but you know better, and you could have gotten yourself killed if any of them had been smart enough to attack.*

As if summoned by her self-criticism, the *ilduce* loomed up in front of her. Smoke rose from his scales, and his hide was scorched and cracked in places. "Magi," he hissed spitefully. "You think yourself great, do you? You're nothing but a child." He drew a clawed hand back. "Now, I take your life in recompense."

Before the claw could fall, the ear-splitting *BOOM* of the Erixan's weapon deafened Arraya again. The *ilduce* staggered backward and fell, utterly limp when he hit the ground, never to rise again.

Arraya found herself on her knees, her hands shaking. Some of it, she knew, was the aftermath of drawing so much power so quickly. She had exceeded her limits, and there was always a price to pay. However, she wasn't too proud to admit to herself that a much larger part of it was adrenaline and fear. "Stupid, stupid, stupid," she berated herself. "The fight wasn't over yet."

"Are you okay?" Naomi asked shakily.

Arraya turned and saw the blonde girl staring at her, her eyes a mix of shock, awe, and fear, tinged with just a shade of satisfaction. "I'll be okay," Arraya said weakly. *Yes, that took more out of me than I thought.*

As the apprentice rose to her feet, she realized that Naomi was still staring at her. She looked up at the blonde girl and saw shock, respect, and a bit of fear all vying for dominance in her eyes.

Arraya gave her the most confident smile she could muster. "I told you."

Naomi stared at her for a long moment, her mouth open and working silently, but no words emerging. Finally she seemed to pull her thoughts back together. "That was...well, I've never even *heard* of a Magi cutting loose before."

Arraya could almost hear Master Shallum's wry advice in her ears. *Never let them see you sweat.* "You still haven't," the apprentice said solemnly, hiding her smile and trying to keep herself from shaking.

"I mean, everyone talks about what kind of power the Magi had," the Erixan continued, the words falling in an uncontrolled babble. "I never really believed it – no one I knew did. None of the shootists, anyway. And there's all kinds of legends about the Magi calling down lightning or conjuring up storms and winds and everything, but to actually *see* it..."

Arraya nodded smoothly, her shakes finally coming under control. "I've heard of your weapons and your kind before, and studied your history," she replied, "but I've never seen one of your kind in action, either. It was quite impressive."

"Sure, I can shoot," Naomi said, "but it's nothing like bringing up fire out of the ground and throwing it at your enemies!"

"We have two concerns, then," Arraya said. The stink of blood filled the air now, and she was acutely aware of the death the other girl had wrought. *Not that it wasn't warranted,* she told herself. "What do we do now, and what do we do with J'Ram?"

The Erixan shootist looked down and seemed to see J'Ram for the first time. She looked back up at Arraya and shrugged. "I was on my way to Jepitsa when I was attacked," she said. "I still have business there."

Arraya nodded in return. "That is my destination as well," she said.

"What is a Magi going to Jeptisa for?" Naomi asked.

The apprentice shook her head. "Now is not the time for such discussions," she said. "While we drove off these bandits, they may have had other allies nearby, and we could still be at risk. If it is agreeable to you, I think we should travel together to the capital."

"I agree," Naomi said. She offered a little smile. "If you're helping me, there's nothing that will stop us from getting there in one piece."

"And then the second point," Arraya continued. "J'Ram."

The young Tillik dropped to his knees before the apprentice and the shootist. "I find myself in dishonor," he rasped. "I tried to set you free, but failed, and was of no use to you in the battle. Further, you saved my life; the *ilduce* would have killed me, had you not intervened."

"I release you from any debt you owe me," Arraya said solemnly. "You can go your own way."

J'Ram offered a toothy smile that was oddly frightening for a friendly expression. "Then I think I shall journey to Jepitsa as well."

"Are you sure?" Naomi asked. "There's not going to be many Tilliks around there."

"The fire-bringer may have released me from debt, but it is owed all the same," he said solemnly. "If you will allow it, I will accompany you."

Arraya reached down and took the lizard's hand, pulled him to his feet. "To Jepitsa, then," she said. *I want to be as far away from this bloodshed as I can. This isn't what my powers are for.*

XI

THE CAPTAIN'S QUARTERS ON THE ship were spacious and airy compared to the cramped below-decks. Long tapestries hung from the walls, and light poured in through the genuine glass windows. The bed against the wall looked freshly stuffed with straw, and books were neatly shelved above the desk nearby. Individual slots in a nearby rack held maps, charts, and bottles of rum.

Ben took all the sights in, observing every detail he could commit to memory, because it was better than thinking about his likely immediate future.

His wrists were bound uncomfortably behind his back, and his legs were bound to the wooden seat where he had been unceremoniously dumped. Corin was still right next to him, similarly bound and seated.

Before them was a large, open wooden table. Across that table, slouched in his chair, was the vessel's captain.

"What are your names, thieves?"

"Ben," the boy said.

"Corin," the girl added.

"Ben and Corin. You two have put me in a difficult position," the man drawled. Instead of sitting, he rose and paced back and forth behind the table. His longcoat trailed behind him, seemingly pulled back by invisible hands whenever he whirled around to change his direction. "What you two have done, we have no rules for. It's not in the charter."

"Charter?" Ben asked.

"Do you know who it is you tried to thieve?" the captain asked.

Ben and Corin both shook their heads mutely.

"I thought not." He abruptly stopped and sat down on a stool directly across from the two Brigands. "Have you no guesses at all?"

Ben shook his head, but Corin answered quietly. "You're pirates."

"Aye, that we are!" the captain exploded, rising to his feet again. "Well done, lass. And how did you figure that?"

Pirates! Ben thought in dismay. *That's worse than I thought.*

"Those weapons," Corin said slowly. "Alan told us there were only a few that you were trying to sell, but they were kept far below decks where no one could get to them easily. If you were trying to sell them to the Royal Guard, they would have been up where you could get at them easily to show them off or move them. Where they were, locked up like that, means you didn't want anyone to see them."

Ben's mind had been scrambling wildly at the new revelation, but it finally found traction. "The trade goods we found in your cargo hold – they were from all over. If you were a trade vessel from a northern port, you'd have been shipping mostly the same things – like a hold full of silk, or mostly spices, or something like that. Your hold was full of a lot of different things – everything you were able to steal."

"I prefer *plunder*, meself," the captain said with a broad smile.

"Those hooks and ropes, you use those for boarding other ships, don't you?" Corin asked.

That made more sense to Ben. Such a device, able to throw a hook or spear into the hull of another ship and then tie them together, would be invaluable to a pirate crew. It would prevent a ship from escaping, and make boarding far easier than more traditional ways. *It also explains how Alan knew about them*, he thought. *He might have a friend on a pirate ship, or just heard about them. Somehow he knew this ship was a pirate ship and he sent us on an expedition to find what he needed.* His heart sank a little. *He was lying to us.* Again. *Well, maybe he was just trying to keep everyone safe in case something went wrong.*

Which it did.

"Boarding harpoons," the pirate captain supplied. "New design, and very hard to come by. Highly illegal, of course."

"So why did we make things difficult for you?" Corin asked.

The pirate laughed. "Only you know the answer to that, lass," he said. "I have no idea why you boarded my ship and tried to steal from my crew."

"*How* did we make things difficult, then?" Corin persisted.

Ben wanted to smack her and tell her to be quiet, but the pirate captain seemed to be in the mood to expound. "It's quite simple, lass. There's nothing about it in the charter."

"What charter?" Ben asked.

"*The* charter," the captain said, as though it should be self-obvious. "Can't be a pirate crew without a charter." He looked from blank look to blank look. "Are ye telling me neither of you know what a pirate's charter is?" He sighed theatrically, seating himself again on the stool as though he were deflating. "And here I thought you were perhaps working for the Jepitsa guard, or on one of me enemies' crews. No, you have no idea what you've stumbled into, none at all."

"Charter?" Ben risked again.

"Tis the agreement between all the crew!" he exclaimed. "Without it we'd be nothing but simple criminals, and I'd not be Captain Japhet."

"What sort of agreement?" Corin asked, curiosity in her voice.

"It's our contract," the captain, apparently Japhet, declared. "All the members of the crew sign onto it, or at least make their mark. It declares how large a share each member takes of the spoils, determines how the captain is elected, and what punishments are met for breakin' the rules."

"It's your law aboard the ship," Corin said reflectively.

"Elected?" Ben asked. "What's that mean?"

"It means the crew selects their own captain," Japhet said. "They choose who is in charge, and can replace the captain should the need arise."

"And you're the captain."

"Aye, captain of the pirate vessel *Tasoth* for three months and two years," he said with a trace of pride. "And that is why I am in such a tight spot now, on account of you two."

Corin put the pieces together. "There's nothing in your charter on how to deal with us."

"Exactly." Captain Japhet pounded his fist on the table, then rose to his feet and began to pace again. "You see, were you members of me crew who tried to steal from us, we'd but maroon you on some island and let you make your own fate. Likewise, were you another pirate, we'd bring you onto the crew to server without reward for our plundering until you had paid your due – two months. But neither of you are sailors, are ye?"

Ben and Corin both shook their heads.

"And that be the problem. Were I to impress you into service, I'd be spendin' my days teachin' you how to sail, and not getting any work from you." He shook his head irritably.

"So why not turn us over to the Jepitsa guard?" Ben asked. *If he would, Alan could use his connections to get us out again. Though if we didn't have that tool, he mightn't get us out.*

"Part of the charter," Captain Japhet said. "We handle all our own law and rule ourselves; we need not some king to tell us how to run our affairs."

"But you can't just let us go, because that wouldn't satisfy your crew, would it?" Corin asked.

"Aye. Were I just to let you loose, the crew might very well elect a new captain. I've come accustomed to the captain's quarters, and would like to stay within them." The pirate slumped down casually in his chair again and kicked his booted feet up on the table. "We must maintain the order of the ship."

"Sounds like Alan," Corin muttered. "Everything's about order."

"So tell me, lad and lass," the pirate said. "What solution have ye to my dilemma?"

"Throw us in the river," Ben suggested. *Corin and I can both swim. Even if our hands our bound, we can make it to safety.*

"Here, with yer king's Royal Guard looking?" Japhet ridiculed. "Hardly a way to keep a low profile. Lad, we be pirates, but it's easier to trade fer our supplies when yer king does not seek us at the end of a rope. Should we throw you overboard, you can bet every gold coin you've e'er set your hands on that they would send troops aboard to find our secrets. No, we need a better way."

"You don't want to hold us prisoner until you're away from port?" Corin asked.

Ben winced before he could stop himself. *Yes, throw us overboard fifty leagues down the river, and then see if we could get ourselves loose and walk back,* he thought sarcastically at the girl. *Great idea, Corin.*

"Hardly, lass. If I have to hold you in the brig, there be too many chances of something happenin' to you both. A girl on a ship full of men? And a thief among pirates who are fond of bloodshed? No, I'd rather not have either of ye on my conscience."

"A pirate with a conscience?" Corin asked skeptically. "You make a living by stealing, and you're all sweetness and light?"

Japhet snorted at her. "Lass, you're a thief yourself. Would ye like to murder each of your marks before you relieve 'im of gold and silver? I hardly think so."

Ben swallowed hard before speaking up. "I have an idea," he said. "You want something to show your crew, right? Something to preserve your status as captain?"

The pirate nodded. "Aye."

"Then what about entertainment?" Ben asked, trying to keep a clamp on his nervousness. "Something for the amusement of your crew?"

Japhet rose and crossed to the racks on the wall and withdrew a bottle of rum. He pulled the cork from the bottle with his teeth and splashed some rum into a battered tankard. He walked back to the table and sat down, putting the bottle on the table beside his feet.

"I mean, you're pirates. You spend weeks or months on the sea. I bet the worst thing out there is getting bored," Ben continued, sweating hard. "I'm sure your crew plays dice or cards or whatnot, but what about something completely different for entertainment?"

"What's that?" Japhet asked as he took a gulp of his rum. "You want to teach us all a new *game*? That'll hardly repay the crew fer your offense."

"No, not a new game," Ben said. "An old one."

"Teach us a game," Japhet repeated. "Lad, you are crazy."

"Not teach," Ben said. "You're pirates. You respect thieves and pirates and strength of arms, right?" He took a deep breath. "Let me fight a challenge match with the youngest man on your crew. If I win, Corin and I go free. If I lose, Corin goes free and you've exacted punishment for both of us."

"You would gamble with yer life?" the pirate asked dubiously. "You'd cross blades with a pirate for your own life? Even the youngest of mine crew has been hardened in battle and bathed in blood, boy."

"Not just with his life, but for the boarding harpoon," Corin spoke up. Ben's head whipped around to meet her eyes. She shrugged helplessly. "If we return without it, Alan will have both our heads," she said.

Ben snorted. "Thanks for gambling with my life," he muttered.

"You were *already* gambling with your life," Corin pointed out. "I just made a win better for us."

Japhet emptied his tankard, slammed it down on the table, and refilled it from his bottle. He produced two more tankards and lazily filled them as well, pushing them across the table toward the two thieves.

"Ye have uncommon courage," he said to the pair. "To try to strike a bargain with yer lives in the balance. Should ye survive, and ever need a job, I would be proud to have such pirates on me crew."

Ben looked down at the tankard. "Hard for me to drink with my hands bound," he pointed out.

The pirate roared in laughter as he stood and circled around behind the pair. "As I said, uncommon courage," he commented as he cut the bonds with a dagger. "Very uncommon."

***

The sun had barely peaked over the eastern horizon when Ben and Corin were led onto the deck of the pirate ship. The vast Jepitsa docks were silent; no doubt dockhands and ship crew alike were in deep, alcohol-induced sleep after a long night of carousing. *Not so different than us*, Ben observed distantly. *Probably the best time to do something this dangerous.*

The pirate vessel's crew was assembled on the deck in a loose circle. They were a rough crowd of men, unshaven, unbathed, and unsober. Clothing was ragged and dirty, and more than a few blades hung from belts, ranging from small daggers to a greatsword slung over one massive sailor's back.

Ben guessed, had he and Corin managed their theft undetected, that the crew would all be fast asleep. They were a rather tired and ragged lot, but no doubt the anticipation of entertainment had them all awake and eager. *And bloodthirsty*, the thief thought uneasily. *No matter what happens, this isn't going to end well for someone. And that someone might be me.*

Captain Japhet held up his hand to the pair of thieves. They stopped at the edge of the circle, while the pirate stepped into the open space left on the deck. "My fellow pirates!" he roared. "Today we have a day of entertainment!" Cheers rose from the assembled pirates.

The captain smiled and waited for the cheers to subside before continuing. "These two talented thieves have agreed to grace us with their presence," he continued, this time accompanied by a roar of laughter. "They understand their trespass – they thought us mere marks to be preyed upon. They did not know us as their kin – they on land, we on sea. But now that we all know the truth, they have agreed to compensate us for their fault!"

More goodhearted roars of approval thundered in Ben's ears. His mouth was dry, and he had difficulty swallowing. *This would be great if they weren't roaring for my blood.*

"The boy has agreed to a match fight against the youngest of our crew, for all our entertainment! So now, let us prepare to witness, nay, *enjoy* the fight to come! And we shall see," Japhet added with a dazzling smile, "which is superior, land or sea!"

"So, what's your plan?" Corin murmured.

Ben shrugged, so slightly that only his fellow Brigand would see it. "I really don't have one."

"You *don't?*" Corin hissed. "You sounded so confident, like you had it all under control."

"Glad it came across that way," Ben said quietly. "It's not the truth."

"Then why did you suggest doing something this *stupid?*" the girl asked. "You're going to get killed!" Her voice was steadily rising, and the nearest sailors were beginning to glance at the thieves.

"Keep your voice down," Ben murmured. "I did this so that you can get away."

Corin looked at him, dumbfounded. "What?"

"If I lose and I die, we've paid for our crime," Ben explained, trying to keep the near-panic out of his voice. "They'll let you go. If I win, we leave with that boarding harpoon. Either way, you get to leave."

"Why did you do something so *stupid?*" the other thief whispered, shaking her head. "You have to look out for *you*. No one looks out for me, and you shouldn't, either. You might have just killed yourself."

"Probably," Ben said.

"Do you even know how to use a sword?" Corin asked, fear creeping into her tone.

"I know which end to hold."

"That's a start. Anything else? I mean, didn't anyone teach you anything about swordplay?"

"I'm a thief, not a soldier or Guard," Ben said quietly.

"You mean you're not part of Alan's little army?" Corin asked. "I thought that's why he brought you in on this."

"Little army?" Ben asked in return, taken aback. "I thought I was imagining it."

"Didn't you see the archers? He's also got a couple of racks of swords he bought somewhere. I know he's been training some of the older Brigands for swordplay." She sighed. "No, of course it wouldn't be you. You're naïve, but you're not a bully."

"I don't understand," Ben muttered. "I mean, I saw the archers at the last Brigands meeting, but I didn't think..."

"No, you didn't," Corin grumbled. "You didn't think at all. Ben, all us Brigands grew up together in Riverfront. Now we're getting old enough that some of us aren't happy with Alan – we can see how he's using us."

"Using us?" Ben interrupted skeptically. "He's never..."

"Naïve," Corin muttered. "Naïve. He has to control us, Ben. When we were all younger, he could do it with words and promises and pats on the head. Now that we're all growing up, that doesn't work anymore. He's building his own little army of loyal rats and he's giving them swords. He's going to use them to keep all of us in line. We step out of line, it's *off with our heads.*"

"That's ridiculous," Ben denied. "He's never done anything to threaten us, or treated us like anything but..."

"Loyal subjects," Corin said bluntly. "And why threaten us outright? He doesn't need to when we're surrounded by his toadies, all wearing swords or carrying bows. He doesn't *need* to make outright threats, Ben – he's far more effective this way, because he doesn't make people who still believe him suspicious, like *you.*"

Ben shook his head. "One way or the other, that doesn't matter right now," he said. "We can have this discussion later. I need to focus on the fight."

Corin nodded. "Don't get yourself killed."

"Yeah. I'm trying very hard not to."

"So, we need a plan," the girl said. "How's..."

"Well, my friends," Japhet materialized between them, an arm around either thief. "The time has come, and the crew awaits their entertainment. Ben, my dear lad, are you prepared?"

Ben looked up into the circle and saw a young pirate, perhaps a year older than himself, swaggering around the circle. He was dressed in only a pair of trousers and boots, his muscular chest gleaming in the early morning light. He held his cutlass easily in one hand, lifting it over his head in dramatic flourishes to draw whistles and cheers from his fellow sailors. His movements were powerful and graceful.

Predatory.

Ben tried to swallow, but couldn't find the spit necessary. "I'm going to need a sword," he managed to say. *This is not going to end well.*

"Of course, of course," Japhet said brightly. "I would not ask you to fight Roche unarmed. It would be unsporting, wouldn't it, lad?" he laughed.

Ben couldn't seem to hear or see past the circle. Haze closed in, and a white roar filled his ears. *I really am going to die,* he thought as a sword was thrust into his hand. His fingers closed around the hilt of their own accord, and the weapon felt heavy in his hand. "Any last minute advice?" he asked the pirate captain.

"Try not to bleed too much on my deck, right, lad?" Japhet said with a roar of laughter. "Go on, lad!"

Ben stepped into the circle of pirates. As the crowd closed ranks around the two combatants, Ben's entire world seemed to narrow to that small expanse of deck. Nothing else mattered; nothing else even *existed* outside that circle. *Win or die,* Ben told himself. *I may not be a warrior or a swordsman, but I'm a survivor. I can survive this, too, even if it means I have to carve up this pirate.* He adjusted his grip on the sword and took a practice swing. *I can do this.*

"To our combatants!" Japhet shouted from above the crowd. Ben had to crane his neck and look up past the blinding dawn to see the pirate captain had climbed the rigging. He held a kerchief in his hand, a brilliant red cloth. "May you fight well. When this cloth touches the deck, you may strike!"

The bit of fabric floated down, both impossibly slow and impossibly fast. Ben held his borrowed sword up, and noted distantly that it was not a short-bladed cutlass like most of the pirates carried, but a longer straight-edged sword with a simple cross guard. His eyes were fixed on the red cloth until it was a handspan above the deck, then locked upon his opponent. *Let him strike first.*

Roche's cutlass flicked at the young thief impossibly fast. Ben swung down with his sword, batting the attack away. The tip of his sword bounced off the deck, and he barely kept the weapon from clattering out of his hand. As he tried to recover to guard, he nearly split Roche in two with the blade, but the young pirate danced back.

They gave me a longer blade. We're about the same height, which means I have more reach than he does. Ben felt like his senses were all heightened as he looked desperately for anything that would warn him of his opponent's intentions. His eyes showed him, with utter clarity, the gleam of the well-oiled cutlass, the sweat dripping down Roche's chest, the sparkle in the pirate's blue eye. *They gave me the longer blade to make the fight more even.*

Then Roche was moving, cutlass swinging in a flashy overhand arc. Ben jumped back and swung with his sword, but the pirate's cutlass was returning to carry Ben's attack away in a parry.

Ben tried to bring his sword back to defend himself, but his young opponent tangled their swords and rotated his back into Ben's chest. The thief started to lose his grip on his sword, but before he could recover, the pirate threw an elbow into the side of his head.

He dropped his sword and tumbled across the deck of the pirate ship, his ears ringing and head spinning from the blow. *Ow, ow, ow,* was all the coherent thought he could manage. Ben finally managed to get his feet back under him and rose to his feet, and saw his sword – on the other side of Roche.

It might as well be a league away, Ben despaired.

Roche thrust his sword up in the air, drawing another round of cheers from the crowd. He strutted in a circle, calling for more applause. Then, with his back still turned, he tossed his sword to another pirate in the crowd. Now unarmed, he turned back to face Ben, a confident smile on his lips. "You're out of your league, little boy," he taunted.

The thief didn't bother with a taunt, just bringing his fists up to protect himself.

The pirate waded in, throwing blows left and right.

Ben had grown up in Riverfront with a band of orphans, both boys and girls. They had been without parents or law, with the only rule in the early days being *don't get caught.* Alan had later brought order to the rough-and-tumble group, forming them into the Brigands. But even among the Brigands, there was plenty of brawls between members of the gang. *We might not have all this swordplay, but I can fight.*

Sort of.

Ben took blows on his forearms and chest, slipping to the side to avoid the worst shots aimed at his softer stomach, groin, and eyes. He fired off punches in return, inflicting as much hurt as he received. *Hey, I can beat him!* Ben thought.

Then a wild haymaker caught him across the jaw. He tasted blood but didn't go down, forcing himself to stay on his feet. Roche stared at him with wide eyes before kicking Ben's legs out, sending him sprawling to the deck.

The thief rolled over onto his back, but the pirate was all over him, straddling his stomach and firing punches left and right. Pinned to the deck and unable to move, Ben struggled to mount any sort of a defense, with blows coming in faster and faster. As more strikes slipped past his guard, dizziness began to overwhelm him, until a final blow brought blackness.

That went well, Ben thought before consciousness slipped away.

XII

IT HAD TAKEN THE APPRENTICE and her new friends some time to catch three horses – they had fled in terror from the rolling thunder of the Erixan's guns and the walls of fire the young Magi had summoned.

Arraya was unhappy she had been unable to find the red roan. *I'm going to be cleaning the stables for a month when I get back*, she thought glumly. *There's no way she'll ever forgive me for losing a horse.*

The Erixan, Naomi, hummed cheerfully as she saddled the coal-black mare she had caught. When she had finished with the tack and filled her saddlebags with what food she could find, she sat down again next to the dying fire. She spent time breaking down her two guns – the long weapon she bore on her back and the small one she wore on her hip – and swabbing them down, cleaning away every bit of dust and grime, occasionally clucking in disapproval to herself.

The single Tillik, J'Ram, saddled his horse far more slowly. The chestnut stud was uneasy, prancing away from the lizard-man. Arraya frowned at the horse's antics, then closed her eyes and touched the creature's mind with her magic.

The horse had been trained to carry any rider, but he hated the reptilian scent emanating from the Tillik. It was an instinctual dislike – the horse's training was at odds with its instincts, and those instincts ran far too deep to be ignored.

Arraya frowned. *Wouldn't a horse trained by the Tilliks already be used to the scent?* She had barely posed herself the question before the answer came as quickly. *Because this horse was stolen by Tillik bandits, not trained by them. Of course.*

She shrugged to herself. *Either way, I can help.* With her power, she soothed the creature's fear, took part of it into herself. As she absorbed it, the horse's fear settled and he grew still, standing to allow the Tillik to saddle him.

J'Ram frowned at the horse's abrupt improvement in behavior, but didn't question it. He quickly finished saddling the stallion. After tying his new mount to a tree, he began to scrounge around for whatever food was left.

Arraya had to admit that the remnants of the food were pitiful, even as she checked her own packs hanging from the bay mare she had caught. *The fire I used burned everything*, she thought glumly. *Master Shallum would tell me*

I need to be more careful and think through my actions. Now we're going to have a lean trip because I started throwing magic around in all directions. It was reckless and foolish.

The flame-haired girl did allow herself a bit of leniency, however. *If I hadn't started using the fire, we both would've died, and a shortage of food now wouldn't have mattered. This way we still have a chance, even if it means we're going to be traveling slower so we can hunt.*

The sun was rising quickly in the east, its brilliance far overtaking the smoldering embers of the fire. Naomi finished reassembling her guns, holstered the smaller one in its place on her hip, and slung the larger one over her shoulder as she rose. "So, what's your plan, crazy girl?" She slung a belt over her shoulder, the leather strip studded with dozens of small pockets bearing small bronze cartridges.

"We go to Jepitsa," Arraya answered reflexively. "From there we can part ways."

"Nothing more specific than that?" Naomi asked dryly.

"There's not much more than that," the apprentice said. "With the three of us, we can stay to the roads. I doubt anyone would risk attacking us."

"Two girls and a lizard-man?" Naomi said disdainfully. "We're going to be walking targets."

"Riding targets," J'Ram sissed as he approached, the stud following reluctantly in his wake. "She is right. We will be seen as easy, weak prey." He bared his teeth in a disturbing hunter's-grin. "It is not so, but we will attract highwaymen like carrion to the dead."

"So we stay off the road," Arraya grumbled. *Aren't we Magi supposed to be the wise ones that everyone looks to for advice?* she thought. *Sure isn't working out the way right now.*

"How far are we from Jepitsa?" the apprentice asked, turning to J'Ram.

"Five days' ride," the Tillik said. "We have food enough, if you are strong."

"Is that an insult?" Naomi asked with a growl.

"Truth," the Tillik said evenly. "Eat little and ride hard, and we need not slow to hunt."

"I can ride harder and faster than you ever would, lizard," the Erixan spat. "And the crazy girl here might not be able to outride us, but she can probably use some spell to keep herself going long after we're both bones in the dust."

Arraya tried to keep her annoyance tamped down. "Can the horses take five days of hard riding?" she asked.

"They are well-fed and used to work," J'Ram declared. "Five days will leave them ill, but the beasts can carry us that far."

"Then we ride," the apprentice declared.

They mounted up without fanfare, riding north. The Tillik took point, clearly more familiar with the terrain than either of the girls. He kept them moving at a brisk trot – fast enough to cover leagues in little time, but not so hard as to tire the horses prematurely.

Arraya fell in behind the Erixi rider, content to cover their backs. She settled into a sort of meditation, her reflexes handling all the work of riding and guiding her steed, while her mind stretched out to feel the currents of the True Magic all around her.

She had never tried the technique before while riding, and she found it vaguely difficult, but not impossible, to manage both riding and *feeling* at the same time. As she gradually fell into the well-practiced meditation, she pushed further and further out, searching for any sign of bandits or patrols from Jepitsa.

Such sensations were difficult to gauge. She had no doubt she'd immediately recognize a soldier or bandit, but distance and sometimes even direction were inaccurate at best, and completely wrong at worst, to sense in that way. She had very clear senses of both J'Ram and Naomi, but past that it was difficult to tell anything except a lack of potential enemies within the range of her senses.

She was startled out of her meditation by Naomi's voice. "So what is a Magi doing out here?" the Erixan asked. "I mean, last I heard, King Hazael didn't like your type at all, and you're heading straight into his stronghold."

"The Magi have been gone for a long time," Arraya said, shaking her head and trying to reach out again, but conducting a conversation was far too distracting. "I doubt he's looking for us."

The blonde girl studied Arraya for a few moments. "So. Assassination attempt?"

Arraya sputtered for a response. "I...no, we're not...could never do that."

Naomi's response was merely a speculative, "Hmmm."

"No, really," the apprentice tried again. "We don't kill. Not like that."

"Is that why you didn't burn any of the Tilliks with your fire?" Naomi asked.

Arraya grimaced. *So she noticed.* "Magi avoid killing whenever we can," she said. "Especially with the True Magic."

"Why?" the other inquired. "I mean, it's just a tool. If I refused to use my guns to kill, I wouldn't be much of an assassin."

That's interesting, Arraya thought. *So she is an assassin. And she's on her way to Jepitsa. Who could her target be?* Aloud, she said, "The True Magic is more than just a tool. It's everywhere and everything. It's life itself."

"Life ends," Naomi said succinctly.

"Yes, it does," Arraya agreed. "But to kill with the power...well, it's not something we do lightly. Any of us."

"Have you ever killed with magic before?" the assassin asked with a speculative smile.

"Never," Arraya admitted solemnly. "I've never needed to. There's always another way."

"Another way isn't always the best way," Naomi replied. "Sometimes killing is the best answer."

"Maybe that's true," the apprentice allowed. "There are certainly evils in the world that cannot be stopped any other way. But I doubt those bandits rose to that level," she added. "Certainly they have done harm, but death?"

"By letting them live, you left the possibility of them doing further evil in the world," Naomi pointed out.

"Granted, I made sure a dozen of them won't. But the rest? They could enslave more travelers, steal more from innocent people, or even kill others. If you would have destroyed them all, they never could have harmed anyone else again."

"Who makes that judgment? Who determines what people should die for their crimes?" Arraya asked, a bit heatedly. "An assassin?"

"The person with the power to do so," Naomi answered. "I have that power. I carry it in my guns every day I bear one. You have that power, too, with your magic."

"Power doesn't make you right," Arraya retorted.

"No, it doesn't. But it means I have the ability to choose. Not just the ability," she amended, "but the *responsibility* to do so."

"You're rather philosophical for an assassin," the flame-haired girl commented.

"And you're rather meek for having the ability to start fires with your *mind*." Naomi shook her head. "You're not what I would have expected from a Magi, crazy girl."

They rode in silence, side by side, for a league before Naomi spoke up again. "You still haven't told me why you're going to Jepitsa."

"Neither have you," Arraya pointed out dryly.

"Of course I haven't," Naomi joked, "because I have no idea why you're going."

Arraya snorted and continued to ride in silence. *It's odd. I thought I'd feel like I'm in constant danger, riding alongside an admitted assassin, and trailing a known highwayman. I feel safer now than I did coming from Cosmane by myself.*

Nightfall eventually caught the riders. They pushed on until the light had completely failed, and only after a near-miss with a sinkhole did J'Ram call the trio to a halt.

Arraya stripped off her saddle and rubbed the horse down before loosing a blanket and finding a dry spot to curl up upon. None of the three built a fire, by unspoken agreement – they were deep in the lawless territory between beacons of civilization, and no doubt other ne'er-do-wells roamed the woods.

Supper was dry jerky and a few cupfuls of water. The meager food left Arraya hungry, but she knew intellectually that it was enough energy to keep her going.

Her stomach still complained.

Sleep was slow in coming. While both J'Ram and Naomi fell asleep quickly, Arraya struggled to find enough peace to doze off. Time passed slowly, and the apprentice finally decided to try meditation in place of sleep.

Meditation was one of the first techniques Arraya had learned; it was, she later learned, often the very first exercise taught to apprentices.

Three-year-old Arraya knelt on the cold floor. Her little knees ached from the unforgiving stone, and her legs longed for release to stand, walk, run – anything to stretch out and move.

"You must learn patience," Master Shallum said. "You are young and undisciplined. You would rather play then stay here, learning lessons. For that reason, it is unusual to take a child to learn at your age. You, however, are special."

"Special?" the little flame-haired girl asked, cocking her head curiously. "How?"

"That does not matter for now. All that matters is that you can do this task."

The little girl blew out a sigh. "I'll try."

"Close your eyes," Master Shallum commanded. "And slow your thoughts. Concentrate only on my voice."

Arraya thought, Easy for you to say. You're so old you probably don't think anymore.

A firm rap on her head brought a protesting, "Hey!" from her lips. She opened her eyes and glared up at the Magi, and at his treacherous stick.

"I heard that," he said firmly.

"I only thought it," Arraya grumbled.

"You have no secrets from me," the master replied reprovingly. "Now, close your eyes and focus."

The girl sighed and closed her eyes, concentrating on the master's voice.

"Focus only on me," Shallum said quietly, forcing Arraya to strain to hear. "Before your training begins, you must learn to feel the True Magic. It is all around you, even within you. It is as common as the light under a bright sun, or the very air around you, or the water in the oceans. And to feel it, you must not seek it — you must let it in."

"How do I let it in?" the three-year-old asked.

"By ceasing to be."

So much of what Master Shallum said didn't make sense to the young mind, but she was tired of asking questions. Instead, she focused on Master Shallum's voice more fully, letting the familiar tone of his voice wash over her.

"To think of yourself, to worry, to concentrate on your discomfort or pain is to keep yourself distant from the True Magic. You must not hold it away from yourself. You have to embrace it all – the pain, the cold, the warmth, the comfort. When you accept it into yourself, you accept the True Magic as well."

"Accept that I hurt?" Arraya asked quizzically.

"Pain is a part of life. You must accept all the facets of life – the good and the bad. You must not create boundaries, or you will wall the magic away from yourself."

The little girl turned that thought over in her head. "But I don't want to hurt," she said at last.

"You should not," Shallum advised. "Nor should you want others to hurt. But when pain is offered, you must accept it into yourself."

Arraya was acutely aware now of the pain in her knees, the uncomfortable tingles in her legs. Don't hurt, she told herself. It doesn't hurt.

Her very skin started to tickle. It was far different from the pain in her limbs; instead, it felt like a warm blanket very lightly wrapping around her.

"Don't shy away from it," Shallum said encouragingly. "Allow it to happen."

The pain in the little girl's legs faded away as she felt warmer, more secure. It feels like sitting next to a fire, she decided. Master Shallum didn't build a fire, did he?

Then she opened her eyes.

Her skin was visibly glowing.

She yelped in fear and scrambled to her feet. The invisible warm blanket seemed to evaporate, and abruptly she was cold, and her legs hurt, and her knees protested at the sudden movement.

And Master Shallum was laughing.

"What? What was that?" Arraya asked in bewilderment. "Why are you laughing at me?"

"You have taken your first step," he said, taking her hand. "You've touched the True Magic."

Years of discipline had taught her far more control. As she fell into her meditation, she did not fear revealing her existence and location by literally lighting up the night.

Meditation was not a substitute for sleep. However, it gave her strength now when her own reserves were failing; it sharpened senses dulled by weariness; and it quieted the rumble of hunger in her belly.

And it brought her a moment of peace.

She understood well that her body had limits – she felt pain, hunger, weariness for a reason. Using the power to exceed those limits was easily within her repertoire of knowledge, but it had a cost that she would pay dearly for later. Still, the soothing warmth of power brought her comfort in the lonely, cold darkness.

That was enough for her to fall asleep.

***

Morning was a somber event. There was no laughter as the three riders ate a bit more of their precious food in a companionable silence. Again they did not risk lighting a fire – either light or smoke could draw unwanted attention in the predawn hour. Arraya noted both Naomi and J'Ram seemed ill-rested, their sleep as uneasy as her own. *At least I have power to rely upon*, she thought. *This must be far harder for them.*

Even the horses seemed restless as the riders saddled and mounted.

And then the ride was on again, three young riders – a daughter of the Magi, an assassin, and a Tillik – pushed toward Jepitsa with all the strength and speed they could muster.

J'Ram led as he had the previous day, seeming to find a trail where none existed. His ability to choose a path seemed to border on supernatural – to the degree that Arraya began to question whether Tilliks were capable of using the True Magic as well.

The very idea was silly from the beginning, but pondering the question gave Arraya something to think about beyond her own fears for Master Shallum and the tiredness that seemed to drag at her very spirit.

Magic has manifested itself outside the Scions before. There's the oracles, for one, even if they are all crazy. The Rune Sages use magic, too, and Master Shallum once told me that the Elvish tribes were capable of it.

What sets the Magi apart is that we're able to use it directly, fully, without going mad. The oracles can tap the same power we do, but they trade sanity for wisdom, and I'm not sure they're on the better side of that trade. The Rune Sages try to capture and use the magic with symbols and paint and ritual, but they can't tap the True Power directly. We drink from the stream, but they need a cup. The Elves, though...I don't know enough about them. They're a number of primitive tribes, so who knows what they're capable of doing?

Maybe the Tilliks are able to do it because they're not doing it consciously. Oracles go mad because they seek knowledge from the magic, directly trying to divine answers out of nothing. If the Tilliks use it to make them better hunters, without being aware of what they're doing, would it affect them the same way?

The question was academic and irrelevant, really. Arraya could propose any number of answers, but she had no way to test those answers for truth.

Still, the mental exercise kept her busy into the afternoon. It distracted her from the hunger gnawing inside her again, from the protests of muscles demanding rest. It was so effective, in fact, that she nearly fell off her horse when J'Ram's horse fell into step beside her.

"Tell me, fire-caller," the Tillik said, his voice as dry and solemn as ever. "Why do you seek the lair of your enemy?"

Arraya spent a moment recovering her balance, and a second moment to unscramble her thoughts. "What do you mean by 'the lair of your enemy'?" she asked instead of answering.

"We live a long time," the young Tillik rasped, "and we are not easily deceived. The High King Hazael has sat upon a throne of blood for ten and two years. The fire-bringers were servants of the King-Before, but have fought time and again against the sitting King. War has been waged and lost, but your kind does not submit." He hissed something Arraya couldn't understand. "Your kind does not accept defeat. Yet you ride into the stronghold of the High King."

Arraya frowned. "Why does it matter to you?" she asked suspiciously.

"I am pledged to your service," J'Ram said. "I will protect you from harm – even should it be from yourself."

"You're not my protector," Arraya said gently. "I am a Magi. I protect myself and others."

"It is not a question," J'Ram insisted. "I am bound to it."

"Why are you so bound?" the apprentice asked.

"Debt must be repaid, even if forgiven," the Tillik said simply.

"Why?" Arraya inquired. "I'm not holding you to any debt. Why do you insist on repaying it?"

"I follow the teachings of Nojalik, the servant of the Aither," the Tillik said reluctantly. "I am a hunter, as is she. I pay my debts in full."

"Nojalik?" Arraya asked in surprise. "I thought the Imposter-King had forbidden all worship of the Aither."

"What use is law that cannot be enforced?" the Tillik said with a toothy smile the apprentice found a bit unsettling. "Do you think all my kind are highwaymen and robbers and murderers?" He shook his head. "The King upon the stolen throne may decree, but he cannot enforce. The home of the Tilliks is far from his seat of power."

Arraya frowned and spent a moment focusing on riding as her horse broke stride to jump over a hole. "So the Tilliks resist the rule of the Imposter-King? Your entire race?"

"Telka is far from the hand of Jepitsa," J'Ram repeated. "Should we be decreed to worship Erebus, who should carry back report that we worship the Aither instead? It is a long, *dangerous* road from Telka to Werbri. Many servants of the King have disappeared when traveling through those lands."

Arraya shook her head in amazement. "I didn't think anyone resisted the Imposter-King anymore," she said. "After the last war..."

"No, no, no," the Tillik contradicted. "We do not resist. We do not march against the King upon the stolen throne. We are who we are. We are Tilliks."

The apprentice offered a small smile. *I suppose it's fair,* she thought. *We're not exactly fighting the Imposter-King ourselves. We're just not submitting to his rule. Fighting right now would be disastrous because we don't have an army at our backs or a rightful ruler to place upon the throne. Still, when the time for war comes, the Tilliks could be useful allies to us. Even if they're not soldiers, they could be great scouts and spies.*

"You have not yet answered," J'Ram said, interrupting her thoughts again. "I have asked, you asked, and I have thus answered, but you have not yet answered in turn."

"I go to Jepitsa because I am needed there," Arraya answered honestly, without a scrap of real information. "I am a Magi. I go where I am needed."

J'Ram sissed, a sound the apprentice was slowly beginning to recognize as laughter. "You speak well, fire-caller."

"Thanks," Arraya said dryly. She reviewed the conversation in her mind, then asked, "What are the teachings of Nojalik?"

"Nojalik is a servant and messenger of the Aither," J'Ram answered after a thoughtful pause. "And the first among the Aither's hunters."

"What does she teach?" Arraya asked.

"The values of the hunt," the Tillik replied, as though the answer were self-evident.

"What values?" the apprentice wanted to know.

"To stalk deliberately, without error," the Tillik said, the words coming out without thought. "To hunt well, and with great intent. To commit and strike completely, with finality. To kill entirely, and with speed."

Arraya swallowed. *Sounds lethal.* "So where's the teaching that insists you're beholden to me, though I've released you from your debt?"

"To kill entirely, and with speed," the Tillik replied, his tone taking on a shade of annoyance.

She spent a few moments turning that over in her mind. "I don't follow," Arraya confessed at last. "It doesn't make sense to me."

The Tillik rolled a reptilian eye to watch her. "Aren't the fire-bringers also the Wise?"

"Wise does not mean all-knowing," Arraya bristled. "Even the Magi have limitations. We do not know everything the Aither knows."

The hunter sissed. "The Tilliks tell many stories of the Wise, but none tell of your jokes."

The apprentice sighed. *I wonder if the other races make as little sense as the Tilliks.*

"The true hunter does not delay in his kill," J'Ram explained. "He does not leave his prey to suffer, and he always, always follows through. To wound and not finish the prey is to dishonor yourself and your prey. Thus, for me to begin an obligation but not complete it would be dishonorable for us both."

Arraya mulled that over as she concentrated on her riding for a few moments. *It makes sense, in its way*, she thought. *It's different than what I've been taught as a Magi, but not really opposing. It's...interesting. And if he's telling me the truth, I shouldn't have to worry about his loyalty, unless I run afoul of something else he believes.*

"Thrice I ask and done," J'Ram said into the steady *clop-clop-clop* of the horses' hooves falling in a steady trot. "Why do you seek the lair of our enemy?"

Our enemy, now, she observed. *He really is committed to this.*

"Will you deny me an answer?" J'Ram asked, disappointment and disapproval obvious even in his reptilian voice.

Arraya closed her eyes for just a moment to consider her options. They were, unfortunately, the same options she always had. *I can tell him nothing, I can lie to him, or I can tell him the truth.* The consequences of each action flitted through her mind in an instant. *Refusing him would cost me his loyalty, as could lying if he discovers the truth. Too much information could endanger Master Shallum. I'm better off risking losing his affection by lying.*

Aren't I?

The logic of the question was cold and implacable, but her instincts screamed at her that it was wrong. *He is an ally, and could be a friend. Trust him.*

Trust.

"My master is in danger," she whispered, so quiet she could hardly hear her own voice. "And I'm his only chance of survival."

XIII

BEN'S HEAD THROBBED AS HE opened his eyes. *What happened?* he wondered.

Slowly, he began to remember. He and Corin had boarded the ship – the *pirate* ship – to steal a tool they needed for a heist. *A boarding harpoon*, he recalled, as more of it came back. They had been captured by the ship's crew and taken before the pirates' captain, a man named Japhet. Ben had agreed to a fight with one of the pirates, with the prize being their lives.

And he had lost.

So why am I still alive? he wondered. His whole body seemed to ache as he turned his head from side to side, taking in his surroundings. *And where am I?* The rack of rum and maps, the desk, the bed all slowly filtered in. *Oh. I'm in the captain's personal quarters on the ship. I just hadn't seen them from this angle before.*

Voices approached the cabin's door. He sprang to his feet and looked around for a weapon or a place to conceal himself.

Or rather, he tried to spring to his feet.

He managed to make it as far as rolling off the soft bad and crashing into the hard, cold wooden floor before the door opened.

" – bargain well, lass."

"I do my best," the familiar voice of Corin rang in Ben's ears.

The thief looked up from his spot on the floor and saw Captain Japhet and Corin both looking at him with bemusement. "He recovered faster than I expected," Japhet said.

"I told you it would take less than half an hour," Corin replied. "Can you walk, Ben? It's time for us to go."

"What happened?" Ben croaked.

Corin frowned. "You don't remember?"

"I remember the fight," Ben said slowly. "Right up until I went down. Then I woke up here. Why am I still...?"

"Breathing?" Japhet offered helpfully. The pirate roared with laughter. "Lad, I'd rather not have to kill, and me crew is the same. You were beaten, and put up quite the entertaining fight. You paid your dues, and now it's time to be on your way."

Ben tried to sit up, but his body vetoed the idea with a fresh burst of pain. "Ow. What about the harpoon?"

"I have it right here, Ben," Corin said, patting an item hanging from her shoulder. "We need to get going. Alan will be waiting for us, no doubt."

"No doubt," Ben agreed, this time firmly telling his body to keep its objections to itself as he sat up.

"Come, lad," Japhet said. "It's time for you to be off me ship. I'd rather me crew didn't decide they want a rematch. You're not weak, boy, but you need to practice with the blade." The pirate captain seemed to consider him as Ben slowly climbed to his feet. "Should you ever be looking for a new career, look me up," he added. "A year with us and you would be a fearsome pirate."

"I'll keep that in mind," Ben rasped. "Thanks."

The thief slowly limped toward the door, his left knee describing in detail his poor decision-making while his ribs voiced their assent. Corin offered him a glowing smile and offered an arm. "I think you're going to need some help if you're going to limp back to Riverfront," she said.

"I think you might be right about that," Ben agreed. He settled his arm around Corin's shoulders and leaned into her to take the pressure off his aching knee.

"Lad, I almost forgot!" Japhet exclaimed as the two thieves began to leave. "Just a moment!" The pirate strode over the floor of the cabin, threw open a chest, and pulled out the first object on top. With it in hand, he returned just as rapidly. "This is yours, boy."

Ben looked down as Japhet extended a sword toward him – the blade he had used in the fight. "Thanks," he said.

"I wouldn't ever want you to be forgetting us," Japhet said with a wink. "Besides, that blade is too long for us. Should you be fighting in close, like the hold of a ship, it's better to have a short blade so you not be hitting the walls."

The thief slowly – and painfully – slung the sheathed weapon over his shoulder. "I'll keep that in mind."

"Now off with you," Japhet shooed them away. "I wouldn't want the Royal Guard to be catchin' a glimpse of your new toys. They wouldn't like them, not one bit."

Ben was surprised to find that he didn't have to walk back to Riverfront. The pirate crew had provided a small boat for their use instead, a bit of wood and tar barely large enough to hold the two of them and powered only by a pair of oars.

Corin settled into the rowing seat after settling Ben in the front. "I'll give you one thing," she said dryly. "You certainly have a way with people."

"Yes, I do," Ben agreed wearily as he tried to make himself comfortable. "I'm going to be hurting for a week."

"Probably," Corin said. "Did you break anything in that fight?"

"I'm not sure," Ben confessed. "I'm bruised head to toe, but nothing has punched through the skin, and I was able to walk this far. I think I just got good and beat."

"That was a stupid plan, by the way," Corin informed him. "You decided, to save our skins, to take on a man who fights and kills for a living. Then you did it with *swords*, which you've never used, and fought him in a circle where you couldn't cheat. You're lucky he thought it would be better to go hand-to-hand rather than just run you through with his blade." She dipped one of the paddles in the water, slowly pushing the boat away from the pirate vessel and up the stream toward Riverfront. She offered him a brilliant smile. "And thank you."

Ben luxuriated in the warmth of that smile. "You're welcome."

"Now, don't ever do anything that stupid again. Ever. Or next time I'll let the pirates dump you overboard after you've been beaten within an inch of your life," she added.

"I could happily live the rest of my life without a beating like that," Ben said. "In fact, I could live three or four lifetimes and be perfectly happy to never be beaten like that again. Hell, I could have done without it the first time."

"In our line of work, I doubt that's the last beating you'll ever get."

"Yeah. Me, too."

***

Riverfront was quiet in the post-dawn hours, as was usual. Corin bumped the boat up against the shoreline, but didn't bother to tie it. As she helped Ben slowly limp up the bank, the boat drifted back into the current and slowly floated away. Ben stopped for a moment to look back at the wandering watercraft and felt a moment of sadness. *Guess it's better this way — less evidence against both us and the pirates. Still, will anyone even believe us when we tell them what we've been through?*

"So," Corin said conversationally, "let's get you back to your shack and get you settled in. I'll take the boarding harpoon to Alan and see if I can find a doctor to look you over and make sure you're going to be okay."

"No," Ben said tiredly.

"No?" Corin asked curiously.

"No. We're going to go talk to Alan together."

"Ben, you need rest. I can handle it," the girl said in exasperation.

"No, you can't," Ben said. "Besides, I got beaten within an inch of my life to get that thing. There's no way I'm not going to turn that into Alan myself."

Corin snorted. "You're such a boy."

"What's that mean?"

The dark-haired girl shook her head. "Never mind. Think you can walk all the way to Alan's castle?"

The last word came out with a heavy overlay of sarcasm that Ben chose to ignore. *She's been through nearly as much as you have been,* he told himself. *Cut her some slack. It's not like Corin is working against Alan, or that she'd backstab him. We're all in this together.*

"Well?" she asked again, interrupting his thoughts.

Ben nodded. "Yes, I can walk that far. I think by walking around I'm loosening up. I'm feeling a little better all the time."

"Liar," was all Corin said as she stepped out to lead the way.

The two thieves took the better part of an hour to reach the island. Ben nearly fell in the crossing, but Corin fished him out before he could be swept away by the current.

They were nearly at the entrance when two figures materialized out of the brush, longbows in hand with arrows nocked and strings drawn. "Who are you?" one of them asked in a low, gruff tone.

"Ben and Corin, here with a package for the boss," Corin said sarcastically. "Really? Don't you recognize us?"

One of the armed guards stepped around in front of them. "You two look like hell," he commented. "I didn't even recognize you. What happened?"

"We were invited in for tea by a noble," Corin bit out, "and she decided it'd be fun to paint us black and blue and smear us with mud. Now, are you going to let us in, or not?"

Without further word, both guards disappeared as suddenly as they had materialized a moment before.

"Bootlickers," Corin muttered as she led Ben into the ruined tower.

Alan was already descending from the upper level. "You have returned," he said calmly as he walked down the broken staircase. "Did you find it?"

"Yes," Corin snarled. "We found the boarding harpoons and brought one back. Had a nice chat with some pirates, too."

Ben watched Alan's expression as his face paled. "Pirates?" he repeated. "What pirates?"

"The pirates who owned the ship and the boarding harpoons," Corin shot back. "The pirates who caught us boarding their ship and decided that we would make splendid entertainment. The same pirates who beat Ben here within an inch of his life and left him for dead. The only reason we're here is because I managed to slip away during Ben's fight and got back in to drag him out when they finished. So, do you want to start telling us the truth now?"

Alan dragged his shocked expression from Ben's injuries to Corin's face. "Truth? What are you talking about?"

"There's more going on here than what you've told us," Corin ground out. "Don't try to pretend otherwise."

"Corin, I've been nothing but forthcoming with you," Alan protested. "You think I would risk two of the best thieves in the Brigands by withholding information? Not to mention the entire plan to steal the crown and make us all fabulously wealthy? That hardly makes sense."

"No, it doesn't make sense, but it's the truth," the girl spat back. "You had to..."

"Enough, Corin," Ben said quietly. "It doesn't matter right now anyway. Give Alan the boarding harpoon and let's get back to Riverfront."

"Ben, he set us up!" she protested.

"No, he didn't," the other said. "It doesn't make sense to set us up. He needed what we brought back, and besides, we're all Brigands – we're family. He wouldn't do that to us." *You know it's true*, Ben thought. *You know that, even if you dislike him, he would never, ever hurt us.*

Corin sighed. "Fine." She pulled the boarding harpoon from her shoulder and dropped it to the stone floor with a clatter. "For your inspection," she said flatly before turning and walking out.

Ben shrugged helplessly at Alan before turning wordlessly to follow the girl.

***

Corin didn't speak the entire walk to Ben's shack, though she walked beside him. Ben could feel the heat of her anger radiating in the cool morning air, but he decided silence was the better of his two options.

The hovel was occupied by three other sleeping bodies when Ben swung the door open. Corin followed him in as he crossed the threshold to his bed. The girl helped him settle into a pile of blankets, still silent and seething. As she turned to leave, Ben finally spoke. "Corin, he's doing what's best for all of us."

"He's doing what's best for Alan," she replied coolly.

Ben shook his head. "This whole job – stealing the crown could bring money into Riverfront like we've never seen."

"You mean it's going to line Alan's pockets with more gold than we've ever dreamed."

"Why don't you trust him?" Ben asked bluntly. "He's kept the Brigands together, he's kept us all out of the dungeons, he's made sure we all have enough to eat and a place to sleep. Seems to me he's been a pretty good leader."

"Is that all life is to you?" Corin turned, her anger now directed at Ben. "Eat and sleep? Living in a little wooden shack that could fall down around you? Ben, we all live in the dirt, and he's living like a king already. He's set himself up in a castle, he's putting together his own Royal Guard, and he's *using* us. We're his peasants. We pay him *taxes* for the *privilege* of pulling off a successful job! You're so loyal to him you can't see what's right in front of you!"

"The money we're giving him is turned around and spent on the Brigands," Ben protested. "Where do you think we get the silver to feed the younger kids?"

"And how much is he taking out of that money for himself?" Corin continued. "How much is he spending on bows and swords and armor and uniforms?" She snorted. "Maybe he's already recruited you into his personal Guard. Is that why you can't see it?"

"Corin..." he protested weakly.

"No, he wouldn't have bribed you that way. You'll give him loyalty for free."

A thought occurred to him. "What sort of king would get his own hands dirty?" he asked Corin.

"*No* king gets his own hands dirty. When was the last time Alan helped with a heist?" she said heatedly. "When was the last time it was *his* neck on the line if something went wrong?"

"He's going with on the crown heist," Ben said, his tone strengthening as his confidence waxed. "He already said as much. If all he wanted to do was play king, why would he risk himself on a job this dangerous?"

"Because it's the biggest payout we'll ever see in our lives?" Corin spat. "He wouldn't risk losing that much gold because one of us screwed it up. No, for this job, of *course* he'll come along."

"You're just looking for a reason to tear him down," Ben said wearily as he settled into his bed. "You hate him for some reason, and you'll find a fault in everything he does."

"And you'll never find a fault in him." The girl shook her head. "Not until it's your head in the noose or under the executioner's axe. Then, maybe, you'll see I was right all along." She turned and started to leave.

"Wait," Ben protested. "Wait. Are you leaving?"

"If you're going to sleep and heal, yes, I'll need to leave," Corin said with a roll of her eyes.

"I meant Riverfront," he replied softly.

The girl froze for a moment, her expression unreadable as only her eyes seemed to dart back and forth like a trapped animal. Finally, she relented with a, "Maybe."

"Don't," Ben said. "Not yet."

"Why?" she asked.

"I'll make you a bet."

"A bet," she repeated warily. "What sort of bet?"

"You think Alan is going to use the crown heist to make himself rich, right?" He took a deep breath. "If you're wrong, you stay with us and admit that Alan really has been looking out for us."

"And if I'm right?" she asked with a cocked eyebrow.

"I'll leave with you."

Corin snorted. "Who said I wanted you to come with me?"

"No one. But there had to be some reason you stayed at the pirate ship until I came to."

Her expression was unreadable. *I wish I knew what she was thinking,* Ben thought. *I've never known what she was thinking.*

"If I'm right," she said slowly, "then we take all the children with us when we leave."

"The children?" he repeated, puzzled. "Why?"

"Because we won't leave them behind to get used by Alan," she snarled. "If we leave them here, he'll just replace us with them. They come with us."

Ben considered the bet. *I already know I'm going to win. These terms won't mean anything.* "Fine," he said. "Deal."

"Deal." Corin shook her head and walked out the door. "Sleep well, Ben."

***

Ben was pleasantly surprised by how quickly he fell asleep. His dreams were fractured things, peaceful and quiet moments with Corin interspersed with savage pirates and sword fights and wrestling and beatings. Alan always seemed to loom in the background, just beyond his sight but clearly watching. Sometimes the master of the Brigands seemed to be as brilliant as the Light One, other times as lifeless and black as the Dark One.

Daylight was fading when the thief opened his eyes.

Sitting on the floor an arm's-length away, cross-legged Zeke was loudly slurping on a bowl of soup. "Good morning, sleepy head," he said.

The bits of daylight leaking through the cracks in the wall showed a sun setting on the horizon. "Good morning," Ben croaked. "Any more of that?"

Zeke jerked a thumb at the door. "The fire and the cooking pot are out there." He frowned. "Can you even stand?"

"Would rather not find out," Ben replied with as much wit as he could manage, which wasn't very much given the pain flooding through his bruised body.

"Stay here, then." Zeke rose and walked out, returning a few moments later with another bowl of soup and spoon. He sat down and offered them to his friend.

Ben extended his arms from under the blankets to accept the meal. "Thanks."

"You're welcome." Zeke smiled. "Way Corin tells it, you're the best thief that ever walked Riverfront."

"How is that?" Ben asked as he looked down at his soup. He fished out a fly with the spoon and flicked it away before settling into eat.

"The two of you stowed away onto a pirate ship, evaded dozens of bloodthirsty pirates, and stole one of their own weapons," Zeke said dramatically. "Then, during your escape, you were forced to fight sword-to-sword with one of them. After disarming him, you offered him a chance at living by throwing away your own weapon, but you had to kill him when he attacked you both again."

Ben choked on his soup, sputtering and coughing. When he could finally manage to talk, he asked, "Is that what she's telling everyone?"

Zeke nodded. "Said it was the stuff of legends. A thief from Riverfront taking on a pirate hand-to-hand and winning. Stealing from the best thieves in the world and taking the prize." He frowned. "I didn't think you knew anything about swordplay."

Ben smiled faintly. "I don't."

"Then how did you...?"

"Just between you, me, and the soup, what do you think?"

Zeke got it. "Oh."

"Yeah." Ben stretched out and readjusted, trying to make himself comfortable again.

"So what actually happened?"

"Corin and I snuck onto this ship at the docks. Alan had told us it was a trader ship from the north, but it wasn't – it was a pirate raider. That thing he sent us after? The pirate captain called it a 'boarding harpoon.' They use them for holding trader ships in place while they loot 'em."

Ben took a spoonful of soup. "We got our hands on one of them right before we got caught."

Zeke nodded, leaning forward to ask, "So how'd you get away?"

"We didn't." Ben spent several moments eating more of his soup before he continued. "The pirate captain didn't know what to do with us, because he didn't want to turn us over to the Guard. So he agreed to pit one of his pirates against me in a fight. If I won, we got to leave with the boarding harpoon, and if I lost, well, Corin got to keep her skin."

"So you beat the pirate and left," Zeke nodded.

"So I lost horribly," Ben replied with a small, pained smile. "I got lucky to even survive the fight. Last thing I remember was being pinned to the deck of the pirate ship when he punched my lanterns out."

"So how are you here, and how are you not dead?"

"Corin really didn't tell me." Ben shrugged. "She got us free passage off the ship and we got to keep the harpoon."

"Even though you lost."

"Even though I lost," Ben repeated between bites of soup.

"That's just like her," Zeke commented. "She doesn't say anything and problems just disappear."

"What do you mean?" the injured thief asked.

"Haven't you noticed? Corin never says anything about herself, or what she's doing." Zeke drained the last swallow from his bowl by raising it to his lips. "She's probably the best lock pick in the Brigands, and she's smart and sees *everything* going on. And you *know* she's doing a lot of things no one ever sees, but she won't say a thing about it." He belched, then shrugged. "I don't get her at all."

Ben mulled that over as he finished his soup. "So what do you think she did?"

"Beats me," Zeke shrugged. "Maybe she bribed the pirates with some gold or something." He smiled. "Your job was supposed to be the easy one, but it was far more exciting than ours."

Ben frowned. "So what did you wind up stealing?"

"I thought we were going to be getting some hammer or pick," Zeke said. "We wound up stealing some sword."

"A sword?" Ben asked curiously.

"Yeah," his friend said with a shudder. "You can tell it has some magic on it. It just *feels* wrong when you pick it up. It's...*unnatural*."

"Where did you find that?"

"The Commander of the Royal Guard," Zeke said with a grin. "We did the whole job in the shadow of the castle itself. We all thought we were going to run into trouble, but it was a simple in-and-out. Even getting out of the city seemed easier than normal."

Ben shuddered. "I'm glad that was you and not me. If I never have to touch something with magic on it, I'll be happy."

The doorway darkened, and both thieves turned to see Alan himself standing in the portal. "Hello Zeke, Ben," he greeted them.

Both offered respectful nods. "Welcome," Ben said. "Sorry if I don't get up."

"That's why I came," Alan said, offering a warm smile. "I wanted to see how badly you had been hurt. You were moving very slow and stiff when you brought me the harpoon."

"Nothing broken," Ben reported. "I should be back to normal in a few days, I think." He hesitated. "I mean, if you need me to, I can be ready to go for the crown heist sooner."

"No, that won't be necessary. It will be four days or so before we're ready to move on the crown. Timing will be important to ensure we can immediately sell the crown to our buyer – we wouldn't want to be caught with it in Riverfront. The Royal Guard would burn it down and kill us all if we are caught." Alan seemed to study Ben for a moment. "Zeke, can you let us have a few minutes?" he asked.

The tall thief nodded and departed without a word.

Alan seated himself in front of Ben. "I need to ask you something," he said hesitantly.

What's going on? Ben wondered. *Alan never hesitates. He's always so sure of himself.*

"I have concerns," the leader of the Brigands said, his voice so quiet Ben had to strain to hear it. "I'm worried about Corin."

"What about her?" Ben asked, striving to hide the nervousness that was already worming to life in his belly.

"Ben, I'm afraid she's trying to turn the Brigands against me," Alan said quietly.

"Why would she do something like that?" Ben asked hesitantly.

"Power," Alan said. "She is jealous of my place, and she seeks to make herself a ruler." He offered a small smile. "Has she tried to turn you against me, too?"

Ben shook his head mutely, trying to forget his conversation with Corin earlier. *She wanted to take me and the children away. Could she be trying to set up a new group of Brigands, with herself as the leader?*

"Of course she wouldn't," Alan said with a small smile of satisfaction. "She knows you're too honest for such a scheme. You would never turn against your fellow Brigands."

"Never," Ben confirmed, striving to keep the tremor from his voice. "I'd never betray the Brigands."

Alan smiled and rose to his feet. "Of course not." He turned and walked to the door. "Four days to rest, and then I'll need you ready to go. After all, without your skills, we wouldn't have the tools we need to make it happen."

Ben watched him leave. *I'm going to have to choose. But who will I stand with?*

XIV

THE SUN STOLE GLIMPSES OVER the horizon as the three riders tiredly pushed the last leagues to Jepitsa. The great plains of Werbri spread out in all directions further than their eyes could see, only broken by the great rivers and the patches of farmland.

The city and the great castle were visible from twenty leagues, a man-made mountain rising from the flatland.

Once, Jepitsa had been a beacon of hope and light for all of Letale. The great castle had been besieged by enemies from across the ocean more than once, but never had fallen to attack. When the Imposter-King had taken the throne, he had done so by deception and subterfuge, rather than leading his armies across the plain in open war.

Now, it brought nothing but a sense of foreboding for Arraya as her horse tiredly trotted the last leagues. *The Imposter-King has corrupted everything*, she thought. *The great beacon of Letale is now a fortress of darkness. The temples of the Aither have been turned to the Dark One. The Magi are hunted as criminals, and no doubt the Dark One's servants have taken the role of the Magi as advisors to the Imposter-King.*

The horses were at the limits of their endurance when the three reached the final river crossing. Instead of pushing across, Arraya dismounted. Naomi and J'Ram both offered puzzled looks before following suit.

"What now?" J'Ram asked. "We rode to our limits to reach the stronghold of the enemy, and now we wait?"

"Patience," Arraya said. "And thank you, for getting us here. But rushing into the Imposter-King's stronghold will give us nothing. You're a hunter, right?" she asked. "It's time we scout. Once we know the lay of the land and the defenses of our prey, we can begin to hunt." *That's more hunting metaphors than I ever thought I'd use,* she thought wryly. *But if it helps him understand and keeps him from racing in with claws out, I can manage it.*

"How long will your business take?" Naomi asked. The Erixan shootist had donned a light cloak. The smaller of her weapons was strapped to her waist and virtually invisible, while the longer weapon was concealed in a bedroll slung from the side of her saddle.

"Likely a day or less," Arraya replied. "Why?"

Naomi shrugged. "Depending on which direction you're going when you leave, I might want to travel with you again. Besides, I don't think either of us are long on resources, are we? After getting hit by the Tilliks, I haven't got more than my guns or the clothes on my back. No coin, no food, nothing."

Arraya's stomach growled as if to punctuate Naomi's point. "I'll keep that in mind."

Silently, J'Ram reached into his pouch and stretched out his scaly hand, offering a small pile of silver coins. "I have little, but perhaps it would be enough."

Naomi's hand flashed for the coins, but Arraya was quicker. "Tsk, tsk," the apprentice said.

"Hey, it'd be just payment for captivity," the Erixan said sharply. "In fact, those might be *my* coins."

Arraya shrugged indifferently at the blonde girl. "And maybe they were mine." She softened. "Let's work together for now, then." The apprentice offered the shootist half the coins. "So, here."

Naomi took the coins, giving the other a puzzled look. "Then why...?"

"I didn't want you to ditch us," Arraya said. "So, we're going to need food, and we're going to need some place to sleep." The apprentice pointed across the river. "Those rickety little hovels? That's probably our best bet."

"Why not one of the inns within the city proper?" the shootist asked.

"Because the city guard probably doesn't come out here. No one official keeps an eye on this place."

J'Ram nodded approvingly. "The river attracts insects, which the thinskins can't tolerate. None are there but those who have nowhere else to be."

"Close enough," Arraya said. "So, how about it? You want to find us some cover?"

The assassin's expression was unreadable. "Fine. My business will need to wait until after nightfall."

What is your business? Arraya wondered. *Are you here to kill someone? Who would you be after? Why would someone hire an assassin to travel all the way from Erixi to Jepitsa for one job?*

She tried to put her questions out of her mind. "Thanks."

Naomi turned and waded across the river without another word, her horse following quietly and exhausted in her wake.

"And me?" J'Ram asked. "What should I do to further your quest?"

Arraya frowned. "Keep your head down. There's not many Tilliks around the capital, so everyone will watch you if you're inside the city." She sighed. "See if you can find us something to eat, and then lie low wherever Naomi finds us someplace to stay."

"And what will you be doing?" J'Ram wanted to know.

"Scouting."

***

Arraya left her horse at a small stable just inside the city gate, paying a pittance for hay and shelter for the tired beast, taking only her staff with her. *Even if I'm leaving slowly enough to retrieve her, I doubt she'll be in any condition to travel*, the apprentice knew. *After that five day ride, she'll need days to recover, and I won't be here that long.*

Assuming I can find Master Shallum.

The apprentice pushed that thought aside violently. *No doubts. I can do this. I will do this.*

After acquiring a loaf of freshly baked bread from a tiny bakery, Arraya began searching for a high, quiet point in the city. It took her three hours to cross the city, looking for a spot that offered both height to see from and seclusion from interruption. She passed up the peaks of several houses as too public, and guard towers as too prone to interruption. Many an alley offered seclusion, but no height for her to look from.

She finally found such a point in the chapel of Aither – now given entirely over to the Dark One. It was a bit unnerving climbing into the bell tower, knowing what it now enshrined, but she contented herself with a touch of irony. *I'll use a temple to the Dark One to serve the will of the Aither.*

She seated herself cross-legged under the giant bell. Instead of immediately stretching out for power, she spent several minutes eating the loaf of bread, easing her own body's hurts and needs. Five days of hard riding and barely sleeping had taken a heavy toll, and while using the True Magic had kept her going, she was tapping a very large portion of her power to keep herself going – strength that she could be using other ways, strength that she could very well need to rescue Master Shallum from whatever unseen threat she had perceived in the vision.

When her hunger was sated, she considered her options wearily. She needed rest – deep, peaceful sleep – to fully recover her strength. The apprentice could go back to whatever flophouse the Erixan had found, sleep hard, and then attempt this weaving. On the other hand, this would require an enormous amount of strength, and she would need rest afterward to recover.

Spell, then sleep, then recover Master Shallum, Arraya decided. *Oh. Master Shallum would cuff me if he heard me call this a spell instead of a weaving.*

There were different ways to use the True Magic, and the Council of Magi were particular about how they classified uses of the power, preferring to avoid the generic definition of "spell." Calling upon the elements, such as the fire Arraya had used against the Tillik highwaymen, was called summoning. Had she used her power to help her allies during the ride to Jepitsa, she would've needed to use an enchantment – creating an unnatural effect, either on an item or person.

Summoning was a quick and simple process – a flexing of will while tapping power could create fire or wind, earth or water. Enchantments required a physical focus – either a singular object or person.

What Arraya was attempting was neither summoning nor enchantment – it was a weaving.

Weavings involved using magic over an area, instead of focus on a single point. Arraya had read a legend of one of the ancient Magi, a lone Scion who employed a weaving so powerful he drove an entire attacking army mad, turning them against each other in a bloodbath. Another Magi had cast a net over all of Letale, using the weaving to find a powerful servant of the Dark One that had been terrorizing the kingdom.

A weaving involved both more strength and more finesse than either enchantments or summons. For that reason alone, the masters of the Magi never tried to teach weavings to apprentices. While a number of apprentices were capable of either the focus or the brute strength necessary for a weaving, no past apprentice had ever managed both at the same time.

And it was dangerous to even attempt such a use of the True Magic. For the untrained, even a simple use of the power could drive a practitioner mad. The Scions were naturally adept and could shape the power to their wills, but drawing on too much of the True Magic could dissolve their natural defenses and destroy them as well.

No master wanted to see an apprentice driven mad.

The red-haired girl laid her staff down, closed her eyes, and began to tap into the True Magic.

She hadn't realized the true depth of her exhaustion. In a moment of clarity, she suspected she tapped into her power unconsciously to some degree, enough to keep her on her feet and moving as long as her will held out.

Now, trying to draw enough power in to manage the weaving felt like trying to drink an ocean.

Arraya struggled to draw in the power. She wrestled with it like she would a mortal opponent, using every technique she knew to gain leverage, every bit of strength she possessed, every drop of willpower she could manage to hold onto the energy she was drawing in.

Some tiny part of her realized that Master Shallum had never taught her to use power like this.

And then, somehow, impossibly, she had it – all of it. The power for the weaving.

She wasn't attempting anything as ambitious as what she had read about, but it strained her mind to the edge of breaking. Without haste, she shaped it in her mind, defining every aspect of it with crystal clarity. Arraya clamped down hard on any unease she felt – she had no time nor concentration to spare for anything but the weaving. Allowing any part of the weaving to wane would create a backlash of pure power that would utterly destroy her.

The apprentice found that sufficient motivation to concentrate.

The weaving crystallized in her mind, and it was as real to Arraya as the bell tower she sat upon.

With most workings, it was simple enough to pour out summoned power into the form she'd already created in her mind. This time, though, it felt like she was trying to exhale the same ocean she'd already swallowed.

She struggled with controlling the power. It hammered against the structure she had shaped, threatening to wash it away under a flow of pure magic. Exhaustion tugged at her, and she nearly released it all in despair. It would be far easier to surrender, to give up her consciousness in the wash of the True Magic, to allow all her worry to vanish.

A heartbeat passed, or a lifetime – Arraya could never tell when she was so deeply into a working. She held onto the power with every scrap of willpower she could manage, allowing the ocean into her weaving drip by single drip. The universe itself grew old while she worked, and she did not relent until the last trickle of power filled her weaving.

She opened her eyes, and the very air thrummed with power. She felt as though she were sitting in a lightning storm, with thunder rolling around her and flashes of light everywhere.

And she was *aware*. She could feel everything through the entire city of Jepitsa. To test her power, she counted every rat, every pig, and every chicken inside the city walls. The answers flowed to her effortlessly, without more effort than simply desiring the answer.

I can't believe I pulled this off, Arraya marveled. *This is absolutely amazing. I've never felt anything like it.* It was a working beyond anything she had managed before – a web of connections, a blanket of power that connected her to every living thing within the city walls. It was the most important gift for any Magi.

Knowledge.

She glanced down at her arms and saw them shine in the falling light. Curiously, she reached up with one hand to feel her opposite arm and found it soaked with sweat, cold and clammy.

Oh. I'm at the limits of my power. I must still be functioning off the power I called up to create the weaving. She swallowed hard. *So find your answers quickly, before this all falls apart.*

She sent a single question out into her web of knowledge. *Where is Master Shallum?*

The web began to fray, and she could feel the weaving itself begin to come apart. Her technique had been less than perfect, and people and creatures alike kept *moving*, forcing the web to continually change to maintain the connections. A full Magi could have maintained the web with mere trickles of power once it had been established, but Arraya had no power left to feed the web.

Understanding tickled at her mind. *He's in the castle. He's at the heart of Jepitsa.*

It was all she could manage before the weaving unraveled entirely.

Arraya slumped in exhaustion. *That was...wow. Okay. Yes, now I'm going to need to sleep.*

Then a hand fell on her shoulder. "What are you doing up here?" a voice asked.

"I'm sorry, priest," she croaked. "I needed to..."

The apprentice's screaming instincts finally caught her attention. The utter *wrongness* of the hand on her shoulder scraped against her senses, the tiny trickle of magic she still felt crying for her attention. She reached out to grab her staff, lying next to her on the wooden floor.

Then the impact against her head left her senseless.

***

"*Master,*" *an eleven-year-old Arraya asked,* "*are the servants of the Dark One like us?*"

"*Why do you ask, apprentice?*" *Master Shallum asked.*

Arraya sighed, vaguely annoyed because he tended to ask questions rather than answer them. "*I just wanted to know.*"

"*The servants of the Dark One are not to be trifled with,*" *Master Shallum warned.* "*In many ways, they are as powerful as the Magi.*"

That thought was enough to set the girl back on her heels. "*As powerful as you?*"

Shallum nodded. "*We serve the Aither, and draw our power from the True Magic. But they serve Erebus, and draw power from the False Magic.*"

"*False Magic?*" *Arraya asked.* "*You've never taught me about that before.*"

"*That's because the False Magic is merely a shadow of what we serve.*" *Shallum nodded.* "*The True Magic is used to heal, to create, to build, to advise, to learn. The power of the Erebus is used to hurt, to tear down, to destroy, to dominate, to control. Those who serve the False Magic are corrupted by the very power they use.*"

"*Corrupted how?*" *Arraya wanted to know.*

"*They lose their mortality in horrible ways. They become predators, destroying mortal lives to sustain themselves, twisted more as they are drawn deeper into their slavery to the Erebus. Some take on hideous forms, like beasts of the field or creatures of the night. Others seem to maintain their forms, but are destroyed mind and soul. None escape unscathed, and all of them hunger for power.*" *Master Shallum smiled sadly.* "*There is no redemption for these creatures. They have chosen their fates, and they cannot turn from their own decisions."*

"Oh." Arraya struggled with the concept for a moment. *"So...what happens if they catch me?"*

The master raised an eyebrow. *"I do not believe in protecting you from the truth. Are you sure you want to know?"*

The flame-haired girl nodded.

"They will take your very power as their own," Shallum said, his voice low and slow. *"They will eat you up entirely and use what they've stolen from you to elevate themselves."*

***

Arraya opened her eyes and, for the second time since leaving Cosmane, found herself bound in chains.

How long was I out? she wondered. *Minutes? Hours? Days? And what happened?*

She spent several minutes unscrambling her thoughts. *I cast the weaving and found Master Shallum. Then there was something wrong...some*one *wrong. And then that person used my head as the bell clapper.* She shook her head. *That's the last time I sit in a bell tower.*

The apprentice took stock of her surroundings. She was chained hand and foot to a table, and the chamber was dark. The little light offered was from a handful of candles scattered around the chilly stone room. The room offered little other adornment: a handful of tapestries, a simple wooden table and handful of stools, a barrel and a trio of pewter mugs.

Arraya was unable to tap into the power, bound as she was, but she didn't need it to remember the *wrongness* of the being that had struck her down. She had been off guard and exhausted from the weaving, but now she had time to think and gather her wits. Now, when she had time to consider, she recognized that slithering power she had felt – it was utterly familiar, and utterly alien.

It was a servant of the Dark One. The power was an echo of the True Magic – the shadow power the slaves of Erebus employed.

"So, Arraya," she whispered to herself. "You traveled from Cosmane to Jepitsa in a week. You escaped the grasp of bandits that would have sold you into slavery. You gained allies in an Erixan shootist and a Tillik hunter. You managed a working that should've been impossible for an apprentice. And then you let yourself get caught by one of the worst enemies of the Magi." She sighed. "Great job, apprentice. Master Shallum would be proud."

The apprentice struggled with the shackles for a few minutes before deciding they weren't going to give. Acutely aware of her body's bruised and exhausted state, she reached deeply for all the serenity Master Shallum had tried to teach her during her apprenticeship.

And fell asleep.

***

Arraya found herself in a single spot of light. The floor was formless, a pool of grey dully illuminated by some light she could not see.

"This is a dream," she said aloud, her voice echoing weirdly.

"Yes, it is," her own voice answered.

She rose from the chair and turned to see herself stepping forward.

"You're not me," Arraya said, narrowing her eyes at her likeness.

The other red-haired girl was her mirror image, but sharper, more beautiful, cleaner, *better*. In contrast to Arraya's battered, dirty brown robes, this new Arraya wore sleek black from head to toe. She lacked the bruises and dirt Arraya had accumulated since leaving Cosmane.

"Of course I'm you," the other girl said calmly. "Or rather, I'm a part of you."

"What part of me would that be?" Arraya asked warily.

"Call me your survival instinct," the doppelganger said. "The part of you concerned with the basic things in life – food, sleep, survival, mating." She shook her head. "You haven't made very good decisions. A Magi? Really? You eat little, sleep not nearly enough, committed yourself to an order that will keep you from ever having children, and now you've begun to risk our life...for what?"

Arraya shook her head. "I'm not talking to you. This is a dream, and you're crazy."

"I'm a part of you, so you'd better hope I'm not crazy," the other said. "And I'm *very* concerned about survival."

The apprentice ignored her and walked toward the darkness. "I'm sure you are."

"Stop," the other girl said. "Please. Stop."

Arraya turned back at the edge of the circle of light. "Why? I'm not foolish. You're some trick to get me to join the Dark One's servants."

"Hardly. If anything Master Shallum has told us is true, a long term commitment will mean our destruction. But that doesn't mean we can't lie, take advantage of it now, and turn our backs on it later."

"No," Arraya said. "We can't."

"Even if you survive this encounter, what about the next one? And the one after? As long as you keep pursuing this path, the dangers will come until we're struck down. You should abandon this path."

"We can't," Arraya repeated. "We...*I* need to follow my path. I won't let you turn me from it."

"You're lonely," the other said bluntly. "I am you, Arraya. I know how much you want a family – a real family, not just teachers. You want true friends. You want a lover. It's only natural. Stop this foolishness. Turn from this path."

"I can't," Arraya said simply, not letting her discomfort rise to her expression. "Master Shallum is counting on me."

She walked into the darkness and woke up.

***

This time the room was not empty.

The apprentice's wrists were chafed from the bindings, but when she opened her eyes she felt surprisingly rested. *I'm not going to ask questions,* she decided. *Something to do with the True Magic, maybe? There are days I wonder how much Master Shallum hasn't told me.*

Her magical senses were still as blind as ever, her power cut off by her captivity. When she looked around with her eyes, the room seemed empty, but her instincts told her she was not alone. *Where?* she wondered.

Movement stirred in her peripheral vision. When she tried to focus on it, there was only still empty shadows.

"Ah, a tasty little mageling," The voice was dry and rough, and it scraped against her ears like its magic had scraped her senses before. "Young and tasty, not dried out and tough like the elder fire-callers."

"What do you want from me?" Arraya called.

"Your power," it laughed. "Your heart. Your soul. Your life."

"You don't want much," the apprentice grumbled under her breath.

The shadows seemed to congeal into a figure in the center of her vision. "It is a rare opportunity to meet with one of you little magelings outside the protection of your masters. They lock you up in stone fortresses, ward us away, create torches to keep us shadows at bay. They fear us, fear what we can offer you."

"Offer me?" Arraya asked. "What would a slave of the Dark One offer a servant of the Aither?"

"What did you think I would do, little one?" the congealed shadow asked. "Eat you?" It laughed, a short and genuinely entertained sound. "Little mageling, I'm offended. Of course, I *could* eat you, but it's hardly my first choice."

"Then what's your first choice?" Arraya asked.

"There is cost to power, little one," the shadow said. "Even your elders teach that. For those of us who live in the shadow, we must feed. Here, in Jepitsa, we feed off mortals – a single one of these prey can sustain me for a month. But you, young mageling..."

The congealed shadows fell away, revealing a tall, impossibly handsome young man. His flesh was pallid; only his lips showed color, a blood red that sharply contrasted his pale skin.

"A young mageling could provide me strength for years, should you choose to stay with me. Your power could sustain us both. Tell me, young mageling, do you not find that appealing?"

His eyes were dark and oh-so-deep, and Arraya found herself slowly drowning in them. "It doesn't sound so bad," she admitted. *Maybe the other-Arraya had a point.*

"It doesn't hurt," the shadow creature said. "In fact, you might find it very pleasurable to offer your strength to me. Just surrender yourself to me, and everything will become simple."

Arraya recognized the trap now. The creature had some power to manipulate minds and weaken resolve. She had no doubt that if she truly did surrender, his will would completely subvert her own, and he would use her in whatever way he saw fit.

A vampire, she finally identified him. *It must be a vampire. It fits what I read about them, what Master Shallum told me.*

And even in all her knowledge, her willpower slowly eroded away. All she could seem to do was stare into those dark eyes.

XV

SIX THIEVES HUNKERED DOWN ON the roof of the tallest house in Jepitsa. The moon was partially obscured by heavy clouds, deepening the concealment offered by the night skies.

Why couldn't we have had this when we knocked over the pirate ship? Ben wondered. *This is nearly perfect.*

Ben looked around the small circle, all its members dressed in black clothes.

Alan stood at the head of the circle, confident as always. He was flanked by Bruiser and Timid, both thieves seeming too large to truly be inconspicuous. Rounding out the circle was Zeke, who had helped steal the sword Alan wore on his back, and Corin.

Ben tried to ignore the uneasiness gnawing at his belly. *Why am I here?* he couldn't help but wonder. *Bruiser and Timid will use the boarding harp, and Zeke can help handle it*

— he's smarter than both of them and can think faster if something goes wrong. Alan will personally lead something this important. Corin is still the best lock pick in the Brigands...but what's my role? Why am I here?

"Alright, let's review," Alan said tightly, his voice barely above a whisper. "Equipment check."

Ben spent a moment reviewing his own equipment. His new dagger hung from his belt, his lock pick kit was bundled tightly in his pocket — even if he wasn't as good with the thing as Corin, and a small coil of light rope and a small grapple hook were looped over his shoulder, securely in place but not restricting his movement. *And that's it. I'm a thief, not a soldier. I don't need much to do my job.*

Alan waited until everyone was looking up at him before he spoke again. "Now, the plan. Part one."

"We fire the harpoon and establish a line," Timid said, his voice even quieter than Alan's.

"Part two," Alan prompted.

"We cross the rope and drop onto the top of the castle wall," Corin answered, her voice distant.

"Who is we?"

"You, me, and Ben," she clarified, her attention still clearly elsewhere.

"Three."

"We retract the line," Zeke answered. "And the three of us escape before we're noticed."

"Four."

"We make our way through the castle and infiltrate the dungeon, which should be empty right now," Ben offered.

"And five," Alan finished with satisfaction, "we steal the crown and escape out the front of the castle."

"You really think you're going to just walk right out with the loot?" Bruiser asked skeptically.

"Castles are built to keep people out, not in," Alan said confidently. "It won't be a problem." He fingered the hilt of the sword, then glanced over at Zeke. "What's our timing?"

Zeke settled cross-legged on the roof and withdrew a long tube from his belt – the purchase that had soaked up most of the gold he had taken as part of the Lord Rittin heist. *A spyglass, he called it*, Ben remembered.

"We'd better setup," Zeke said. "Our best gap is coming in just a couple of minutes."

Alan nodded his assent. Bruiser and Timid immediately began preparing the boarding harpoon, setting it up on three steel legs to give it stability, loading the hook, and ensuring the rope fed freely when it was tugged.

They've been practicing since Corin and I brought it back, Ben observed distantly. *If they screw this up, the whole thing could be over before it starts.*

"Steady," Zeke said quietly. "Wait for my signal."

Ben caught a flash of annoyance on Alan's face. *He's ready to go and doesn't want to wait*, the thief thought. *He's just as eager as any of us.*

"Go," Zeke said without a trace of urgency.

The weapon fired a heartbeat later, a too-loud *whump* that set Ben's nerves on edge. "That was louder than I expected," he grumbled. "They're going to hear us coming."

"We'll be fine," Alan assured him just as the hook cleared the wall. Timid jerked the rope, dropping the hook into position. Zeke immediately took hold of the winder, cranking it to pull the rope snug in place.

"We're on the clock," Alan said. "Let's go. Corin, you're first."

Wordlessly, the girl dropped down to hang from the rope. Hand-over-hand, she pulled herself along the rope, almost invisible in her dark clothes over the darkened city. She seemed to vanish into the night as she hauled herself toward the castle.

Ben's heart seemed to be stuck in his throat for a moment. *If she falls...* He cut off his own thought viciously. *She won't fall. Neither will you.* Without prompting, he followed her lead, swinging over the city with nothing between his dangling feet and the ground, far below. He tried to focus only on the rope ahead of him, on the slow ache growing in his hands as the rope stretched out beyond his sight. And then he glanced down.

It was utterly terrifying.

His mind seemed to stop at the sight of the ground so far below. *Don't fall, don't fall, don't fall, don't fall.*

His hands kept him swinging along, even as he considered his own mortality and the absolute doom that seemed to reach up and grab at his legs, attempting to drag him down.

Then the castle wall was in front of him, and Corin was reaching over the wall to help him up. In spite of her smaller stature, she hauled him up and over the edge. He barely had time to breathe before he and Corin were both back at the edge and grabbing Alan's hands to bring him up as well.

The three thieves dropped in a crouch, leaning heavily against the wall and panting for breath. Alan reached up and took hold of the hook. "Now we're committed," he murmured as he tossed the harpoon and the rope off the edge.

There goes our safety line. Not that it was very safe, Ben observed distantly, his heart still pounding in his ears.

"Let's move," Alan said, rising to his feet far too soon. "Before the guards come around again."

The guards patrolled the walls in opposing circuits, with four pair walking continual circles atop the wall and meeting another pair every quarter-circuit. The thieves were operating in a very narrow gap as they ran hunched over, depending on the darkness and their black clothes to conceal themselves from any watchful eyes.

The trick now was to get down from the wall and into the deeper shadows cast by the high stone fortifications. The wall was nearly twenty feet high – too far to safely jump, and Alan had not wanted to risk using another rope. Should the hook hang up when they had reached the ground, they would be leaving behind irrefutable evidence of their presence – evidence the guards would not ignore, for fear of a spy or assassin within the castle walls. Instead, they had to reach one of the eight towers rising above the wall – the only place where stairs or ladders would allow them to descend.

The towers were no doubt useful in a siege – they would provide an extra-thick layer of stone for defenders to hide behind, and extra altitude from which to shower an attacker with arrows. More fortunately for the thieves, they also broke the line of sight for patrolling guards, opening the window of opportunity that had allowed them to breach the walls at all.

They reached the tower, Alan in the lead, and ducked into the portal nearly blind.

Which is when the plan fell apart.

Alan, still hunched over as he ran, bowled over a guard just stepping out. The guard didn't yell or shout; he barely managed a strangled gasp of surprise as he and Alan both went down in a heap just inside the tower.

Corin, a few steps behind Alan, slowed to try to evaluate the unexpected situation, but Ben raced past her to leap for the guard.

Alan was already wrestling with his opponent on the floor. "Ben! Dagger!" he hissed.

The young thief's hand fell on the hilt of his weapon and it was out of his sheath before his mind caught up. *I don't want to kill anyone*, he thought in dismay as Alan and the guard grappled on the stone, each trying to find the advantage.

Then the second guard smacked Ben in the back with the wooden shaft of his spear.

Ben stumbled, pain sending him to his knees. The dagger slipped from his grasp and clattered among the dark stones, and he lost sight of it. He twisted around in time to meet the guard's follow-up charge, catching the blunt end of the weapon as it swung toward his head.

His palms screamed in pain as the weapon slapped into his hands, but he held onto it with all his strength. *If I lose my grip, we might all die here!* He and the guard wrestled for the weapon and for their lives.

An eternity or a heartbeat later, the guard gave a strangled gasp and crumbled to the floor. As he fell face-first, the hilt of a dagger protruding from his back seemed to burn itself into Ben's eyes. *That's my dagger. But...how?*

Alan loomed above him. "Come on," he hissed. "We don't have much time." He pulled the dagger from the man's back and handed it to the younger man.

"What?" Ben asked dumbly as he sheathed the still-bloody blade.

"Quickly. Grab the arms."

Alan was already reaching down to grip the man's ankles. Ben followed suit without thinking, grabbing the man's hands and lifting. The guard's dead eyes met Ben's for a moment, and the young thief nearly let go. Somehow he managed to hang on and follow Alan back out onto the wall, helping him swing the body over the edge and let go.

A lifetime later, he heard the body quietly thump against the ground. Then Alan and Corin were dragging the second guard out, this one's throat slit open. It, too, took a lifetime to fall.

Everything had happened so fast.

"Come *on*," Alan hissed. "This shortens our window. We don't have much time before they notice missing guards. We have to go!"

Ben found himself following automatically as Alan led them into a race down the stairs. *His footsteps are so loud the King himself is going to wake up*, was all he could think.

Then they were concealed in the friendly shadows of the walls. As the comforting darkness wrapped around him, Ben could finally begin to think. *We killed two guards. No*, Alan *killed two guards. He had to do it. If he hadn't, we would've been captured for sure. He was trying to protect us, wasn't he? He didn't have a choice.*

The dungeon was little more than a hole in the ground. Given its lack of occupants, no guards were posted around the entrance – there was little use in guarding an empty prison. By design, the dungeon had been constructed with its only portal in the deepest shadow, with the intention of ensuring prisoners there would see the least daylight possible. The choice served the thieves well, ensuring no one could possibly see them as they descended into the prison.

Ben's chest loosened as the dungeon swallowed them whole. *Even if someone finds those dead guards, no one would look for us in here*, he decided. *It's funny, really. The prison is the safest place for us in the entire castle right now, I'd wager.*

Alan didn't stop until they were deep inside the dungeon, so dark that Ben could no longer see his own feet. "Corin, light?" Alan asked quietly.

The girl withdrew the makings of a torch from her pouch – an oil-wrapped rag, a set of flint and steel, and a still-green stick the length of her forearm. All three sat down and waited in the darkness until Corin had built and lit a blazing light, illuminating their grim surroundings.

Ben wished it were still dark.

"Why did you hesitate?" Alan growled at Ben, fire reflected in his eyes that had nothing to do with the torch. "We got damned lucky when you dropped your blade; it fell where I could reach it. You should have stabbed him while I had him on the ground."

"I'm a thief, not a murderer," Ben said hotly.

"Is that so?" Alan spat. "That's not what I heard about your little adventure on the pirate ship. Didn't you kill someone there?"

"It wasn't like that at all," Ben said defensively.

"You can't hesitate like that," the leader of the Brigands said irritably. "You could have cost me my life. What if it had been Corin or Zeke on the ground there? Would you have acted then, or let them die?"

"I..." Ben stopped. *I don't know*, he realized. *I'm not sure.*

"Fine. Don't answer," Alan said. "Come on, we still have work to do."

Ben slowly rose to his feet, following Alan's lead. Corin silently handed Alan the torch and let him lead the way deeper into the dungeon.

I could have gotten Alan killed, he realized. *All because I didn't act. But...how far can I go? When is it okay for me to kill someone? I mean, we're not murderers, we're thieves. We don't get a payout for killing someone, only stealing from them. So it's better if we can manage it without blood, right?*

"Here's the spot," Alan said at last. "Ben, Corin, back up and keep an eye out. Ben, I'll need your rope."

"For what?" he asked.

"What do you think?" Alan said, his tone brooking no question.

"Oh. Right." Ben handed over the rope without further protest. *He'll need it to climb into the store room after he's opened a hole.*

Alan waited until both Corin and Ben had retreated thirty paces back toward the dungeon's entrance before he unsheathed the sword. The blade seemed to glow with some unnatural light, casting weird shadows that danced across the walls and floor. Ben watched with equal parts fascination and disgust. *Magic weapons*, he thought. *Magic can drive any man insane, and now we're risking using a weapon that's imbued with the stuff. What will that do to someone who carries or uses that sword?*

The leader of the Brigands seemed to study the roof for an eternity while he held the blade in one hand.

"What is he doing?" Corin whispered.

Ben nearly jumped out of his skin. "I don't know," he confessed. "It's like he's trying to find something. If I were him, I'd start chipping away – it's going to take time to chip away at the stone roof, and the enchantment should keep anyone from hearing, right?"

Corin didn't immediately reply, her eyes never flinching from the sword. Ben found his own gaze drawn back in morbid curiosity. *Maybe the magic is already starting to addle his mind*, he thought, his concern starting to weigh against his curiosity. *We should have found a different way. Maybe that sword is already driving him mad.*

"Who thought using a sword for breaking through a stone roof would be a good idea?" Corin muttered. "He's going to wreck the blade before he gets through, magic or not."

"I don't know," Ben confessed. "None of this adds up."

"What do you mean?" Corin asked.

The boy shrugged uncomfortably. "I'd rather not – "

Alan struck with the sword.

With a deafening *boom*, the ceiling itself seemed to collapse. Stone dropped from the ceiling like a hailstorm of impossible proportions; dirt rolled up from the floor in a choking wave. The suddenness of it all drove every thought from Ben's head but one very clear, possibly manic observation. *That wasn't silent.*

Ben coughed on the dust cloud; right beside him, Corin was gasping for breath in the choking dirt. The torch had vanished somewhere in the collapse, plunging them into total darkness save the dim glimmer of the magical sword.

Minutes passed before the dirt began to settle back to the floor. When the air had cleared enough for Ben to see, he was greeted by the sight of Alan climbing up the rope he had taken a few minutes earlier. "Come on," he gasped to Corin, leading the way over the floor now littered with debris. "Come on."

The two stumbling thieves finally reached the hole leading up to the storeroom, only to find the rope gone.

"I'm sorry it had to be this way, Ben," Alan's voice echoed down from overhead.

Ben looked up and could just make out the dim figure standing above them. "Alan? What's going on?" he asked. "The whole castle had to have heard that. They'll be coming for us. Where's the rope?"

"Ben, Ben, Ben," Alan said sadly, shaking his head. "I had such high hopes for you, but it's become very clear that your allegiance does not lie with me."

"What are you talking about?" Ben asked, a bit frantic. "Throw the rope down!"

"He's not going to do it, Ben," Corin said from beside him. Bitterness colored her tone. "I warned you about him, but you wouldn't listen." She turned her attention upward. "I should've known better than to follow you into here, Alan. Not after you lied about the pirate ship."

"And that's exactly why I'm leaving you where you are," Alan said smugly. "You've been dangerous for a long time. I know you've wanted to take my place, and Ben was your first pawn in the game."

"What are you two talking about?" Ben asked in frustration.

"He's leaving us here," Corin said tiredly. "He's going to let the guards catch us while he makes off with the crown. Or is this even about the crown? Did you lie about that, too?"

"Hardly," Alan said with a snort. "This crown is worth far more than either of your lives."

"And what, you expect us not to tell the Royal Guard while you leave us to rot?" Ben asked, a deep-seated anger beginning to grow.

"Of course I do. If you betray me, you *know* the Guard will kill everyone in Riverfront to get it back," Alan said with mock cheerfulness. "Now, neither of you wants to see everyone there die – all the younger Brigands, your friends, the merchants. So you're going to keep your mouths shut to save all those lives."

"There never was a weapon to break us in silently, was there?" Ben asked.

"Oh, thank you for reminding me," Alan said. The sword flashed with its unnatural light and fell at Ben's feet, the blade plunging a third of its length into the dirt floor. "I almost forgot I'd need to leave you with that."

"And what is this?" Corin asked.

"The only tool in Jepitsa that could have gotten me in here," he said. "The Sword-That-Never-Fails."

Ben gasped. *It's a legend*, he thought as he stared at the hilt. *It's the one weapon that always strikes its target. That's how he brought down the whole ceiling with one blow!*

"Why, Alan? Why leave us here?" Ben asked.

"The guards needed to find someone," he said with a shrug. "I'd intended to leave just Corin behind, but you've shown very clearly you are loyal to her, not me. Your dagger soaked in the blood of the guards makes it that much easier."

"You're a bastard," Corin growled. "You think we'll let you get away with this?"

"You'll never leave that dungeon alive," Alan said calmly. "The Royal Guard is no doubt waiting for you at the dungeon entrance, and there's no other way out of that hole." He laughed. "With that, I'll take my leave. With any luck, I'll sell the crown and be out of Jepitsa before anyone realizes it's gone. And then I'm gone. And it's all thanks to you." His smile flashed in the dusty gloom. "Thank you both."

"One more question," Ben said.

"No, Ben, I won't indulge you again. Time grows too short; the guards will be coming soon." Alan offered a mocking wave. "Goodbye, and enjoy your life without me – it's what you both have wanted."

And then he was gone.

Ben felt a thousand emotions – heartbreak, hurt, anger, rage, hatred, and so many more that he could not name. And in their wake, he felt only numb weariness.

Everything I did for the Brigands, all the thefts, all the jobs, all the sacrifices I made – it's all nothing. Alan left me behind to die while he goes on to live like a king. He glanced over at Corin and saw only resignation on her visage. *I should have listened to Corin. I was wrong about Alan the whole time, and Corin was the only one who saw through him. She knew what he really was all this time.*

Ben's very heart seemed to be ash; it begged him to lie down and die. *What's the point in going on? Even if we aren't executed for killing two guards, we'll never leave this dungeon alive. We'll rot down here until there's nothing left. Even if the Brigands would want to bribe guards to get us set free, the most corrupt member of the Royal Guard would never let it happen. It's over...it's all over.*

But one small part of his heart remained, burning brightly at the center of his being. *If you give up and die down here, Alan will get away with all of it. And when they find the crown is gone, they'll burn Riverfront to the ground. They'll kill everyone. It's going to happen regardless of whether we tell the Guard about what's happening.*

Alan betrayed us. We can't let him get away with it.

His gaze fell on Corin again. "Are you ready?" he asked quietly.

"Ready for what?" she asked. There was no strength left in her voice. "He won, Ben."

"Maybe, but that doesn't mean we shouldn't fight it."

She laughed, but there was no mirth – only venom. "Fight it how? We can't escape. We can't win. You know why I came with on this heist, Ben?" When he shook his head, she snarled, "To protect *you*. You haven't been able to see Alan for what he is, and I knew if something went wrong he'd use you in a heartbeat to escape. I was sure if I came along, I could prevent that from happening." It was her turn to shake her head. "He must have had this planned from the beginning. He wanted to be rid of me."

"Why?" Ben asked.

"Because he can't risk anyone exposing him for the lying snake he really is," Corin said flatly. "Anyone who might make him look bad disappears."

"That wasn't what I was asking."

Corin looked at him with confusion.

"Why did you want to protect me?" he asked quietly.

"Because you deserve better than this," Corin said. The words held something intangible – something besides the deep-seated loathing she felt for Alan. "If anyone in Riverfront deserves better, it's you."

"What? Why me?" he asked in confusion.

"Ben, you're the one thief in the Brigands who isn't just looking out for himself," she explained slowly. "You're always concerned about someone else. You're one of the best thieves in Jepitsa, but you're just as poor as the rest of us because you give away most of what you steal. The Rittin heist? You spent most of it on gifts for your friends." She shook her head. "You always try to see the best in people. You always have a kind word to say, a compliment to offer. That's why you're a threat to Alan. Not because you're planning to overthrow him, but because you're *better* than he is. And everyone in Riverfront can see it." She sighed. "Even if he hadn't believed you to be working with me, he would have betrayed you for that reason, sooner or later."

Ben opened his mouth to answer, but the flicker of torches caught the corner of his eye. He swallowed and turned to face the coming guards. "I'm sorry, Corin," he said quietly. "I wish you weren't here."

"I wish I wasn't, too," Corin said wryly. "It should be Alan standing here, not us."

Ben unsheathed his dagger and tossed it into the dirt beside the Sword-That-Never-Fails. "Yes, it should be." He swallowed as the guards came into view, their forms only partly obscured by the dust still hanging in the air. "And someday, it will be."

"Someday," Corin repeated. "Someday."

XVI

ARRAYA'S BETTER JUDGMENT SCREAMED AT her as she stared up at the vampire. *Fight it, fight it, burn it down, run, escape!*

The rest of her simply couldn't find the will to do anything but stare up at the servant of the Dark One.

The vampire smiled, an almost-normal gesture that set off even more warnings in the apprentice's mind. "That's right, little mageling. Just surrender yourself to me. No more fighting, no more struggling, just a comfortable life with me. You have such power that you can feed me for years to come. I will take care of you like the pet you will become."

The shackles holding her to the table clicked open. The apprentice tried to look at her arms, stretched back over her head, but she couldn't bring herself to look away from the creature's too-dark eyes.

"Choose," the vampire said. "Choose to flee, or stay here with me."

Arraya found she could do little but stare dully into those eyes.

"Well chosen," the vampire said with another smile. "All that remains is for me to feed upon you but once. Then you will be bound to me forever."

No! Flee! her instincts screamed. Still she could do nothing as the creature loomed over her, preparing to draw on her life and magic.

Then a blur of lizard scales hurtled from the shadows, accompanied by a terrifying roar. The vampire looked up, startled, and vanished from her vision as J'Ram smashed into him with all the deadly grace of a cougar striking a deer.

Arraya felt something snap in her mind, and suddenly she could move again. "What?" she mumbled aloud as she lifted her hand, staring at her palm as though she had never seen it. Her thoughts jumbled around, as though the vampire had dammed them all up and now they were bursting free. *Vampire. Manipulator. Avoid the eyes. Twists thoughts.*

She rolled off the table, landing in a crouch. The Tillik wrestled with the vampire on the floor, blows flashing faster than her eyes could follow. A particularly brutal strike drew a spray of blood, but Arraya couldn't tell which of the combatants had been wounded. The vampire was inhumanly strong and fast, but J'Ram's reptilian strength evened the match.

The vampire slipped a blow beneath the Tillik's guard, and suddenly J'Ram was tumbling through the air. He smashed into a barrel, which promptly burst into a wash of ale. The lizard-man tumbled once, twice, and then was on his feet in a crouch, an angry hiss at his lips.

It was all the opportunity Arraya needed.

Fire lashed out from her open palm, enveloping the vampire in fire. The creature screamed, and it was enough to make Arraya hesitate.

Mistake, she thought, as the vampire turned and leaped at her. She was a daughter of the Magi, heir to the True Magic, but she wasn't fast or strong enough to meet the vampire hand-to-hand.

J'Ram smashed into the vampire, sending them both sprawling across the stone. The reversal seemed to stun the dark creature for a moment, giving the Tillik his opportunity. Not bothering to rise, he grabbed both the vampire's ankles and swung with all the strength of his race.

The vampire smashed into the floor on his back, his expression dazed. J'Ram didn't stop there, though, swinging him again to smash on his stomach. Then again on his back. And again. And again.

When the Tillik had finished, the vampire's visage was smashed beyond recognition. The Dark One's servant lay utterly still.

J'Ram rose to his feet, half-panting and half-hissing. He flipped the vampire over, then plunged his hunting claws into the vampire's belly and sliced it open. Blood geysered up, a sickening warm red rain. The Tillik hissed and spat upon the corpse before finally turning to Arraya.

The apprentice stared at J'Ram with a slackened jaw. "How did you...?"

"I pledged to protect you," the Tillik half-growled. "When you did not return, I followed your trail and found you here."

"The vampire..." Arraya managed.

"Excellent prey," J'Ram replied with some satisfaction, his rage seeming to cool. "As hatchlings we are taught to hunt them in packs – they are too dangerous to hunt alone. For my *sarka-prina*, my..." he struggled for a moment to find the word, "blood-trial, I slew my first." He nodded back at the corpse. "They are difficult to kill. Should a hunter fail to puncture the blood sack, they can recover from the most grievous of wounds."

Arraya shook her head. "If you hadn't come along, he would've had me," she said quietly. "He had me completely."

J'Ram bowed his head. "You are the Wise. He would not have entrapped you so easily." He frowned at her. "Did you find what you were seeking?"

Arraya nodded. "I know where he is. It's just going to be difficult to get in." She smiled at the Tillik. "I'm going to need to find an entrance."

"No," the Tillik said simply. "If you are going to hunt, you need to gather your strength. Allow me to be your forerunner, to find a way to your prey."

The apprentice turned the thought over. "I guess it makes sense," she said begrudgingly. "Did Naomi find us a place to stay?"

"I will guide you there," J'Ram promised. "And then I will find your path."

The apprentice recovered her staff where it had been discarded in a corner by the vampire. *No respect for the Magi among the vampires*, she decided. "Lead on," she said.

***

The rickety little shack boasted little more than a pile of raggedy blankets in a corner. The sun was reaching its peak, and she was tempted to wrap up in the cleanest of the blankets outside in the sun. *I'm a stranger here, and maybe that vampire had allies. If he did, they may be looking for me...even in the light, when they are weakest. If they catch me asleep, they may decide just to kill me rather than trying to take me again.*

Arraya shuddered at the thought.

"I could not find any other wrappings for you, fire-caller," J'Ram said apologetically, misinterpreting her reaction. "This place is what the Erixan demanded. She is quite insistent."

The blonde-haired girl dropped down from the roof, landing in a crouch. Arraya didn't so much as blink, but she did glance upward to see the small shelf just under the ceiling that had concealed the shootist. *No doubt it would allow her to climb onto the roof, if necessary. With those guns, she could defend this place against any stray guards that might wander by.*

"This is the best place we can find to hide out until nightfall," Naomi declared, her voice low. "No one's going to come poking around here. It's close to where – " she cut herself off. "Never mind."

What is she here to do, anyway? Arraya wondered. The assassin had very nearly revealed her business in Jepitsa. *I doubt there's anyone in this slum that would be worth sending an assassin all the way from Erixi. I doubt she's going to tell me anytime soon, though.*

"I'm not going to wait that long," Arraya decided aloud. "Until nightfall, I mean."

"Do not rush to face your prey," J'Ram cautioned. "Move before you are prepared, and you may fail your hunt."

"Time is not on my side," Arraya said quietly.

The Erixan looked between the Tillik and the apprentice. "I don't even know what you're talking about, and frankly, I don't care. You're *still* crazy."

A small smile reached Arraya's lips. "You know, maybe I am. Doesn't change the fact that I need to do this."

"Crazy girl."

Arraya shook her head and picked up one of the blankets. Wrapping herself in it, she sat down and laid her head back against one of the dirty walls. She ensured her staff rested upright next to her, at hand if she needed it. "I need rest," she said slowly. "J'Ram, you're going to scout for me, right?"

The Tillik nodded and offered her a disturbing, fang-filled smile. "It will be my pleasure to scout your hunting ground."

"Good. Give me five hours to sleep," she decided, "and then wake me up. I should have recovered enough by then to be ready to go."

J'Ram disappeared, and Arraya curled up under the blanket. Naomi climbed back up to the shelf under the roof and quietly began to work.

The apprentice drifted on the edge of unconsciousness. Time passed, but she could not quite slip into the void of sleep. She found rejuvenation there, but not all she desired. *I'll take what I can get*, she decided. *The True Magic will sustain me.*

"Your friend is late." Naomi's voice snapped the apprentice awake.

"How late?" Arraya asked, blinking away the sleep. *Has it been five hours already?*

"About half an hour," the Erixan said calmly.

The apprentice looked up to the shelf and saw the shootist sitting cross-legged, a variety of objects spread out on the little open space. "What are you doing?" she asked.

"Reloading," Naomi said dryly. "I didn't leave Erixi with much for ammunition. Didn't think I'd need it. Including what I used when we escaped the Tilliks, I burned more than half of the rounds I was carrying."

"Rounds?" Arraya asked.

Naomi cocked her head and looked at the apprentice. "I thought you already knew all about us," she said. "Didn't they teach you everything at crazy-school?"

The apprentice snorted. "They focused on restraint, to make sure we didn't start fires around smart-mouthed shootists."

"Better for both of us if you didn't," Naomi said with a grin. "You might take me down, but you'll go with me."

"Hardly," Arraya said. "You've got both your guns pulled apart."

The shootist looked down. "Yes, I do. I also have a mostly full bag of powder here."

The apprentice frowned. "Powder?"

Naomi shrugged. "This part isn't much of a secret," she said. "I'm surprised the Magi don't know about it already."

"Some of the Magi do. I don't," Arraya replied, a bit testy. *Patience*, she told herself. *She's trying to get under your skin. Don't let her succeed.*

The shootist held up a small brass cylinder, long and straight, in her right hand. "Casing," she said succinctly. In her left hand she held up a smaller, lead object shaped vaguely like a rounded cone. "Bullet." She dropped the bullet in her lap and picked up a bag. "Powder." She mimed pouring the powder into the casing, then picked up the bullet and slid it into the open end of the case. "Round," she said, holding up the object.

"How's it work?" the apprentice asked. In spite of the continual danger around them, her curiosity – the same trait that drove her to read endlessly – demanded answers.

The shootist brandished the smaller of her weapons. She picked up a piece from the shelf, a metal cylinder with holes bored entirely through. "Cylinder," she said.

"I can see that," Arraya said dryly.

Naomi picked up the round and slid it into the cylinder, then held it up for the apprentice to see. "I can put six rounds in this cylinder," she said. She snapped it into the gun, then turned it to face the wall. "I pull back on this lever," she continued, "to bring the next round into place and to prime the weapon. When I pull the trigger, it falls and ignites the powder, sending my bullet down the barrel. Pull the hammer back again, and it rotates the cylinder."

Arraya nodded grudgingly. "Clever weapon. But if it's so great, why do only Erixans use it?"

"The secret's in the powder," Naomi explained. "No one except the Erixans know how to make it." She smiled. "Even I don't know how to make it – only the Armorer and his apprentice know the secret."

The apprentice rolled her eyes. "Only two people in all of Letale?" she asked skeptically.

"Yes," the shootist said. "The rest of it the best blacksmiths already understand and could probably duplicate, with a little effort. I bet the King's armory has a stock of guns they've stolen or captured from Erixans in the last century. But without the secret of the powder, guns are nothing but big and hard to make clubs."

Arraya eyed the bag of powder. "So how's it work?"

Naomi shrugged. "It goes boom. All I know is that it needs a spark, and then watch out. Beyond that, it's never really mattered to me."

"Still, it's interesting," Arraya murmured. "Amazing it's managed to stay secret so long. You have to know every place in Letale, from Prona to Cosmane, have been trying to make it." She raised an eyebrow. "Really, given how effective guns are, I'm surprised Erixi hasn't mounted an army and conquered the entire land. The way you fought against those Tillik bandits, there's not another army that could stand up to you."

The shootist eyed her warily. "There's plenty of good reason," she said. "Like the fact that we're not all hell-bent on ruling. The Erixan shootists exist to protect Erixi, not to lead conquests." She smiled. "In fact, that's the legend of how the shootists came to be in the first place."

"Oh?" Arraya's attention was wandering, but she thought it polite to continue.

"Yes. The legend says that, in the early days, Erixi was too isolated from Letale. Pirates and warlords and bandits would attack and loot the island from end to end. Because it was far off the shores of Letale, the armies of Werbri struggled to defend it – and worse, when it fell under the rule of some would-be king, it was almost impossible to recapture.

"So the Aither himself intervened. To keep the faithful people of Erixi safe, he showed the most virtuous man on the island the secret of the powder, and taught him how to forge a weapon to use it. The powder's booming sound is sign of the Aither's blessing on it. And with the new weapon, the gun, that noble man founded the Order of Thunder – the home of all the shootists."

Arraya nodded. "The Order of the Magi was founded similarly," she said.

"Similarly? How so?" Naomi asked.

The apprentice shrugged, a little uncomfortable. "I'm not a storyteller."

"Tell me anyway," the blonde-haired girl said.

Arraya cast back into her memory, dragging half-forgotten stories into the light. "When Letale was settled, it was first divided into many kingdoms – all the places we now call Cosmane, Werbri, and all the rest. And all the kings fought over the throne at Werbri, because whoever held it could conquer the other kingdoms. *If* they could hold it, that is.

"The early kings waged brutal war for the throne. Sometimes the reign of a ruler of Werbri was measured in weeks, or even days. Warriors fought and died in service to their kings, and the plains were forever stained red from all the bloodshed."

She sighed. As the words tumbled out, it started to sound ridiculous to her own ears. "The Aither wasn't happy with all the war. Letale was a large, open, beautiful land that should have had room for all without war. Instead, we had turned it into a battleground.

"So he chose a few of the Scions and showed them how to use the True Magic. He gifted them with the ability to manipulate it, project it, all without going mad like all the others who try such things. And more than that, he gave them *wisdom* – the discernment they would need to settle the wars.

"Those few Magi convened a council with all the kings of Letale, and from among them, judged the most worthy and placed him upon the throne. They took up the roles of adviser and councilor, using their power to help maintain the peace – but without ruling themselves."

"Which is why my kind call you the Wise," a voice rasped from the doorway. Arraya jerked, her hand falling on her staff before she could gather her wits.

J'Ram laughed, a sissing sound too disturbingly like a snake's hiss for the apprentice to draw any comfort from it. "Sorry. It is funny to catch a hunter unaware."

"Thanks," Arraya growled. "Next time you fall asleep, I'm going to jerk your tail and we'll see who's *unaware*."

"Sleep," the Tillik sissed again. "Too funny, fire-caller."

"What time is it?" the apprentice asked.

"An hour before the sun falls out of sight," the Tillik replied.

"Then I guess it's time to get moving," the apprentice said, climbing to her feet. "Did you find me a way in?"

"Of course," the Tillik said with a bow. "I found you a path worthy of a hunter."

***

The apprentice studied the collapsed drain tunnel with mild skepticism. *J'Ram insisted this was the best way into the castle. It was how the Imposter-King's team of assassins entered and put him on the throne.*

Back then, though, the tunnel was passable.

Arraya studied the debris-clogged entrance and nodded slowly to herself. *Of course the Impostor-King would destroy this entrance. He knows well the vulnerability this route represented. He wouldn't make it so easy for someone else to repeat his own trick for elevation to the throne.*

Her head still throbbed from her confrontation with the vampire. The blow had raised a large welt, and while she knew she could heal the injury, it would take an extra night of meditation. And now, this close to Master Shallum, she did not dare hesitate. *If I take the time to heal, it could mean his death*, she told herself. *If he's within the castle, he's already held by the Imposter-King. They could execute him at any time.*

The apprentice swallowed hard at the thought. *You know the servants of the Dark One are about. No doubt they are in league with the Imposter-King, else he could not have captured a Magi as powerful and wise as my master.*

She studied the tunnel again. *Though getting into the castle may be more difficult than I had first anticipated.*

Arraya considered her options. An enchantment of some sort might allow her to walk into the castle unseen by mortal eyes and unheard by mortal ears, but there was no guarantee that a creature of darkness would not see through such a disguise. While her combat skills had improved greatly, and been tested against her foes on the journey, she knew that attacking a castle single-handedly was beyond the power of any Magi. Stealing a guard's uniform could work, as her magic would not betray her to the Dark One's servants, but she had yet to see a skinny red-haired girl among the legions of the Royal Guard.

No, this tunnel was the best possibility.

If she could manage a weaving twice.

The fact that she'd managed it once was hardly short of miraculous in itself – after all, she had survived with her mind intact. *Well, I think so, anyway*, she told herself wryly, trying to break her own tension. *That was a weaving over an entire city. This will just be one small tunnel.*

Arraya lowered herself into a kneeling posture before beginning her meditation.

Drawing in the power was both harder and easier than the first time. Her senses were scraped raw by the energy she'd used before, far more sensitive to the flows of the True Magic than they usually were. It felt as though the very act of breathing inflicted some small pain on her.

But holding onto the power was far easier than before. It was as though she had been *stretched* in some way she could not define – her very being broader, more elastic than she had ever been. The power flowed into her with pain, yes, but it did not overwhelm her ability to hold it. *It's like my very ability to do magic is more than before.*

She hoped, with an idle thought, that it hadn't weakened her ability to maintain her focus. *Rupturing the structure of the spell would be...bad.*

Very bad.

When she had gathered up the power she needed, she opened her eyes and studied the tunnel. Had she seen the passageway before its destruction, her weaving would have been far easier. Now, she had only her imagination to draw upon.

In her mind's eye, she could *see* the currents of the True Magic. Like fine threads of silk, they wrapped around the untold tons of stone and dirt, forming a fine but unbreakable mesh. And then, with the slow, unstoppable might of a river, the magic lifted the debris away, crushing it back into place at the top of the tunnel.

When the image was clear in her mind, as real as her own limbs and life, she began to pour the magic into the form she had created.

She had thought it hurt to draw in so much power for her second weaving in a single day.

Now she knew what pain really was.

As she tried to guide her gathered magic into the weaving, she felt as though her heart was being ripped from her chest. Her limbs seemed to be stretched by mighty cords, her flame-colored hair jerked from its roots. It was *painful.*

And Arraya refused to relent.

Her body screamed at her to relent. Her mind withered under the strain. Her heart despaired at the impossibility of the task. *After all,* a small voice whispered to her, *you're just an apprentice. No apprentice could manage this much power.*

But she still did not give up.

Inch by inch, the dirt and stone began to lift.

The pain was too much to bear. Her body had suffered too much, her mind too tired, her heart too lost.

"Tell me, apprentice," Master Shallum commanded. *"Why do we learn to harness the True Power? Why do we become Magi at all?"*

"To serve," Arraya answered.

"To serve what? Whom?"

"To serve the people. To serve the king. To serve each other." Cold air bit shrewdly at the apprentice through her thin clothing, but she held it at bay with a simple use of the power.

"To what end? Your own destruction?" the master asked.

"If necessary," Arraya answered.

"How could your destruction be of service?" he asked.

"If I trade my life for another, I would be serving the one I saved," she replied.

"Perhaps, but would that be in the interest of the kingdom?"

"Master?" she asked, puzzled.

"Think, Arraya, of what you can do. Imagine all the good you can do in a lifetime of service to the kingdom. Imagine the servants of the Dark One you could stop, the hurts you could heal, the wisdom you could provide, the knowledge you could teach. Imagine all that you can and will do for the kingdom." His smile was small. *"Now imagine sacrificing yourself for another. Remember all that you could have done, but now won't, because of your sacrifice."*

"Others would take my place," Arraya said.

"Will they?" Master Shallum shook his head. *"Do not be eager to self-destruction. Always weigh the totality of your decision, beyond the moment. Be wary of your decision."*

Arraya had made her decision.

The haze of pain slowly faded away, and when she opened her eyes, the tunnel stretched out in inky blackness before her.

She picked up her staff and slowly climbed to her feet. An odd euphoria overtook her as she stared down the tunnel. *Residual power from the weaving?* she wondered. Either way, it didn't matter – she was going into the tunnel.

XVII

N OW, WHAT SHALL WE DO with you?" the
Commander of the Royal Guard asked.

Ben stared up at the man balefully. *If he has a
name, I've never heard of it*, the thief thought dully.

"Two thieves somehow make it into the castle," the
Commander continued, "and break into the dungeon of all
places. Then they use *my sword*, the most powerful weapon
in Jepitsa, to bring down the ceiling and break a hole into a
store room. And apparently, these same thieves that were
smart enough to raid my own home *and* to kill two guards
and to break into the king's own fortress didn't have a way
to climb up into that room?" The tall man, resplendent in
his purple armor, snorted in disbelief.

Ben didn't answer. *Alan, if I ever get out of here, you're
going to regret leaving us behind.*

"See, thief, I'm not stupid. You were after something – or someone. Who are you working for?"

"Myself," Ben said flatly.

The Commander's blow snapped his head around, and he bounced his cheek off the cold stone wall. "Don't lie to me, boy. You're not smart enough to manage something like this yourself. You were after something specific. What was your target?"

"We were here for the King's underwear," he said with a wry smile. "I wanted to see if the royal britches really are better than what we have."

The blow came from the other direction this time, and suddenly the aches in Ben's face were mirror images. "I have no time for your silly games," the interrogator growled. "Tell me the truth."

"And what?" Ben asked with all the energy he could muster. "You'll let us go?"

"You wouldn't believe me even if I promised that," the Commander said coldly. "But tell me the truth and this will end. There is no reason you cannot live peacefully in these walls."

"That sounds wonderful," Ben said with as much sarcasm as he could manage. "How could I resist such a great offer?"

This time the Commander's fist buried itself in Ben's stomach. He would have doubled over, had he not been shackled to the wall. The blow seemed to reach all the way to his spine, leaving the thief gasping for breath. "Your alternatives are much worse," the Commander warned. He seemed to stop and consider for a moment. "Perhaps I should let you recover for a moment."

Leaving Ben leaning against the wall and struggling to breathe, the Commander crossed to the other side of the dimly-lit chamber where Corin was similarly shackled.

"This is the deepest and darkest part of the dungeon," the Commander said with a small smile. "If you cooperate, I'll move you to the cells nearest the entrance. Then you will be allowed to see some small amount of light each day. Continue to resist, and you will stay down here and live your days out in darkness."

He offered a smile back at Ben. "This is quite simple. I'm going to ask you questions. Refuse to answer, and your friend here suffers the consequences."

Bastard! Ben thought as the entirety of the threat sunk in. Hate he hadn't even thought himself capable of flooded his heart and mind alike. *You're going to use her against me to try to break me.* It was a brilliant, cold, horrid tactic, and Ben wasn't sure if his resolve would hold.

"Don't tell him anything," Corin said with a slight nod.

"Shut up," the Commander said, raising his hand to strike her.

"Ask," Ben said quickly, before the blow could fall.

The interrogator offered him a grim smile. "Very good. What are your names, thief?"

Corin caught his eye and shook her head fractionally, but Ben couldn't resist. *What harm could our names do?* he asked himself. "I'm Ben," he said softly. "She is Corin."

"You see, it's easier just to answer, isn't it?" the Commander affirmed with a smile. "No one needs further harm today. Now, what were you after?"

Once they know, they'll tear Riverfront apart, Ben thought. "The King's recipe for roasted chicken," he said.

The Commander's fist began to fall toward Corin's stomach when a voice of authority rang out, filling the entire chamber with power and purpose. "Stop!"

Ben looked to the door leading into the chamber. Two new guards had already stepped through to flank the portal before the source of the voice stepped inside.

The man was dressed in white and purple robes and carried a scepter in his right hand, and a jeweled band of gold encircled his head. "Commander," the man said, "why do you use such primitive methods?"

"My King," the Commander said, dropping to his knees.

King Hazael! Ben thought in shock. The ruler of Letale looked from Corin to Ben, seeming to consider them both. After a long silent moment, he walked toward Ben, authority and power floating in his wake.

Don't tell him anything, Ben told himself. *The worst he can do is kill you.*

The thief kept his eyes fixed on King Hazael as the monarch approached. The King stopped before him and reached out with his scepter, turning Ben's head to the side, first one way, than the other. "You are unusual for an assassin," Hazael mused. "And for a thief. You found a way into my fortress, but you allowed yourself to be captured. No one wise enough to make it as far as you and your partner did would make such a foolish mistake." His eyes narrowed. "There was a third member of your team, wasn't there?"

Ben's mouth was suddenly so dry he couldn't seem to answer.

"You two were the decoys," Hazael stated.

No, he doesn't know, Ben told himself. *He's guessing.*

"You are unlike any other thief I've dealt with," Hazael continued. "You meet my gaze when any other would cower. You defy me even in the face of death. Yet you are no assassin."

"How do you know that?" the thief managed to rasp dryly.

"If you were an assassin, you would've come to kill me, not break into my store room. You used your greatest weapon to create a path, not destroy me." The King smiled. "I could use someone as creative as you as an adviser. Tell me what you were after – the entire truth – and I will not only free you and your young lady here, but I will elevate you to power and riches you've never known."

Riverfront, Ben thought, and all the appeal of the offer faded away as images of fire and death danced in his head. "I wanted a pair of royal boots," Ben said. "I've heard they're like walking on air."

The King smiled. "Fortunately, we have methods for dealing with recalcitrant prisoners," Hazael said. "You could have been elevated to great heights by my hand.

Instead, you'll be destroyed by it. And you *will* tell us everything."

Ben tried to find some witty reply, but the weariness and the terror had bled out his strength.

Hazael abruptly turned and walked back to the door. Ben watched him depart, wondering what new terror the King could unleash on them. *After all, in the last week I've nearly drowned escaping Lord Rittin's estate, been beaten senseless by a pirate, and betrayed by my own leader. What can a King manage to top all that?*

A figure dressed in rough-spun robes with a purple overcloak was standing in the doorway now – an unassuming, greying man that had been present for...? *Did he come in with the king? Or did he just arrive?* Ben couldn't decide, but ultimately, it didn't really matter.

"We will need answers," the King said. "How long will it take?"

The man offered a small smile to his ruler. "I can offer you some answers now," he said, "but the rest will take time. To extract answers from such prisoners is delicate work, and I will need time to prepare the proper magic."

"What can you offer me now?" the King demanded.

"The smallest of details," the man said. "You are right in that these are thieves, not assassins."

"What about the two dead guards?" the Commander demanded.

"Patience," the adviser said calmly. "These two are both from Jepitsa. The clothing they wear is simple hand-weave, and I've seen the same material among the poor here. It is locally made and sold."

"If they are outside assassins," the Commander interjected, "the first action they would take would be to acquire local clothes to blend in."

The man gave the Commander a patronizing look. "Please, don't interrupt," he said mildly. "You may learn something." He looked back at the thieves, his gaze alternating from Corin to Ben and back. "Their accents are local as well. And yes, an accent can be faked," he added with a significant look at the leader of the Guards. "But their eyes betray more. Both of them are terrified, far more than a professional assassin would be."

"Then what were they after?" the King asked. To Ben's ear, his voice sounded just a touch impressed.

"I can speculate," the adviser said. "Until I have extracted the answers from their minds, I will not know for certain."

"Your best guess, then," the Commander said, his tone far more respectful than it had been moments before.

"These thieves knew far more than they should have," the adviser mused. "Not only did they find a way to enter the castle undetected, but they knew precisely the place to strike to get into the king's own stores. And to do *that*, they stole a weapon of such power that it could have made them wealthy, had they chosen to sell it. It stands to reason, then, that their goal had to be more valuable than one of the greatest swords to ever exist."

The King and the Commander exchanged looks, before they both turned to look at the adviser.

The simply-robed man nodded. "My best guess it that they were after the Queen's Crown."

"Then there was a third thief," the Commander stated.

"There must have been," the adviser confirmed. "He left these two behind as decoys to cover his tracks while he escaped."

The King turned to the two guards standing stock-still at the door. "Go, and see if the other crown is still in its resting place," he barked. "Quickly!" Hazael turned back to his adviser. "How long until you can give me the identity of the third thief?"

"I will need time to prepare myself." He shrugged. "It is not often I have had reason to invade the mind of another. Half an hour, perhaps, to gather up the power I will need and to ensure I am ready."

"Fine," the King said. "Go, and prepare. We will need answers before the third thief can escape with the crown."

"My liege," the Commander said with a deferential bow, "if these thieves are from Jepitsa, they no doubt came from the slums outside the city wall. I can take the Guard and march on it now and flush out the scum that took the crown."

The King shook his head. "To find the thief, you would have to burn Riverfront to the ground," he said. "It serves its purposes, and I would rather it stand. If my adviser cannot find the identity, we will have no other choice, but first we pursue this path."

"With your leave, Majesty," the adviser said.

The King nodded his assent, and the man vanished back through the portal. The King and the Commander followed after a few moments of quiet, terse conversation that Ben couldn't quite hear.

And then Corin and Ben were alone with only a few lit torches in wall sconces for company.

When Corin locked gazes with him, Ben could see the terror in her eyes even across the dimly lit room. "That man...the adviser..." Corin swallowed. "He's going to use magic to invade our *minds.*"

Ben shuddered. "It'll be okay," he tried to comfort her.

"Magic drives people mad," Corin said tightly. "Everyone knows it. If he uses it on us, he'll leave us..." she shuddered. "We might as well be dead."

"What do we do?" Ben asked.

"The King said he doesn't want to burn Riverfront, right?" Corin asked with just a touch of hope. "We should tell them who Al...the third thief is."

Corin's stumble was enough to remind Ben that someone could still be listening. "People who use magic are already crazy," he said. "Even if we tell them who the third thief is, he'll probably rip our minds apart anyway to make sure we're telling the truth. They won't risk us misleading them with the crown at stake."

"Oh," Corin deflated. "You're right."

"When he comes back," Ben said, "I'll ask him to start with me. After he's ripped everything he wants out of my head, maybe..." he swallowed, "maybe he'll leave you alone. They won't need to break your mind, too."

"Ben," Corin tried to start.

"No, it's better that way," Ben said quietly. "You would have already left if it weren't for me. It's my fault you're still here and you got caught."

"That's not true," the girl protested. "I couldn't just leave and let Alan keep control over everyone. It's not your fault, Ben."

"I guess it doesn't matter anymore," the thief despaired. "The ultimate heist, and Alan got away with it. For all we know, he already sold the crown and has fled Jepitsa. He's had hours to do it, hasn't he?"

Corin shrugged. "I don't know," she said honestly. "Down here there's no light, and the guards had knocked us both out. I don't even know if it's night or day out. How long ago did we bring the roof down? A couple hours? A day?"

It was the most unnerving part of the dungeon, Ben had found. He had always been most comfortable in the dark: it hid him from prying eyes, offered him the opportunity to steal, and had been his faithful friend for nearly as long as he could remember. But in the utter blackness of the dungeon, his old friend had turned against him. It played tricks on his mind, concealed his enemies instead of himself, and confused the passage of time.

"Ben," Corin said quietly.

"Huh?" he looked up at her, startled out of his reverie.

"Thank you," she said simply.

"For what?" Ben asked in confusion.

"Ben, I've been with the Brigands just as long as you. And in all that time, no one's ever treated me like you," she said softly. "You've given me gifts, and now you're willing to sacrifice yourself to save me. No one has *ever* done that for *anyone* else in the Brigands." She sighed softly. "You've treated me like a princess – like I'm royalty. And you've done it without even thinking about it."

The thief shrugged uncomfortably. "I...Corin..."

"No," she said. "Let me finish. I'm sorry I haven't treated you better after all this time. You deserved better. And now that I've *realized* that, I can't do anything about it. It's too late. We'll never get out of here alive."

As though stirred by Corin's words, a scraping sound echoed from the corner of the chamber.

Ben frowned. "What's making that noise?" he muttered. "A rat?"

He tried to focus on source of the noise, but it was impossible to make out in the dim light. And then *something* was moving, drawing itself out of the ground.

***

Even with her weaving having cleared the debris, Arraya would have found the tunnel impassable without the Magi's staff. The darkness was close and cloying, and tried to trip her on the uneven ground, but she held the staff aloft and pushed just a tiny trickle of magic through it. Its tip glowed with incandescent light, allowing her to see a half dozen steps ahead.

The tunnel ended abruptly. "This must be the spot," the apprentice muttered. She lifted the staff to examine the ceiling and found a narrow seam in the stone. In the low tunnel, it was no effort at all to reach up with her free hand and heave against the stone.

It didn't budge.

Reluctantly, Arraya set her staff aside. The light faded away as she heaved with both arms, trying to push the portal open. In spite of the seam, it did not move at all — not even a fraction.

She considered her options for a moment. *Could I use magic to break the stone open? Of course I could, but it could draw attention. Brute force is still the best bet.*

As the last of her light faded, she threw her entire body into the effort. Reluctantly, the stone began to move with an unpleasant grinding. She redoubled her efforts, and the stone finally yielded, allowing her to slide it along the floor above.

Arraya breathed slow and shallow, trying not to choke on the freshly disturbed dust. She picked up the staff and was surprised to note that light filtered through the newly opened hole. With an effort, she heaved herself up into the chamber beyond.

Her eyes slowly adjusted to the dimly-lit chamber. A handful of torches lined the walls, and two figures dressed in battered, dirty black clothes were chained to the walls.

Deja vu swept over her. "I've been here," she murmured. "Or...I've *seen* this."

Memory flooded her, and she staggered. "This is where Master Shallum dies," she murmured. "This is the room I saw in my vision."

"Who are you?" the girl bound to the wall asked.

Arraya focused immediately on her. *Concentrate on the moment. Leave the future to itself.* "I'm Arraya," the flame-haired girl introduced herself. More details of the vision flickered through his mind. *Which means...*

The apprentice turned to focus on the second chained figure. "The heir," she breathed. "You're the heir to the throne."

Both prisoners stared at her with uncomprehending gazes. "I'm sorry," Arraya said. She stepped over to the heir first, focusing on his shackles. "Let me unbind you, and then I'll explain everything." She closed her eyes, and it took only a whisper of power to turn the locks. The cuffs fell away from hands and feet, and the dark-haired boy fell without the support.

He landed heavily on his hands and knees. Arraya knelt to offer him help, but he shook his head. "Free Corin," he rasped.

The girl, the apprentice realized. It took only a moment for Arraya to free the other thief with a similarly small effort. The dark-haired girl immediately rushed across the tiny chamber to help the heir rise to his feet.

"I didn't expect to find you here," Arraya said. "Not now, not like this."

"Do you know us?" the heir asked.

"I know who you are, yes," the apprentice said. "You are the heir to throne of Letale. *You* are the rightful king."

***

"Who *are* you?" Ben breathed.

"I am Arraya, an apprentice of the Magi," the red-headed girl said with a deep bow.

Corin elbowed him in the ribs. "How do we know we can trust her?" she hissed.

"She let us out of the shackles, didn't she?" Ben retorted. He turned his attention back to her. "Did you just say you're a Magi?"

The girl nodded. "Yes," she said simply. "I'm an apprentice, but yes, a Magi."

Ben's unease returned. "I thought the Magi were all slaves of the Dark One," he said cautiously. "Everything I've heard about you said you're all crazy, and King Hazael fought a war just to drive you out and protect Letale from you."

The girl's brilliant green eyes flashed dangerously in the dim light. "The Imposter-King has told many lies about us," she said fiercely. "He usurped the throne from the rightful line of kings and drove us out. For centuries the Magi served the kingdom as advisers and protectors, until his coup."

The thief swallowed hard. *Okay, so maybe she is a little crazy. She's a magic-user, after all. So play nice with the crazy girl who let us out but could kill us both.*

"So what are you doing here?" Corin asked cautiously.

She definitely can see the danger, too, Ben thought.

"I came here to find my master," the Magi said gravely. "I had a vision of his death here in Jepitsa, at the hands of a servant of the Dark One. Here, in Jepitsa, with the Imposter-King upon the throne, they are nearly unchecked in power."

"Why would your master be here?" Corin wanted to know. "If there's such danger here, why would he step into it?"

"He came here to find *you*," Arraya said, focusing intently on Ben. "He came here to find the heir to the throne. He had a vision of a surviving heir, someone the Magi could support to restore truth and order to the kingdom."

"Me?" Ben said, starting to laugh. "Me? The *heir to the throne?*" He couldn't seem to stop laughing. "I'm no prince, and I'm definitely no king."

"You may believe that," the girl said with serenity, "but it does not change the truth. You *are* the rightful king of Letale."

"Yeah. Right." Ben shook his head. "No wonder people say magic users are crazy. You're living proof."

The Magi's emerald eyes flared hotly again. "I am *not* crazy," she ground out through gritted teeth. There was a line of moisture on her cheek, and she half-whispered, "I wish people would quit calling me that."

"So, now what?" Corin asked gently. "If Ben's the rightful king, what do we do now? Are you going to lead us up to the throne room and kill King Hazael?"

The question seemed to focus the strange girl. "No. I'm merely an apprentice, and I don't have the power nor the ability to fight the army that no doubt stands between here and there." She hesitated. "I came here to find my master, but now I have you instead." She swallowed. "I'll lead you to safety, and then return for my master." Her eyes took on a faraway look for a moment, and then she asked, "Have you seen my master? Down here, in the dungeon?"

"There were no prisoners when we came," Ben answered. "The dungeon was empty when we..."

"That doesn't make any sense," Arraya muttered. "I could feel that he was here somewhere in the castle. I was so *sure* of it. Unless he was just scouting, and he left again. Maybe he hasn't been captured yet."

"People can't just walk in and out of the castle," Corin pointed out. "We're the best thieves in Jepitsa, and we barely made it in, and that was with weeks of planning and special gear we stole."

Arraya pointed silently to the hole she had used to enter the chamber.

"Oh," Corin said awkwardly. "Right. Magic."

"How am I going to find my master?" she muttered. "Even if I can manage another weaving, he could move from where I sense him. I just don't have the power to keep it going until I find him."

"So, what's your plan?" Ben asked when the apprentice's words became unintelligible mumbles. "What do we do now?"

Arraya looked up at him. "Right. Priorities." She took a deep breath. "First, I guide you two to safety," she said. "Once you're free, I'm going to come back and scout the whole dungeon. My vision was very clear, and it was *here*. My master must be here somewhere – maybe in some cell you had not seen when you were imprisoned." She gestured with her staff toward the hole.

Corin and Ben reached the hole together, a step in front of the Magi. "Where does this lead?" Ben asked.

"Out," the apprentice said.

"I know what this is," Corin muttered. "It's the drainage tunnel that Alan talked about. But he said it was collapsed."

"This passage was indeed collapsed," the Magi said gravely. "It took a powerful weaving to remove the obstruction, and in time it will fail again. Quickly, into the tunnel."

"In time?" Ben repeated. "How long?"

The Magi seemed uncomfortable when she shrugged. "Perhaps an hour, or less. Weavings are difficult and do not last unassisted." Not-so-distant footsteps began to echo in the small dungeon chamber. "Quickly," she urged. "Into the passage."

Ben snagged a torch from the wall before walking to the small hole in the floor, Corin right behind him. He reached back and took her hand, squeezing it tightly as he looked down into the darkness. "It's safe?" he asked dubiously.

Arraya nodded. "The weaving will hold," she said firmly. "For a little while, at least. Enough time for us to escape."

The thief crouched down and prepared to drop into the hole blindly, when a new voice echoed into the dungeon chamber. It rang with strength and authority, calling, "Arraya!"

XVIII

ARRAYA TURNED SLOWLY AS HER name echoed off the cold dungeon walls.

Her master, Shallum, stood at the entrance of the prison. A cloak of purple was wrapped around his rough robes, falling heavily from his shoulders. "Arraya!" he called again, a hard edge in his voice.

"Master!" she called, her heart beating faster. "You're alive! And you haven't been captured!"

"Arraya, what are you doing here?" Shallum asked in puzzlement. "Why are you here and not in Cosmane?" The Magi began to slowly walk across the dirt and stone floor, his pace unhurried.

"I had a vision, Master," Arraya confessed, turning her back on the heir and the girl. She eagerly stepped forward to meet her mentor. "I saw you dying here, in this dungeon. And I saw the heir. The Council agreed to send me to find you and warn you."

Shallum's torpid pace slowed further. "Warn me?" he asked quietly.

"Yes, about the danger I saw in my vision!" Arraya said, her excitement fading to puzzlement. "You...Master, what are you doing here?"

Shallum stopped, and Arraya's instincts brought her to a halt a double arm's-length away from her teacher. "Master?" she asked again, softly.

The Magi sighed, long and slow. "You shouldn't have come here, Arraya."

"No, it's okay," she said quickly. "We can free the heir, and we can escape. I used my power to clear a tunnel under the castle. I have allies waiting outside. We can take him and escape, and the Imposter-King will never catch us. We can be out of Jepitsa in minutes."

Shallum shook his head, slow and sad. "You don't understand, Arraya."

"Master?" she whispered. The whole dungeon seemed to spin around her, and a feeling of utter *wrongness* pervaded her senses. The moment stretched out impossibly, twisting around her in such a way that she refused to believe it was reality. *This is a dream*, she told herself. *A nightmare, even.*

This can't be happening.

"You shouldn't have come, Arraya."

"What are you doing here?" she asked quietly. "Why did you come here? And what are you doing in that cloak?"

"I came here to fulfill the purpose of the Magi, Arraya," Shallum said, his voice velvet wrapped steel. "Do you know why we exist, apprentice?"

"To serve," she replied reflexively. "We were given our powers to serve the kingdom. To advise the king, to offer wisdom, to correct injustice, and to turn aside the servants of the Dark One."

Shallum nodded. "Apprentice, we have spent years hiding in the mountains. We locked ourselves away, training and studying but never acting. The Magi exist to *serve*, but we have spent your lifetime in seclusion. We have lost our way." He took a deep breath. "Apprentice, I came here to serve the people of this kingdom."

"To pledge your loyalty to the Imposter-King," Arraya breathed. "To betray the Magi."

"No!" Shallum thundered, his voice suddenly a storm of power and certainty. "I have not betrayed the Magi! I came here to *be* a Magi. I will no longer squander my power in futile hiding, far away from the very people we pledged to serve and protect. It is *they* who betrayed the purpose of the Magi, not I!"

"You *have* pledged yourself to the Imposter-King," Arraya said quietly. "You swore an oath, haven't you?"

"Apprentice..." Shallum began.

"You have betrayed the people you claim to serve," Arraya said, her voice finally rising. "You betrayed the

317

order of the Magi. You came here and made yourself a vassal of a usurper, a power-hungry madman who killed the true King and tried to destroy his heirs! You chose to become a servant to a murderer!"

"You are young," the master said, his voice surprisingly soft. "You still see the world in sharp contrasts. How do you think the last line of kings ascended to the throne? With the tip of a spear and the edge of a sword. Power is taken, not granted. The Order of the Magi has forgotten that, and in its self-righteous judgment withdrew from its proper role in the kingdom. They've abandoned the kingdom instead of adjusting to the new reality."

Arraya trembled as she listened to the words of her master. She still wasn't sure what emotions she felt; anger, certainly; betrayal, definitely; but underneath the hottest and most immediate of her feelings, there lurked more feelings she struggled to identify. *No*, she told herself. *I do know what I'm feeling. I just don't want to admit it.*

Uncertainty. All her life, all her apprenticeship, she had bedrock certainty. She *knew* she was destined to be a Magi. She *knew* she would succeed where so many other apprentices failed. She *knew* she served an order of Magi that existed solely to protect the people of the kingdom, an order that sought to keep the Dark One at bay, an order that had been forced into seclusion by the rise of an illegitimate king – a king they would help overthrow.

Now, a soft voice whispered to her. *Maybe the Order of the Magi is wrong. Maybe there is more to be had by serving the Imposter-King. Maybe we have done far more harm than good by locking ourselves away.*

No. No. Master Shallum may have betrayed the Order – betrayed me – but that doesn't change the truth.

The apprentice met the master's eyes squarely. "I will leave here with the heir."

"The heir?" Shallum asked, his tone puzzled. "What...ah, the thieves caught trying to steal the crown."

"If you speak the truth, he is only reclaiming what is already rightfully his," Arraya said sharply.

Shallum sighed and shook his head. "You know I can't let you leave here."

"Then you'll have to stop me," Arraya said, her voice low and defiant.

The master shook his head again. "Apprentice, do you know why I chose you as my learner?"

The flame-haired girl eyed Shallum with uncertainty. *Why the change in subject?* she thought. *Is he trying to take me off-guard? Preparing some spell?*

"No, you've never told me," Arraya said as she started to draw power into herself. *If it comes to blows, I can't match him strength for strength,* she told herself. *He's a Master and had years of experience and training to shape his power. I've had a fraction of the time. I have to find something unexpected if I'm going to win.* She swallowed hard. *Or survive.*

"Arraya," he said softly, "I took you as an apprentice because I had a vision."

She frowned, but didn't let his words distract her from subtly drawing more and more power into herself. "A vision? Of what?"

"Of you killing me."

The shock of the statement nearly caused her to lose her grip on the magic. "What?" she asked dumbly.

"Mistress Esther and I had decided to make a journey to one of the Scion villages," he explained slowly. "It was dangerous, of course – worse than it is now. The Magi were declared enemies of the King, and we were hunted as dangerous brigands. But many of the apprentices had been killed when we fled Jepitsa, and we needed new students."

In spite of herself and the impending danger, Arraya was held enrapt by the story – a fundamental part of her own tale that she did not know.

"We found several children with power enough to train as Magi, though there was no guarantee of success. We spent two days there with the Scions, eating and drinking with them, speaking to the people, healing their hurts and binding their wounds."

Shallum's eyes were distant as he reflected on the memory. "The children we had chosen to train were given their parting rituals and prepared to travel with us. It took an additional day, of course, before they were ready to leave. On the evening of the third day, the Scions prepared a parting feast for us, with the new initiates sitting with us at the head table."

His voice softened. "Mistress Esther and I sat together, speaking with the newest of our Order, when a three-year-old girl walked up to give her big brother a parting hug. As she climbed up on his lap, she brushed against my arm. And in that moment, I had the most vivid, clear vision I have ever experienced in all my centuries."

"Vision?" Arraya asked. She was starting to lose her grip on the power she had hoarded, her concentration no longer on her magic.

"Yes. I had a vision of this little three-year-old flame-haired child as a young woman, drawing on her power to strike me down. And in that vision, I did not know whether she would succeed or fail – whether I was witnessing the moment of my death.

"The vision passed – indeed, it had only lasted an eye blink – but I knew immediately what I had to do."

"Why didn't you kill me?" Arraya asked, her voice hoarse. "You knew it would come down to that."

Shallum's eyes grew wide, and his jaw dropped open. "Murder a child in cold blood? Apprentice, I am a *Magi*. Even if I were inclined to kill someone – which I'm not – I would not have raised a hand against a child. Do you think so little of me, my apprentice? Do you think I am a servant of the Dark One?" He shook his head sadly. "You know I have decided to serve the King, and you think I have turned my back on every part of my being?"

Arraya swallowed hard. "So why?"

"I did not understand the context of my vision, but I believed the best thing I could do was bring you into the Order of the Magi. There you could be shielded from the influences of the Dark One and his servants. You could be taught not only *how* to use your power, but *why* and *when* to wield the True Magic." Shallum shook his head. "I thought I would prevent you from becoming an enemy of the Magi, a servant of the Dark One, and my doom. And now I have brought my own vision to pass, in a way I never imagined." He searched his apprentice's eyes. "I cannot prevent what is about to come to pass — only you can do that."

"What do you mean?" Arraya asked, her voice alien in her own ears as her mind spun from the revelation.

"You can choose to join me in service here to the King," Shallum offered. "I could use your help, and he will accept you as he accepted me. My service would be doubly effective with you at my side. Your training can continue uninterrupted, until you are ready to come into the power of a true Magi."

The apprentice could barely stand up, wave after wave of dizziness crashing down on her. *He's right. I could stay here with him and train. We could advise the Imposter-King...the King. We could ensure his rule is just and fair. Master Shallum could continue to train me until I'm a full Magi.*

But I would be turning my back on the rest of the Order. I know the man sitting on the throne doesn't deserve the crown. He's a usurper and murderer, and I would be choosing to assist him. The realization of her own motives shocked her out of her revere. *I would be assisting him for selfish reasons. It would all be about what's best for me, not about what's right or what's best for the kingdom.*

If I choose that path, I would never truly become a Magi. The Magi exist to serve others. I would be serving others because it benefits me, not because of my commitment to the Magi.

She straightened and closed her eyes. "I stand in your way," she whispered.

When the apprentice opened her eyes and looked up at her mentor, she expected to see anger or hate – the expressions of a servant of the Dark One. Instead, his eyes were weary and sad, filled with pain. "You are like my daughter, Arraya," he said quietly. "The daughter I never had."

"It's not too late to return to Cosmane," Arraya offered hoarsely.

"Yes, it is." Shallum said.

The apprentice turned her back on her master for just a moment. The two thieves still stood at the edge of the hole in the floor, their expressions tinged with fear and hope. "Go," she ordered quietly. "While I live, the pathways will remain open. If I lose, my magics will dissipate into the wind and be gone. Hurry."

She turned back to face her master as the boy and the girl fled into the passageway she had opened. Arraya was a bit surprised to see Master Shallum make no attempt to stop them. *Why would he let an heir escape?* she wondered. Her heart couldn't sink much further when the answer came a moment later. *Because he'll have all the time in the world to hunt him down when he's killed me.*

Master and apprentice stood apart perhaps twenty paces. Arraya could sense the currents of the True Magic as her master began to draw power into himself. She, too, tapped into the power. Instinctively, she took Esther's staff – now *her* staff – in her right hand and smote it down on the dirty floor. The power continued to fill her as a trickle filled a cup – not swiftly, but with utter surety.

She stretched out the staff in her right hand and pointed it at Master Shallum. The tip began to glow with an ancient, hot light. The master stretched out his hand as well, little flickers of light dancing between his spread fingers. The very air between them seemed to grow hot, like the minutes before a powerful storm broke loose.

They stood posed in opposition in a moment that seemed to stretch into eternity, neither willing to strike first. Arraya knew to unleash her power would burn her own heart to ash. At some level, she knew that regardless of the outcome of the duel, she would never be a Magi now. If she failed, her master's fire would cook the flesh from her bones. If she succeeded, the Council would likely never believe her story and would, at the least, cast her out.

So do what is right, she told herself. *In the service of the people of Letale, I will not let a Magi aid the Imposter-King.*

What stayed her master's hand, she did not know.

Then the moment was dashed against the stones and shattered into a million shards.

She never knew if she struck first, or if Shallum finally gave up on her surrendering. Fire lashed out from the staff, even as fire leaped from his fingertips toward her.

Arraya had chosen the most dangerous tactic she could imagine. She knew Shallum's strike could destroy her, but chose to focus her first blow against him, rather than preparing to parry his attack. *He's stronger than me, both striking and defending. My best chance is to attack from the first. Even if he kills me, I may take him with me.*

The attack seemed to surprise Shallum, and his own gout of fire faltered as he stumbled away from Arraya's attack. The apprentice swept the staff right to left, trying to create a wall of flames to entrap her master.

She was too slow; the master finally summoned the wind in a swirl around himself, extinguishing the flames licking at his clothes and forcing the rest of the summoned fire away.

Arraya cut off her own magic, then, preserving her strength. As the flames died away, darkness plunged into the dungeon. Shallum's frantic defense had extinguished the torches, leaving almost no light.

The apprentice dove to the floor to her right, sprawling in the dirt. A fireball flashed out of the darkness and splashed against the wall where her head had been. *Close. Too close.*

Shallum didn't immediately strike again, and Arraya laid absolutely still. Her own motion had disoriented her, and she wasn't sure precisely where in the darkness her master was standing.

Then he began to walk, slow and deliberate. His footsteps echoed in the dungeon, and Arraya struggled to suppress a curse when she realized she still didn't know where he was, or even which way he was moving. *Patience*, she told herself. *Lie still. Let him make a mistake. Don't betray yourself.*

"I did not want this for you," Shallum's disembodied voice echoed off the walls. "No apprentice should be forced to fight her own master. No apprentice should be forced to make these decisions. But these times are strange, when light is dark and dark is light. Even now, it is not too late, Arraya. You can still join me."

And then his foot fell upon the staff, still gripped in her right hand but laid flat against the floor. He stumbled, and Arraya called upon her power again to strike.

Somehow Shallum conjured the wind again in time to hold her flames at bay. The firelight tinted their faces blood red, and Arraya strained to break through the magics of her master. He seemed almost dismissive of her now, stretching out his left hand to keep her attack at bay while the right leisurely gestured to the torches. They flared to life again, and the chamber was suddenly aglow in light.

The apprentice finally yielded her attack, dropping the point of the staff. "I will never surrender to you."

He shook his head. "You could have been a powerful Magi, one of the greatest our Order has ever known. Instead, you will die here like a servant of the Dark One, burned to nothing like an abomination. I'm sorry, Arraya."

The apprentice barely had time to get the staff up, this time summoning all the wind she could manage.

As master and apprentice, they had sparred continually with magic. Arraya understood, at some level, that he had held himself back during her training. Had he unleashed his full power upon her, he would have utterly destroyed her – not a productive end for the training of a promising young Scion. Similarly, she knew she had held herself back as well when striking. He was her master, her teacher, her *father*. She had never truly tested her strength against his all the years of her training.

Now, neither held anything in reserve.

She unleashed a windstorm, a gale that snapped his purple cloak and blew clouds of dust up, almost obscuring her view of her opponent.

He unleashed a blast of fire as hot as the sun, a burst intended to end her life.

Arraya's furious defense just barely held it at bay. She felt the heat of it even through her defenses. The tip of the staff began to glow and smoke with heat, and her skin erupted in pain as though she had been in the sun too long.

"You," she snarled through gritted teeth, "are no longer of the Magi, *Shallum!* I may be only an apprentice, a daughter of the True Power and servant of the Aither, but I *cast you out!*"

She wasn't even sure if he could hear her words through the roar of his fire and her wind. Fresh determination kept her spell flowing, the magic rushing through her outstretched hand and staff, but her strength was beginning to ebb. In moments, her wind would no longer keep his fire at bay, and the battle would end.

But strangely, her strength did *not* ebb. It seemed a mighty weight settled over her head and shoulders, and the True Magic itself seemed to wrap itself around her like a suit of armor, steadied her trembling knees and shaking outstretched arm.

There were only twelve Magi on the Council. Only twelve beings walked the world with the power of the Aither, of the True Magic, of the Ancient Fire. There were many disciples – students who learned of the power, understood it, even manipulated it.

But only twelve embodied it.

The strain of holding the power of the wind eased, but the gale holding the fire at bay did not lessen. In that moment, Arraya realized.

I'm a Magi. A full *Magi. One of the twelve.*

Somehow, Shallum did not seem to sense the cosmic shift, the elevation of his own student's raw strength. His own attack did not lessen, though strain was beginning to show in the tremble of his fingers and the sweat rolling down his brow.

Even with the new power wrapping itself around Arraya, power she could feel permeating her bones, she did not strike. *He is my master, and I love him. He is the father I left behind. I can't strike him down – not now, not ever.*

Instead, she poured all her newfound strength back into the wind.

Shallum didn't, *couldn't* expect the change. How could he know his own student would double and redouble in power in the span of a few heartbeats? How could he know that everything he remembered from training her would abruptly become worthless?

The wind carried the fire back into Shallum's own hands.

The sun-hot fire engulfed the Magi before he could react as his own attack was turned back on him. He screamed, once, as the flames flashed up his robes and over his flesh, but the fire he had conjured was so destructive he had time for little else.

Arraya lowered the staff to the floor, then leaned heavily down on it as she watched what little remained of her master turn to ash.

Realization flooded her mind. *I've killed with the True Magic.* Some glimmer of foresight whispered to her that it may have been the first time, but it would not be the last.

"I'm sorry, Master," she whispered. "But you had to be stopped. For everyone."

Tears dripped down her face, cool streaks over the scorched skin demanding her attention. "Thank you," she continued, "for teaching me all that I know. But you had lost your way, Master."

The fire began to die as quickly as it had been conjured. The remains provided little more fuel, and Arraya no longer fed it magic to keep it lit. Flickers of orange reduced themselves to glowing embers, which in turn began to darken all-too-quickly.

She wanted to dally, but cold facts began to pour through her mind. *The guards will be here soon. I need to get back out the tunnel, seal the path to prevent them from following me, and find the heir. And most of all, I need to get the heir back to Cosmane, so the Council can determine what to do next.*

Arraya closed her eyes for a long moment to recover her wits. When she looked again, her master was little more than ash.

"Be at peace, master," she managed through her tight throat. With a whisper of power, she scattered the ashes with a burst of wind before turning to the tunnel.

Distantly she could hear the steady clank-clank-clank of approaching armored soldiers – the Royal Guard, no doubt. A small, irrational part of her mind told her to stay and fight. With the power of the Magi coursing through her very blood, she could destroy all comers, take revenge upon the evil that had turned her master against his own student, persuaded him to betray his own Order and oaths.

Instead, she stepped over and dropped into the small sewer tunnel.

She began to run as the guards entered the dungeon. With her newfound power, she reached out and considered the spells she had woven to secure this entrance – and exit – in place. And like a child worrying a loose thread on a tunic, she found a weakness in her own spell and began to unravel it, bit by bit.

Far ahead of her, she could sense faintly the heir and the girl. They were in no danger as she ran faster, stretching out her legs into the best sprint she could manage in the low, dark tunnel.

As the spell began to unwind in earnest, earth and stone fell from the ceiling and choked the passageway behind her.

XIX

BEN SKIDDED TO A HALT as the failing sunlight assaulted his eyes. After the dim dungeon and the even darker tunnel, the last rays of sunlight were still bright enough to jab needles into his eyes.

He squinted, trying to see just where he and Corin had emerged from the tunnel. He stumbled forward a step as the girl ran into him, apparently as blinded as he.

"Where are we?" Corin asked.

Ben continued to look around, his eyes slowly adjusting. "We're outside the city walls," he said at last. "Maybe a league from Riverfront."

A distant rumble began to reverberate. *Is that thunder?* he wondered. As the noise continued unabated, and in fact began to grow, he realized the truth. "The tunnel's coming down," he hissed.

Corin turned back to look. "Do you think that Magi girl...?" she half-asked.

Ben grimaced. "She saved our lives." He stared down the tunnel, but now that his eyes had adjusted to the twilight, he could no longer make out anything but the inky black.

The other thief caught his arm. "Don't even think about it, Ben."

"She saved us," he repeated. "Can we just let her die in there?"

"Stop and think," Corin demanded. "You don't know if she's alive. You don't know where she is. If you run down that tunnel, the only thing you know for sure is that it's collapsing. For all we know, she's making her way back out through the castle."

Ben forced himself to think through her words. *She's right. Yes, she's right. You don't know, and throwing yourself in there is a good way to get killed.*

Dust began to pour out of the tunnel's mouth, a choking cloud that forced both thieves to step back from the entrance. As the rumble reached its crescendo, a dust-covered figure threw herself through the portal an instant before dirt and stone collapsed entirely, sealing it shut.

The red-haired figure slowly climbed to her feet and shook herself off. "I'm glad to see you waited for me," she said nonchalantly, as though escaping certain crushing death was an everyday occurrence.

Ben gaped at her for a moment. *She is a Magi, I guess. Maybe that* is *an everyday occurrence.* "It only seemed polite," he managed, trying not to cough from the still-rising dust. "Given you broke us out and all."

"There are few enough polite people in Jepitsa," the Magi said dryly.

"We don't have a lot of time," Corin murmured, coming up to Ben's elbow. "If we're going to get to Alan in time."

Ben grimaced. "If we're not too late already."

"Come," the Magi said urgently. "We have little time before the Royal Guard begin their hunt. We must be well away from here before they reach this place."

"What are you talking about?" Corin asked. "You're coming with *us*, not the other way around."

The Magi ignored Corin, focusing her attention solely on Ben. "You are the heir to the throne. Now that you've escaped, with the help of a Magi, the Imposter-King will want you dead. There is no time to dally; we must escape from Jepitsa immediately, and make for Cosmane."

Ben shook his head. "No. We can't leave yet."

The flame-haired girl stared. "If you stay, it will mean certain death."

"We can't leave yet," Ben repeated. "What was your name? Raya?"

"Arraya," the Magi corrected.

"Arraya, then. Alan has the crown, and he's going to sell it off and disappear with all the gold." Ben tamped down his anger, but it simmered at the mere memory of the betrayal. "The Royal Guard will burn Riverfront to the ground, and that bastard is going to live in riches the rest of his life while everyone else dies."

He stared hard at the Magi. "Now, I don't know if I'm some king-to-be or not, but right now it doesn't matter. I'm not going to let my friends all die and Alan get away with it. Now, you can come with me to Riverfront and help me, or you can run off to Cosmane or wherever else you want to go. You can't stop me."

The Magi, Arraya, stared hard at him. Ben had the unnatural feeling that she could see *through* him, right to his heart. He had no idea what she saw, but he damned well didn't care right now.

It was still a creepy feeling, though.

"Very well," Arraya said reluctantly. "I will go with you to this Riverfront. But after, you must promise to flee with me. If you remain here, the Imposter-King will surely put you to death."

Ben nodded. "Agreed."

Corin grabbed his arm and leaned in close to whisper, "Ben, she's a Magi. Is this safe?"

The thief stopped dead in his tracks for a moment. Finally, he said, "Have you ever met a Magi before?"

"I've never met any magic users," Corin said derisively. "They're all dangerous. Magic does bad things to the head."

"That may be true," Ben allowed. "That's everything I've heard, too. But she *did* save us from the dungeon, and she seems to be pretty anxious to keep us safe."

"Keep *you* safe, you mean," the girl replied darkly. "Since you're now the next king or something."

"That doesn't matter right now," Ben said with a shake of his head. "She's on our side, or near enough. Right now, that's all that matters. Besides," he added as an afterthought, "we might need her help to get to Alan. Who knows what he's told everyone else by now?"

"He probably told them all that we were captured," Corin said. "I don't see how that changes anything."

Ben shook his head. "No, he didn't. If he told the Brigands we were prisoners, they would want to help us break out – especially if he showed up to Riverfront with crown in hand. He either told them that we tried to backstab him and he barely escaped with the goods, or he told them we're dead."

Corin caught on almost immediately. "And he probably told them all we turned on him, just in case we got away somehow and showed up in Riverfront." Her expression was bleak. "He's probably turned everyone against us."

Ben nodded. "And if he has, we're going to need every friend we can get. Even a maybe-crazy Magi."

"I hate it when you make sense," she complained.

"Me, too."

***

As night declared dominance over day, the two thieves and the Magi began to run toward Riverfront. As the light failed, the three runners were forced to slow or risk a disastrous fall on the unfamiliar footing. Arraya immediately moved out into the lead, seeming to find a trail even in the darkness.

Corin stumbled, and Ben slowed. "I'm fine," Corin gasped through gritted teeth. "Twisted the ankle a bit, but I'm fine."

The Magi stopped and looked back at them, confusion evident on her face. "What's wrong?"

"Just stepped wrong on a rock," Corin growled. "I'm fine."

Arraya shook her head. "How foolish of me. I forgot."

"Forgot what?" Corin asked with a glare.

In response, the Magi lifted the staff she carried in her right hand. Light abruptly burst from the end of it, a blue-white fire that did not seem to consume the wooden stave.

"Neat trick," Ben said, accompanied by a grudging nod from Corin.

"Quickly," Arraya said simply, turning and beginning to run again.

Ben and Corin fell into stride behind her again, legs stretched out and running more confidently in the dim light radiating from the staff.

As they began to close on Riverfront, Ben's heart began to fall. *The Royal Guard isn't looking for us,* he realized. *Even though we escaped. The king has to know a Magi was there, too. Why wouldn't he be searching for us?*

Because the Guard is already busy. And the only thing that would be more important than tracking down a rogue Magi would be recovering the crown.

It took the trio just over a third of an hour to cover the league separating them from Riverfront. As they drew close, Ben could see an indistinct glow over the shantytown. He knew, in his heart, what he would see when they closed the final strides, but he refused to admit it until he saw it with his own eyes. He pressed on harder, running as fast as he ever had. His fast-moving, long-legged strides drew him even with the flame-haired Magi, then past even her and her Magic.

And when Ben crested the final ridge, three strides ahead of Arraya and thirty ahead of Corin, he nearly fell to his knees at the sight.

Riverfront was in flames.

The rows of small shacks were all aflame; some of the flimsy wooden huts had clearly just begun to burn, while others were hardly more than embers. *My home*, Ben wailed silently. *Zeke's home. Corin's home. Everything up in flames. It's all gone.*

From his vantage point on the hill, he could see torchlight moving in the Market, no doubt the Royal Guard continuing to spread destruction. *They'll keep going until everything's burned down, even if they get the crown back.* He swallowed hard. *They're probably going to kill everyone they can find.*

Something in his heart snapped. *No.*

"Where will your traitor have taken the crown?" Arraya asked urgently.

Corin finally reached the ridge, doubled over and gasping for breath. "What...what have they done?"

338

"What Alan always knew they would do," Ben snarled. "He *knew* the guards would do this. He knew what would happen if we pulled it off. He knew it, and we did it anyway." Anger bubbled up, an unstoppable wave of rage originating from the hard pit in his stomach. "He *knew* the Royal Guard would retaliate. He *knew* it."

"King-to-Be," Arraya said urgently, "where would this traitor have taken the crown? We have little time, and I cannot protect you from an army."

Ben didn't answer with words. His anger was white-hot now, and every fiber of his being told him to charge to the dark island in the stream, to the tower where Alan no doubt was laired. *That's why some of the Brigands had bows. He was ready for this. He planned to defend his little castle until he could escape. He had to make sure he was ready just in case everything went wrong.*

Instead, however, he charged down toward the Market and the disaster slowly unfolding there.

Ben had expected the entire Market to be engulfed in fire before he could intervene – *not that I have any idea what I'm going to do* – but he was surprised to find it still standing unharmed as he began to weave between the stalls. He glanced back to see Arraya and Corin a half dozen strides back, and ran straight into the hulking figure of Corpakle.

Pak didn't even turn to look. As Ben picked himself off the ground, he realized it wasn't just the tool genius standing in his path. Standing in a half circle were the merchants of the Market: Fats, Feathers, Cowardly Wade,

Plain Jane, and all the rest. Scattered among them were some of the Brigands, including Zeke. Alan was nowhere to be seen.

Standing opposite his old friends, the Royal Guard stood armed and prepared for battle. Finely polished swords shone in the torchlight. Their armor, blood red in the daylight, were a dark contrast to their weapons in the dim light of the torches. The forty soldiers were a fearsome sight, and Ben couldn't help but shudder as their very appearance evoked the thousand nightmares of every Brigand, the nightmares of every thief in Jepitsa.

Only one of the Royal Guard was sans helmet. As he spoke, Ben guessed he must be the Commander of the Guard.

"We have tolerated your presence for these long years since King Hazael was seated upon the throne," the Commander intoned. "You pay no taxes and steal from within the city walls. You deal in goods you neither paid for nor earned. And now, with this last offense, the King's patience is at an end."

Silence prevailed from the Market-goers. The Commander seemed taken aback by the silence, but he cleared his throat and continued. "King Hazael is not without mercy, however. I have no doubt the crown is here. If one of you turns it over to me, he shall be spared the bloodletting to come. If you all refuse, we will burn the Market to the ground and find the crown in the ashes."

"We don't have it!" Cowardly Wade shouted.

The Commander silently shook his head and replaced his helmet. "You've made your choice."

Ben swallowed hard. *We did this. Everyone's going to die because of what we did.*

The Royal Guard began to march forward, weapons drawn. Ben began to draw back. *There's nothing I can do*, he told himself. *Nothing I can do to stop this. All I can do is try to find Alan and make him pay for what he did.*

Then Pak stepped out in front of the rest of the merchants.

The big man walked out five paces in front of the crowd and halted. In his hands he held a gigantic battle axe; from the blade to the end of the shaft it stood as tall as a man, and a half more.

"I am Corpakle of the Rephaim!" he shouted, his voice filling the night. There was confidence and fire that Ben had never heard in the man before. "I am an heir of those you call the giants! I have understood your offer and rejected it, and now offer you an agreement in return: turn and leave this place, and all of you shall return to your homes. But if you take one further step forward, or set but one fire, not one of you shall leave here alive."

"You are no Rephaim," the Commander sneered. "You are naught but a man like any other."

Pak hefted the mighty battle axe. "Come forward and find out."

The Royal Guard hesitated at the sight. "He's a single man!" the Commander shouted. "Kill him, and burn it all to the ground! For King Hazael!"

Ben wanted nothing more than to sink deeper into the shadows and vanish, but shock dissolved his will to decide.

Every Market-goer drew a blade or axe or mace of steel as the Royal Guard began to charge.

Some of the weapons were clearly Pak's make; his fine craftsmanship was unmistakable. Others were weapons from afar, drawn liberally from the carefully hoarded inventory of Feathers. Still more were local weapons, likely stolen from within the Jepitsa walls, or forged by local blacksmiths in secret.

The Royal Guard had been expecting a slaughter; now, in the face of men and women armed and willing to defend themselves, they faltered: their unstoppable charge broke down, strides became uneven, and their momentum vanished as the denizens of the Market rushed forward to face them in battle.

Arrows began to rain down from the stalls and shanties around them. Ben stole a glance upward. *Alan's guards!* he thought in surprise.

A hand fell on Ben's shoulder. He turned and found the flame-haired Magi staring him squarely in the eye. "There is nothing you can do here," she said bluntly. "We must flee while ti – "

A loud *boom* cracked through the night. It was a single strike of lightning without the flash of light, only the rolling report of thunder. The Magi's head jerked away, looking up. "Naomi is...here?" she asked aloud.

"What...that noise...?" Ben asked, trying to put a thought together.

"One of my allies," was all the Magi offered in explanation. "Come with me. Hurry!"

Shouts and screams and the clash of steel assaulted Ben's ears as the battle erupted in all its fury. The sheer noise of it was overpowering, and he found himself stumbling along in Arraya's wake by instinct. Corin was beside him, similarly dazed and following.

Another crack of thunder assaulted his ears, and Ben nearly lost his footing. *This is insane. I've never imagined a battle is anything like this.*

At the end of the row of stalls, a door stood ajar. Before it was a Tillik, one of the lizard-men of the swamps, short swords held in either hand. Atop the stall was a slim cloaked figure holding a long metal staff, pointing its end toward the battle. *A Tillik, here?* Ben wondered. *Everything else has gone to hell, so why not?*

Fire seemed to flash from the end of the cloaked figure's staff, accompanied by another roll of thunder, this one so loud it left ringing in Ben's ears. "Is that another Magi?" he asked Arraya, his own voice oddly distant.

She shook her head and spoke, her answer barely audible. "She's a friend, though."

Arraya turned her back and began to speak to the Tillik. Fear began to overcome Ben. *Need some place out of sight. Someplace to hide until the Royal Guard is gone. Stay out in the open like this and die.*

He brushed past the Tillik and jerked the door open.

And found himself face-to-face with Alan.

"You!" he cried.

Alan seemed just as shocked to see the thief. "Ben!"

"Where is it?" Ben snarled, his hearing slowly returning.

Alan shook his head. "It's not yours."

"It's as much mine as it is yours," Ben replied. "And as much Corin's as either of ours."

"Wrong," Arraya said from behind him. "It is yours and only yours, King-to-Be. It is a part of your inheritance."

"Who is this?" Alan asked skeptically. "Some girl driven mad by the Dark One?"

"She's a Magi," Ben replied, watching as Alan's face grew pale. "She is the one who freed Corin and me from the King's dungeons and guided me back safely in time to find you, before you could sell the crown and vanish with all the gold that should belong to the Brigands."

Alan's glare was venomous. *I guessed right*, Ben thought. *He was going to sell it and get out and leave everyone else to twist in the wind.* "So you *do* conspire with the Dark One," the leader of the Brigands said at last. "Making allies of a Magi? What other surprises have you waited to spring on me, to steal the crown and make your own fortune?"

"I'm not here to steal anything, you traitor," Ben hissed. "You left us to rot while you made off with a fortune!"

"A fortune I would have used to free you," Alan replied smugly. "I could do nothing to ensure you and Corin escaped with me from the castle."

"You set us up to be captured!" Ben shouted.

"Hardly." Alan sniffed. "It's not *my* fault you two were so clumsy, and even then, I would have freed you. But now you come with some new ally who has twisted your minds against me."

Ben was so furious he didn't see the blow coming.

Alan's punch sent him stumbling back, falling through the open door and into the dirt under the night sky.

The leader of the Brigands stepped through the door, advancing on the fallen thief. Corin leaped at him, but Alan's swift backhand felled her as well.

Ben's mind was reeling as he tried to climb to his feet. Then there was a dagger in Alan's hand – the brilliant blade that had been forged by Corpakle. The young thief tried to scramble backward, to find his balance, but his head still spun too fast to allow him to defend himself.

Then Arraya turned and lifted her staff.

The night air seemed to crackle with power, and Alan stood stock-still, held in place by the power of the Magi.

"You shall not lay another hand on the King-to-Be," she announced with absolute authority. Her very voice rang like a trumpet in the night air, reverberating with power.

Ben finally found his balance and rose to his feet. "Let him go," he told the Magi.

Her green eyes flashed with *something* Ben did not recognize, but she lowered her staff. The power dissolved, and Alan fell to a knee before recovering. He straightened and squared off with the younger man.

"No more lies," Ben said quietly, coldly. "You set me and Corin up to take the fall while you made off with the crown."

Alan did not reply.

"You used us. All of us, all these years. You made yourself a king of your own little domain," Ben accused. "You found yourself a nice little castle and made us all into your peasants. You called us all family, but you made us all your *slaves*. That's all we were to you – tools, vessels to bring you wealth and power."

"And what were you without me?" Alan countered. "Urchin children, street rats begging for scraps to survive. All of Riverfront is *my* creation. I am the reason it stands here today, a city of its own outside the walls. Would you rather be as you are, a capable thief, or would you prefer to be a starved child buried ten years ago instead?"

"Then you found the ultimate heist: steal a royal crown out of the castle and sell it to your patron for enough gold to live like royalty the rest of your life," Ben continued, ignoring Alan's reply. "Use your slaves to get all the things you need for the job: the plans for the castle and the tools you'll need to get inside. As soon as the crown is in your hands, you escape and leave those slaves to twist, thinking you'll be well gone before anyone can react."

Alan glowered silently at Ben.

"If not for the Magi, you would've pulled it off," Ben said. "But now...now, we're going to have this out. You and me, Alan."

The Brigand barked a laugh. "You want to fight me? Here, and now?"

"Right here, right now." Ben rolled his shoulders. "Winner walks away with the crown."

Alan snorted. "You won't lose. Not with your tame Magi to strike me down should I win."

"Arraya, do you promise not to interfere?" Ben asked.

The Magi's expression clearly displayed her displeasure. "I will not interfere, short of him attempting to end your life."

"You don't try to kill me, we're fine," Ben said, switching his gaze back to Alan.

"Fine. I'm not going to get a better deal from you, am I?"

"No. I'm being more than fair."

Corin was at his side then, turning her back on Alan. "Why are you doing this? There's no reason to fight him. We can take the crown and go. Even if you beat him, it won't save Riverfront."

Ben stopped and processed her words, thinking it through. "I'm doing it for three reasons," he said at last. "First, because he left us to rot in the dungeon. Second, to show everyone else that he has no real power — I don't want anyone else to follow him like I did. And third, I'm doing this for *me*. He used me for years, and I'm going to take it back out of his hide." Ben rolled his head from side to side, cracking his neck. "Just keep an eye on the fight with the Royal Guard."

"That's not a problem anymore," Corin said dryly.

Ben looked around for the first time since he had entered the stall and found Alan.

Many of the wooden stalls were on fire, the flames licking the moon as they towered into the sky. Bodies were strewn through the Market – some wearing armor, many clad in simple homespun clothes. The survivors were gathering in a loose circle around the confrontation between Ben and Alan.

Alan seemed to sense the change as well. With a flash of insight, Ben knew what he must be thinking. *He'll need to discredit me – make me into a madman seduced by a Magi. If he loses the fight, no one will listen to him anymore. Heck, at this point even if he wins, he might have lost.*

Ben stepped forward into the loose ring. The imposing figure of Corpakle offered him a smile of reassurance, but Ben felt a moment of dread as he sized up his opponent. *Alan is no taller than I am, but he's three or four stones heavier than I am. If we get into a grapple, I'll lose.*

A strategy blossomed in his mind. *It's risky, but it's my best chance. I doubt he'll see it coming.*

Alan raised his fists and stepped forward to attack. Ben held up his hands, palms outward. "Wait, wait, wait, not until we get the rules straight."

"Rules?" Alan straightened, disbelief evident on his face. "In a fight like this? There's no rules!"

Before the other could react, Ben kicked out as hard as he could, right between Alan's legs. "Well, if there's no rules, let's get the fight started!" he called out as Alan doubled over. "Someone call the start!"

"Three, two, one, start!" Arraya called, a tinge of glee in her otherwise somber voice.

Alan was just starting to straighten when Ben's fist connected with his jaw, sending him sprawling senselessly into the dirt.

Ben shook his hand as he stepped over his fallen foe, flicked open the bag hanging from his belt, and withdrew the crown. *That hurt.* The pain grew as his adrenaline faded. *That really, really hurt. That was rather dumb. Never hit someone's face with your fist, Ben. You're more likely to break fingers than his face.*

Pak was chuckling. "Never hit someone's face with your fist, Ben. You're more likely to break fingers than his face." The big man crouched down and recovered Alan's dagger, slipping it into his own belt.

"Yeah, but it was worth it."

Arraya stepped over Alan's unconscious body and touched Ben's arm. "King-to-Be, we have already dallied too long. We need to flee before the Royal Guard recovers and sends more soldiers after us."

Ben turned to look at Riverfront, the euphoria of beating Alan giving way to the sickening reality around him. Zeke and Corin were in the circle, as were a few of the merchants, Pak the most conspicuous. Far more were missing from the circle, either run off or dead at the hands of the Royal Guard. Few of the Riverfront hovels still stood, and fire still threatened those remaining.

There's no going back, Ben realized. *After everything that happened, there's no way we can go back to the way things were.*

He looked down at the crown in his hand. *Everything has changed, and no wishing will make it change.*

He looked up at Arraya and met those intense green eyes squarely for the first time. "Then lead on."

XX

THE SHIP SLOWLY ROCKED UNDER Ben's feet as he walked to the stern. Corin stood silently with her back to him, leaning heavily against a rail as she looked north.

The pirate vessel *Tasoth* swayed gently in the breeze, its sails catching the wind and harnessing its power to move the ship against the current. Jepitsa had faded from view some leagues ago, but the girl had not moved from her self-appointed spot since they left the docks.

Ben struggled to find something to say, but at last settled for leaning silently against the rail beside her. They stood side-by-side, watching the passing shores for some time before Corin finally spoke.

"I've wanted to leave Jepitsa for a long time," she said softly. "I wanted to leave Alan behind. But I didn't want it to be like this."

"Like what?" Ben asked.

"Riverfront is ashes," she said, and there were tears streaking her cheeks. "The Brigands are scattered or dead. The children..."

"Are under the care of the merchants," Ben consoled her. "It may be better for them now. I talked to Fats before we fled, and he was going to take the kids somewhere far away from Jepitsa and try to teach them an honest trade. And with the rest of the old stall keepers, they have enough gold to manage it."

"Why did Pak decide to come with us?" Corin asked.

Ben frowned. "I'm not sure. Corpakle said he wanted to keep an eye on me. It doesn't make much sense to me, but he's probably the biggest, toughest guy I've ever met."

"That's what happens when you're a giant."

"He's not really a giant, you know," Ben said.

"I know. Giants are twice his size. But he's still a monster." She considered. "Maybe he's a half-giant."

"I didn't think there even *were* any half-giants," Ben mused.

"I've never heard of one, but who knows?" Corin shrugged. "And at least Zeke decided to come with us."

"Yes," Ben said gratefully. "I have a feeling I'm going to need all the friends I can get."

"This Magi girl..." Corin hesitated. "Are you sure she's not going to kill us all, or something?"

"No," he said bluntly. "But she's...well, she's not what we've all been told. You've heard all the stories about the Magi, and how they abused the people and made the king

352

a puppet and how they were really the ones ruling everything, and how they're all crazy and kill on a whim. She's not really like any of that."

"No, she's not," Corin conceded. "I'm just worried. At least when we were in Jepitsa and dealing with Alan, we knew what we were dealing with. We knew who the players and what the rules were. Now, everything's changing."

"What about..." Ben hesitated.

"What?" Corin asked, finally turning to look at him.

He swallowed. "What you said when we were in the dungeon under Key Castle."

The girl looked away. "I don't regret saying anything," she said at last, her voice barely audible over the breeze and the slap of waves against hull. "I meant every word I said. But now..." she stumbled over her words. "Everything's changed. I'm just a thief, and you're the royal heir. If the Magi can put you on the throne, I'm nothing – just another peasant who breaks the law."

"You're more than that to me," Ben said softly.

"It won't matter, Ben. If you're the king, you have rules and traditions you have to abide by." More tears wet her face. "I'm sorry, but there's nothing else I can do."

They both were silent for long minutes as the riverbanks continued to roll by. Ben wanted to deny her words, wanted to tell her that, yes, they *could* be together, traditions be damned. But he wasn't sure if he could effect such change. *It's better to wait*, he told himself. *Until I know I won't be breaking her heart.*

"Corin," Ben finally broke the silence, "why did you tell everyone I had won the fight with the pirate?"

Her eyes sparkled and a smile tugged at her lips. "Because it was true, of course."

"But it wasn't true. Last thing I remember, he had me pinned to the deck of the ship and beat me senseless."

"Yes, he did," Corin acknowledged, "but you won the fight."

"How did I win the fight?" Ben asked. "Did I heroically fight back in my sleep?"

"The fight was for entertainment," she pointed out. "The pirates all thought he'd run you through with a sword in the first five seconds of the match, and it'd be over. You actually stood up to him and, even if you lost, put on a good accounting for yourself. It also gave the crew a good opinion of you – a land-locked thief nearly beat a pirate in a fight. After you passed out, there was heated debate about whether you would still have lost if the fight had been on shore instead of the deck of the ship."

Ben raised an eyebrow. "Really?"

"Really. Captain Japhet was so impressed he wanted to offer you a job aboard the ship, but I turned him down on your behalf."

"Speaking of the captain," Ben said dryly, "how did you convince him to sail us *south* toward Cosmane instead of *north* toward the ocean?"

Corin blushed bright red. "Um, are you sure you want to hear this?"

Ben nodded. "Every word."

"I, uh, I told him there might be a job for him if he did it."

"What do you mean?" Ben asked. "There's not many ships on the river, and there's really not going to be anything or any place to rob here."

She shook her head. "You're thinking about this like a thief, not a king."

"Like a king?" Ben repeated. "Now I'm really lost."

"Japhet is a captain. The next step up would be *commodore.*"

"Commodore." Ben scratched his forehead, thinking through the implications. "Wait. You promised Captain Japhet that I'd make him a commodore?"

"You *are* a king, after all," Corin said sagely. "You're going to need your own navy, and a navy needs a commodore."

"A commodore commands a group of ships," Ben said pointedly. "I don't have *one* ship."

"Yes, you do," the girl disagreed. "You have the *Tasoth.*"

Ben couldn't help but start laughing. "This is the craziest thing you've ever done."

She grinned. "You have no idea." They both laughed for several moments before Corin asked, "So...what happens now?"

"I'm not sure," Ben confessed. "Arraya said she is taking us to the hidden fortress of the Magi, so I can go before their Council. She seems to think they'll raise an army and march on Jepitsa."

"Another war," Corin said flatly.

Ben nodded. "Another war."

***

Arraya sat cross-legged in the foul smelling hold of the pirate vessel, meditating on all the events that had transpired in such a short time. *My master had a vision of an heir to the throne, and went to Jepitsa to find him. My own vision of his death sent me stumbling after him, and I made mistakes – bad mistakes. I also made new allies.* A smile quirked at her lips. *J'Ram will make an interesting friend. He's no Magi, but he has wisdom of his own.*

The gentle rocking of the ship was soothing to the young Magi. It seemed to bring her in tune with the very world around her – the whisper of the breeze and the pull of the river current. The True Magic flowed more easily than it ever had, and she found peace in the power around her.

The peace held in spite of other events. *I was captured by the Tilliks, nearly destroyed by a vampire, and betrayed by my own master. I killed with the True Magic. And I found the heir – the rightful ruler of Letale. With a new contender for the throne, the Magi can rally around him and act. With the Council of the Magi behind him, we can raise armies and finally overthrow the Imposter-King.*

"Hey, girl," the pirate captain said. "Are you hungry?"

356

Arraya opened her eyes. The man stood in front of her, his eyes studying her carefully. "Yes," she answered honestly. "Thank you, Captain Japhet."

"Don't thank me," the pirate said. "How long has it been since you ate?"

The Magi had to consider for several moments to provide an answer. "Yesterday, in the afternoon," she said. "So nearly a day ago."

"I thought it might be something like that," Japhet said dryly. "That lizard-man of yours has been salivating over some of our cargo – apparently smoked fish is a big delicacy for them. If I don't feed him soon, he'll eat up a big part of our profit."

Arraya chuckled at that. "You just need to give him something to hunt," she suggested.

"I tried that," Japhet said irritably. "Thought he'd be interested in a match with the best fighter on my crew."

"He didn't want to fight?" Arraya asked in surprise.

"No, he did. Now my best man is going to be laid up for a week recovering."

The Magi laughed. "He's surprised me a few times since I met him. I saw him go hand-to-hand with a vampire and tear it limb from limb."

"A vampire?" Japhet asked with a raised eyebrow. "They actually exist?"

The Magi nodded. "There are dark forces at work in Letale," she said.

"Hmmm. Well, gather your friends and meet me in my cabin," Japhet said. "We'll take our meal there."

Arraya nodded. "It won't take long." She rose to her feet to begin gathering her allies.

She found the Erixan first, the blonde-haired girl hidden behind a stack of barrels. She was cleaning her guns again, the parts scattered in a semicircle around her. *I'm starting to think it's a compulsion with her*, Arraya observed wryly. "Chow time," she announced.

"Sounds good," Naomi said. "I'm just finishing up here." As she spoke, she started snapping parts together with practiced ease.

Arraya watched her for a moment before asking, "Naomi, why are you still here? I thought we would be parting ways after Jepitsa."

"That had been my plan, yes," the assassin confirmed. "But after what happened, well..." she hesitated. "I left bullet holes in a lot of bodies. The Royal Guard will be looking for me on the roads to Erixi. I think I'm safer traveling with you for now, until I can find a boat to take me directly home."

"That's not all of it," Arraya stated, not asking, her eyes narrowing. "There's something else, too."

Naomi shrugged and offered a smile. "I don't need any more reason than that." She finished assembling her rifle and started on the pistol. "Where's the food?"

"Captain's quarters." Arraya shook her head and left, resolving to watch the Erixan carefully in the coming days.

As she expected, the Magi found her Tillik companion near a barrel of smoked fish in the cargo hold. Less expected, however, was his current activity.

"Why are you chewing on a timber?" Arraya asked, trying to hide her bemusement.

J'Ram looked up from plank in his claws, offering a toothy smile to his friend. "Good for the teeth."

"Good for the teeth," she repeated.

The lizard-man nodded. "Our teeth grow endlessly and must be wore down," he said. "The last few days, I have had little time for personal care. You, Wise One, take so much looking after. Now I am just catching up on lost time."

"I heard you've been causing trouble," Arraya said with a smile.

"I took only a little fish," J'Ram protested. "There is no fresh prey to hunt here. And the thinskins pretend to hunt, but they struggle against even a young Tillik." The last words came out with an overture of amusement. "There is only one here who would be a challenge, but he has no interest in fighting."

The Magi frowned. "Who is that?"

"The Rephaim," the Tillik answered.

"Rephaim? There's no giant on the boat. I think I would have noticed."

J'Ram shook his head. "He is here, but he avoids me."

Arraya shrugged. "It's time to eat. Are you hungry?"

"A hunter always eats when there is food," the Tillik said. "He never knows when he will find prey again."

"I'll take that as a yes. Captain's quarters," she said.

"Are you coming?" the Tillik asked as he rose.

"In a few minutes," Arraya said. "Go ahead, I'll be along shortly."

The Tillik left the plank sitting on the barrel when he left. The Magi studied the tooth marks and shook her head. "No wonder people are afraid of the Tilliks," she murmured. "They could quite literally bite someone's head off."

"They are very dangerous," a voice answered her.

"He's gone. You can come out," she said.

The massive figure of Corpakle stepped out from behind a stack of crates. "You wish to speak with me, young Magi?"

"There's food," she said dryly. "Thought you would want to know."

"I do, thank you." He bowed his head deeply.

"Why were you hiding in Jepitsa?" she asked him.

"Not hiding," Pak said.

"You really are from the Raphaim, aren't you?"

Corpakle smiled. "As I tell everyone who will listen."

"I listen, but I don't always believe," Arraya replied with a wink. "If you're really a Raphaim and not a big human, why were you in Jepitsa and not Cosmane?"

"Exile," Pak said.

"I've never heard of the giants exiling anyone," Arraya countered.

"Self-imposed," he answered. "In Cosmane, I am too small to help my family. I am a burden on them. In Jepitsa, I care for myself and impose on no one."

Arraya sighed. "And why did you come with us, then?"

"To watch after."

"Watch after who?"

"The thieves. Ben, Corin, Zeke. Good youth, badly misled by the Brigands. Tried to protect them from Alan, but I failed." The man's expression was resolute. "I will not fail them again."

"You think you can protect them from what's to come?"

"Maybe, maybe not. But if I don't try, I know I will fail."

Arraya nodded at him. "I respect your decision."

"Thank you."

***

Ben and Corin were both surprised to find the captain's table nearly filled when they stepped into the cabin. Friends and allies were clustered around, devouring food as fast as it could be dished out. It was an unusual crowd – a pirate captain, a lizard-man, a beautiful Erixi girl, the largest man in Jepitsa, and one of their fellow thieves. Zeke was the only one who turned to greet them, but was promptly distracted by the Tillik attempting to steal a hard biscuit from his plate.

"Where's the Magi?" Ben asked.

No one bothered to answer. He gestured for Corin to sit, and the dark-haired girl promptly sat down and started to dish herself a plate of food from the pots in the center of the table. Ben ducked back out of the cabin and headed for the ship's bow.

The flame-haired girl was standing at the very front of the ship, looking south toward the distantly rising Cosmane mountains.

"Arraya?" he asked tentatively.

She seemed to not even hear him. He started to turn away, but she spoke. "Wait. Come here."

Cautiously, he stepped closer to her. She whispered, "Let me share this with you." She reached out and grasped his hand. Images began to flood his sight.

An army encamped around Jepitsa. Ships crashing together on a raging sea, warriors armed with swords swinging on long ropes between vessels. Fires raging across a dry forest. The skies stretched out in all directions, the kingdom far below. Hideous creatures attacking a camp at night, hardly visible in the darkness.

And at the center of it all was Ben. No, not everything –– there was a second center, opposite Ben, working against him. Wherever their borders met, conflict broke out and blood was shed. King Hazael, *he realized. Or was it Arraya realizing?*

It was the future, or many possible futures. Ben was on one side, Hazael on the other, each vying for control of the kingdom.

And it was then that Ben realized he could hear Arraya's thoughts, her desires, her innermost being. And he could feel he was intimately open to her as well. There were no secrets between them.

He could feel her pride, white-hot. She had fought powerful foes and overcame. She had come into her power and become a Magi, not merely an apprentice.

Her pain was ice-cold in contrast. She had been betrayed by her own master, and forced to destroy him to save herself and the King-To-Be. She felt as though her own heart had been plucked out and shredded, with a hard, smooth stone replacing it in her chest.

Accompanying the pain was bitter-tasting loneliness. The life as an apprentice of the Magi was a solitary one. She had a few distant friends among the other students, but no true close friend. There was no family in a Magi's life. The only true bond she had was the relationship between Master and apprentice, and that, too, had been severed.

Underneath all of that was a single spark of hope. Hope for a better life, hope for a united kingdom, hope for the last true heir to sit upon the throne of Letale.

As suddenly as it had come, it was gone as the Magi released his hand. Ben staggered for a moment, trying to comprehend everything he had seen and felt.

"The path that destiny has set before you will be hard," Arraya said quietly. "And I think you deserve to know that truth."

"I didn't know Magi could do that," Ben gasped.

"We can, but we usually don't. It's not difficult, but we don't like to share such visions."

"And what I felt from you?" Ben asked. "Is that just a side effect?"

The redhead's cheeks blushed bright enough to match her hair. "Not usually." She took a deep breath. "I needed to know that you were strong enough to endure. And..." she hesitated. "And I wanted you to know that I will stand by your side. It is my duty, as a Magi."

"Thank you," was all Ben could think to say.

"Now, there was something about food?" Arraya said with a smile.

Ben nodded. "You may be a Magi, but you're not that different from the rest of us," he said with a smile. "Come on, let's eat before there's nothing left."

***

Arraya smiled as she walked beside the King-to-Be. Dangers known and unknown loomed in the future. War and blood would darken Letale again before the Imposter-King would be overthrown.

But today, she would enjoy food and company. The future would come soon enough.

A PERSONAL NOTE FROM THE AUTHOR

Thank you for buying *Destiny's Heir*. It has been a labor of love, my own meager contribution to the realm of fantasy populated by such greats as JRR Tolkien and CS Lewis. I'm either standing on the shoulders of giants or in their shadow, depending on your opinion of the book.

Please take a minute to review *Destiny's Heir* on Amazon. Every new review helps my book's visibility on Amazon, which means I can commit more time to writing exciting new stories!

Lastly, if you'd like to know when I have new stories coming out, sign up for my mailing list or visit www.WritingUnderDuress.com so I can keep you up-to-date with the latest happenings.

Thanks again, and happy reading!

ABOUT THE AUTHOR

CASEY NEUMILLER is a full-time author who grew up in North Dakota. In 2008 he graduated from Dickinson State University with degrees in Computer Science and English. After five years working in Information Technology, he decided to start using his second degree.

He currently resides in North Dakota with his wife. In his non-writing time he hunts and fishes, enjoys online gaming, and plays amateur mechanic and carpenter.

Destiny's Heir is Neumiller's second novel and the first in his new fantasy series. His current writing projects include a sequel, *Destiny's Mantle*, and the next Shattered Expanse novel, *Contract Hunt*.